The Crystal Flame

by

Shirley McCoy

This is a work of fiction. Names, characters, places, and incidents are either the product of the author's imagination or are used fictitiously, and any resemblance to actual persons living or dead, business establishments, events, or locales, is entirely coincidental.

The Crystal Flame

Cover Art by *Kristian Norris*

The Wild Rose Press, Inc.
PO Box 708
Adams Basin, NY 14410-0708
Visit us at www.thewildrosepress.com

Publishing History
First Fantasy Rose Edition, 2017
Print ISBN 978-1-5092-1588-1
Digital ISBN 978-1-5092-1589-8

Published in the United States of America

"Finn, no."

"You can't hold it back all the time and you shouldn't. Damn it, Lyssa, that's how people get hurt."

His words had the exact opposite effect from what he'd intended. Instead of bolstering her courage, she remembered and feared her own power. She shook her head and tried to jerk her arm from his hold. "Finn, let me go."

"Not yet. Show me first."

"Show you what? You've seen my power before."

"But not your full power. Show me. All of it, as much as you like, as much as you have. You can't hurt me; you know that. You are safe here. Let your power do what it wants. Better still, do what *you* want."

Goaded beyond reason and tempted beyond bearing, wrapped in fear and anger and an unfamiliar excitement, she did as he asked. Her ice burst from her hands to the floor, creating a small frozen wall about a foot high which encircled them both.

"Good. That's a start anyway," he murmured. "But there are other ways. It's all right to touch me. It's what you want. I know it is."

Unable to resist his lure, she let sheer temptation rule her and stepped one inch closer. Close enough to touch.

Praise for Shirley McCoy

Chapter One

Even Finn Hale, strong as he was, fire lord of Ravenstone though he was, could not withstand such bitter cold for long. If only he could sleep, just lie down and sleep. *No.* From somewhere deep inside, his indomitable will conjured that one word. Right now, sleep was death to him so he had to keep going. He must reach her, the beautiful snow queen. Failing that, he had to find shelter, but there was nothing, had been nothing, not for miles. He might well die, but he swore he would die fighting. He would not give up until his very last breath. Clinging to consciousness, he wrapped his heavy wool cloak about him and stumbled on.

Though it hardly seemed possible, the snow increased while the temperature decreased. Visibility dropped from slight to nil, presenting a whole other host of problems. It would be very easy for him to walk right into a tree or place one foot wrong and end in a crevice with a broken leg. Worse yet, he might even fall right off of the bloody mountain.

It focused his mind a trifle to concentrate on her, his possible future wife. The fact that she was surely aware of his presence and was clearly trying to keep him from going any farther motivated him more than a little. Well, by all the gods, he had come this far and he would not be deterred. Yet even his resolute spirit could not resist the inevitable. His sense of reality began to waver then it fractured. Then a deep shiver wracked his frame and brought him back to the whirling snow.

His flame rose higher by some small degree; he'd simply have to hope it would be enough because he'd be damned if he'd give up now. Not after weeks of traveling across half the world. Not after days spent in this frigid misery. More than once in his eventful life his obstinate, not to say stubborn, nature had done him good. When his father had died it was that and that alone which had sustained him in those first days.

Once more he was rewarded. One tiny gleam of light shone through the trees and the swirl of snow. He fixed his gaze on it, pointed himself in that direction and prayed he would make it there in time. Hoped when he did, it would be no mirage.

The swirling snow half-blinded him, but at last the reflection of the moon and stars showed him her palace. For palace it was, complete with turrets, towers and ramparts all made entirely of ice. Barely able to register this marvel, he approached and entered a sort of forecourt which offered some moderate protection from the wind.

"Hello," he called in a hoarse voice. As the echo of his words died away, icy doors creaked open to allow him inside. With a grateful prayer to the gods, he entered.

****

As soon as he stepped foot upon her ground, Lyssa Jennings had known. Although, truth be told, she had not at first recognized the sensation, as it had been so long since she had experienced it. No one had approached her home in years. Most knew better. This man did not. With a shrug, she conjured a storm and so did her utmost to ensure he got no farther.

Nevertheless, he made it through in spite of her, which meant he was very strong, though he did not look it as he stumbled in. Perhaps it was that strength which compelled her to open her doors to him rather than leave him to die. Or perhaps it was mere curiosity. Either way, the damage was done and since it was, she might as well speak to him, even question him. Still, she remained cautious and stayed on the stairs, out of the light so she might see but not be seen.

"Who are you? Why are you here?"

When he merely stood there dazed and panting, she repeated the question in more strident tones, with the added inquiry of who did he think he was disturbing her, but got no response.

Far beyond mere curiosity now and headed straight into fury, she prepared to show herself and her power to him when a small sound stopped her.

"My lady, please help me."

Unable to utter even one word more, the stranger held out his once strong hand in entreaty then fainted dead away.

After staring at him, mouth agape, for a moment, she swung into action. For some reason unknown to her, she could not allow him to freeze as she had so many others before him. Instead, she gave orders to her self-made companions, her ice servants, for his care. She directed a chamber be made ready for him. She chose the only one with a hearth and ordered a fire lit there.

While tending him she could not help but observe his beauty. Hair black as a raven's wing, straight nose, strong jaw and full sensuous lips, her eager senses catalogued. In addition, he was tall, all muscle and sinew, with golden skin only faintly paled by his ordeal, skin which she saw more than a little of as she did what she could to revive him. Silken skin she touched as she divested him of his wet clothing then wrapped him in thick blankets in an attempt to warm him. As alluring as that all was, it was nothing to the piercing green of the eyes which had held hers for one instant before his lapse into unconsciousness. Even clouded with pain his eyes were riveting.

It was that gaze which told her she must stay well away from him no matter her attraction. She must stay far from him in the same manner she had stayed away from men all of her life. Yet if she was so very determined on this course, then why save him at all?

For the first time in years she was unsure of the motivation underlying a particular action and it unsettled if not downright terrified her. Another reason to leave him, she determined. On the thought, she started a fire in the hearth. Task complete and sure she had done all she could, Lyssa left the rest in the hands of the gods and sought her own chamber.

****

The first thing Finn was aware of was warmth all through him. He was no longer as deathly cold as he had been, nor terribly heated as he so often was. Instead he was comfortable, more comfortable than he had been in years. And naked. Considering his unclad state and his lack of a sword—his own was nowhere to be seen—he was, thank the gods, also alone. Since there was no one in sight and he discovered his own clothing was dry and folded neatly on a small chair nearby, he saw no reason to rise just yet. For a time he did nothing more than bask in the feeling of contentment flowing through him.

Then, unbidden, his full memory rushed back to him. Soon he recalled leaving his kingdom behind in search of the so-called snow queen. He managed to reach her, then concentrate as he might, it all went black. He must have passed out, he reasoned. Shrugging, he admitted he felt fine now and what was more, he'd completed at least part of his mission. He'd found the snow queen.

He lay there, taking in the room in which he found himself. The bed he was in was large enough to accommodate his over six-foot frame and very soft. Its large frame was made of oak, he noted. There was a wash stand to his left and a screen, behind which he assumed was a chamber pot. A fire burned in the hearth but it was not quite large enough to heat the entire room. So far he could see nothing out of the ordinary. Until he discerned that the walls and floor were made of solid ice.

He looked around in wonder. The place was cold certainly, but all things considered, it ought to have been like living inside a block of ice. It wasn't. The fire burning in the hearth made the room seem cheerful and it carried only a little chill. What was most fascinating, however, was that the fire in the hearth did not melt the ice of the walls or chimney. Amazing. Perhaps she could protect her ice from the unaccustomed warmth. Experimentally, he slid his feet to the floor. Cool but not freezing.

He also discovered he was steady enough on his feet. That being the case, he ought to greet his hostess and savior properly. Dressing, he readied himself then left to explore.

Finn soon learned that the palace he found himself in was vast. There were some few sticks of furniture, but many of the rooms were empty; the walls were all made of ice just as those in his own chamber had been. The tables, cabinets and beds had once been very fine, but though well-cared for, were now aged. In addition, the corridors held very little to distinguish them from one another. It was only his habit of committing the location of his chambers in a strange place to memory which kept him from becoming lost. Even so, he had no idea where the entrance hall he had seen before his collapse was located.

After a time, he at last stumbled upon it and what a sight to behold it was. The roof was fully one hundred feet high. The walls narrowed as they went up and were formed of beautiful panes of clear thin ice. As it rose, the dawning sun made the very chamber itself a prism. Finn suppressed a gasp, but couldn't stop himself from looking all around with wide eyes. To his left were the stairs which his vague memory informed him lead to a shadowed balcony. A noise from above made him swing about and reach for his sword.

****

Lyssa observed him from the upper gallery yet remained concealed. Being so near to death did not seem to have harmed him in the least. From all she could see he was more than recovered.

Sensing her presence, it was his turn to ask who was there.

"If you do not wish to see me or speak with me, I understand," he continued when she maintained her silence. "It's only I would like to thank you for saving

6

my life."

She continued to gaze down on him unable, or perhaps unwilling, to make herself known. To observe him without being observed herself was surely the safest course. Getting a good sense of his inherent vitality and a chance to admire his good looks, to see him so open and alert was an added, if dangerous, bonus.

Yet when he spoke again, it was with the first hint of impatience. "I would like to express my gratitude face to face and I dislike talking to walls. You might do me the courtesy of revealing yourself." He gave her a few moments more then turned back the way he had come. "Well, I can see you are not at all interested in conversing, so perhaps I should take my leave."

"Wait." The word was out of Lyssa's mouth before she discerned she had any intention of speaking. She found she could not let him go, not without talking with him face-to-face. So, trembling slightly, she walked down her icy steps. "Understand this; you will leave, not just this room, but this castle at once. You are alive only because I wish it and now I wish for you to be gone." She stopped halfway down the spiral staircase and studied him.

"Of that I am well aware. If I could just—"

"You are alive only because I wish it," she repeated. "And I have told you to leave. Do not make me ask again."

"At least allow me to express my thanks—"

"Spare me your gratitude. I have no need of it. Don't you know who I am?"

****

The snow queen gazed down at him, imperious and

regal, but at first he did not speak. In truth, he was a bit awed by her beauty and even more so by her demeanor. So haughty and proud, a cool exterior which masked he knew not what. Her long blonde hair was piled high on her head in an intricate chignon and her eyes were as light a blue as some of the ice she created. She was only an inch or two shorter than six feet, slim yet still lightly curvaceous. The long cotehardie gown she wore must have been of her own creation, for the simple garment made of what he took to be dark blue silk sparkled. The soft candlelight glinted on minute fragments of ice which clung to the silk in spiral patterns. The sleeves trailed from the elbow, the neckline was low and scooped to show off her figure. She wore a belt of silver which rested on her hips and with an end which trailed down the front of her dress.

He shook his head just a bit to clear it and tried to respond with some coherence. "I know well who you are, majesty, and I have never seen anything or anyone so beautiful. I have crossed half the world to find you."

Something very like astonishment passed over her face. "You were searching for me?" she asked, incredulous.

"Just so, highness."

Unable to contain her fascination, or so it seemed when he took in the arrested expression on her face, she made her way toward him.

Her brows rose until they all but disappeared beneath her blonde hair. "You know what I am yet you sought me? You are a fool." She turned away from him with an impatient twitch of her skirts, dismissing him, and began to pace.

He could feel the first stirrings of temper, but held

it grimly in check. "I am many things, my lady, but a fool is not one of them. Even as far as Ravenstone, my country, there are tales of you. I have also sought out those who knew you long ago, before you came into your own. Believe me, I am more than aware of who you are. It is *because* of who you are I have come."

Her agitated pacing ceased. For the first time he sensed he had her complete and undivided attention.

"Are you one of those rash enough to wish for death at my hands? Tire me further and I may give it to you."

She could, of that he had no doubt. Her gaze told him as much. Yet somehow the knowledge did not trouble him unduly. He could not, would not, live as he was any longer. If she could not save him, surely there were far worse ways to die than at her hands.

She surveyed him for a long moment. "You're one of those then." She sighed.

"One of what?"

"One who thinks to change me. You think you're the man I'll warm to at last. How tedious." Even so, she cast him a speculative glance. "Still, you are pretty, well-mannered, and you do not lack for courage. If you go now and leave me in peace, I'll not harm you. Moreover, I'll see you safely off of my mountain and on your way."

When his response was not immediate, she continued, "Come, come, that's the best offer you'll get and more than I've offered any man in years."

Choosing his words with great care, he answered her at last. "I don't think you understand. I'm not like other men."

She laughed, just a small burst of sound, like frost-coated bells ringing. "Men. You all think you are different. Be disabused of that notion right now. No man can touch me and live."

Her challenge was clear and he could not resist it. "Really?" The word was a challenge of its own. With no more verbal sparring, he stretched out a hand and conjured fire. Set free, he let the flame build until it was mere inches away from her.

A shocked gasp escaped her then she reacted faster than he ever dreamed possible. From her raised palm, a shield of ice blocked his flame, but could not consume it or quench it. Acting on instinct, she raised her free hand in further defense, but the sound of his voice stayed her.

"Wait. I have no wish to harm you." By tiny increments, he lowered his flame until it was doused. Once he did, he hoped she would dispense with her ice, but instead she continued to regard him with complete distrust. He approached her as deliberately, as calmly as he would have some wounded creature which might strike out at any moment. "It occurred to me, all things considered, we might help each other."

"Who are you?" she demanded. "Or should I say what are you?"

"My name is Finn Hale, King of Ravenstone. I am a fire lord. A misnomer if ever there was one, for I am not its master, but its servant. I cannot fully control it any more than you can control your ice, my queen."

"Whatever makes you say that?"

"'No man can touch me and live,'" he murmured. "Your words," he reminded her.

The deep warm timbre of his voice sent a shiver down her spine, which she steadfastly ignored. With another far less controlled gesture, she transformed the ice to harmless snow which fell at his feet then she turned away once more, consistently avoiding his gaze. "What is it you want?"

"To try," he said. "To experiment. I would someday like to touch and be touched without fear. I have to believe it is possible with you. I've tried everything else."

For the first time in years, in decades, heat rushed to her cheeks. "You can't mean you actually wish to bed me? Very few are bold enough even to think of it. I could kill you."

****

In a deliberate move, his gaze travelled down her body, taking in every detail. "With respect, I disagree on every count, majesty. First, if there is a man who can gaze upon you and not wonder what it would be like to have you, then I would like to meet such a unique individual. Second, I don't believe you can kill me. As I think I've amply demonstrated, I'm no ordinary man. But we're getting ahead of ourselves. We need to take this one step at a time."

As he closed the distance between them, he focused his entire being on her. Gods, but she was amazing, truly brave. How could any man resist her? He would attempt this much at least. Even if he died, it would be worth it. "Take my hand." He offered her his, palm up. "I long to draw you to me, I admit, but for now just a touch will suffice."

****

His countenance, not to mention his tone, were both so mesmerizing, she nearly did as he asked. Only the age-old fear of causing harm stopped her. "You forget yourself. What makes you think I would offer you such a privilege?"

"Curiosity. Aren't you curious? I am what I am; you are what you are. You've seen what I can do. I don't think we can hurt each other. Perhaps this is meant. Don't you think we owe it to ourselves to find out?"

"That sort of 'curiosity' is what gets people into serious trouble," she informed him as she somehow managed to look down her nose at him despite his greater height.

"I'm not asking for much, little more than a handshake, unless you're too frightened." His air, at first teasing, gentled. "Perfectly understandable after all you've been through."

"I am my mother's daughter. I am not afraid of anything."

"I can see that. It's in your eyes. They glitter when you are roused and shards of silver shimmer in the blue. It's quite captivating.

"Take my hand," he repeated.

The fear was so old and deeply embedded in her psyche she could not set it aside straightaway. Still, he had asked for this; if any harm came to him it would be at his own request, so why not? Why not prove to him he was no different than any of the others who came before him?

"Let it be on your head then." Before she could change her mind, she grasped his palm firmly in hers, wholly prepared for some sort of explosion. Nothing whatsoever happened.

No, that wasn't entirely true, she realized. She could feel a slight warmth radiating from where their fingers joined, warmth which did not grow cold, unlike every other human she had ever touched.

When she extended her hand to him, he braced himself. Despite his protests to the contrary, she understood then that he half expected some catastrophe. When nothing of the sort occurred, a slow delicious smile of triumph spread over his face. He closed his eyes a moment, whether to thank the gods or the fates, she could not say. Then his gaze found hers again.

Trapped by his gaze, her hand held in his, she could not move a muscle or utter even one syllable. She had no idea how long she stood there with him, hands clasped, but at last she found her voice. "How?"

"I'm not sure, but it's wonderful isn't it?"

Her normally unshakeable composure wholly rattled, for a moment she didn't answer and when she did it wasn't in words, not at first. Instead, she lifted her other hand and turned up her power as high and as strong as it would go. When he lifted one arrogant eyebrow and punched up his own with unshakeable confidence, she couldn't help but smile. "Oh, yes. It is quite wonderful."

With admirable self-control she reined herself in, jerked back from his endless warmth. "But we mustn't tempt the gods for too long, not just yet at any rate. One step at a time, as you said."

"I did say that," he granted. "More fool me."

As one they extinguished their powers.

"The matter requires some further discussion, don't you agree?"

"Is that your way of asking me to stay?" When she said nothing, he offered her a broad grin. "If it is, I accept most gratefully."

"You may remain here for the present," she conceded. "I'll see a meal is prepared. You may have use of the chamber you woke in for as long as you remain."

"Lovely." He started toward the door then turned back. "One question, might I beg the favor of your given name?"

Lyssa's eyes widened at the inquiry. She couldn't help it. No one had asked her name, not in decades. "L-Lyssa," she stammered. "It's Lyssa Jennings."

Finn bowed with elegant grace and took his leave.

Chapter Two

For the rest of the evening, they avoided contact with one another. Finn kept to his chamber and Lyssa kept to hers. But when morning arrived, she could no longer avoid him.

"Good morning," Finn greeted her in the antechamber off the dining hall the next day. Together, they walked the short distance to the well-appointed room and sat down to breakfast together.

The table made of oak was meant for as many as twelve. In the normal course of things, she enjoyed her meals alone but today, a new place was set on her right. Chairs with intricate swirls and spirals carved into their backs and cushioned seats covered in white brocade stood empty. A sideboard was set off to the right with simple fare ready upon it. Baked ham, scones and a pot of piping hot chocolate she'd ordered specifically for him stood waiting.

He was dressed in a different set of clothes, she noted. Instead of the red doublet made of warm wool, he wore a white linen shirt beneath a leather vest and brown pants of a lighter wool tucked into sturdy knee-high leather boots. She wondered that he did not require something warmer, perhaps the red doublet or even the warm cloak he'd worn during the storm. Then recalled the events of the evening before and reminded herself that, indeed, he was most unlike other men.

She gestured for him to help himself and they filled their plates. After they were settled and enjoying their meal, Lyssa decided she had certain questions and as long as the man was still here, infuriating as well as distracting her, he might as well answer some of them.

She dredged up long forgotten geography lessons and came up with a vague idea of his land's location. "You are a fire lord from Ravenstone in the south."

He nodded and sipped his chocolate.

"Which, if memory serves, is prone to near constant chaos."

"Chaos which has been ameliorated somewhat by my royal presence and my rule I must point out."

She signaled her acknowledgement with a nod of her own, but countered, "If this is so, why are you here?"

"To find you of course, as I said."

"Would you not do better to go and rule your own kingdom instead of coming here to disturb mine?" she inquired with a feigned, almost frigid sweetness.

"Go and turn my back upon the legend? No, not while I live."

"Legend? What legend?"

"Surely you know the legend of our two kingdoms, of the time when your kind and mine came together?"

Lyssa shook her head. "I was a child when I was taken to the little village of Brimbury to be fostered. I was never told the story."

Finn's eyes widened and he began the tale. "In my country, and many others come to that, it is said only a queen of ice can live happily with a lord of fire," he said. "Long ago, the country of Ravenstone and the country of Halstad were one and the people lived together in harmony. This came about when the greatest of the fire lords, Malcolm, married the most magnificent snow queen, Ingrid. Their love was the stuff of legend. Neither his parents nor hers wanted them together. The two kingdoms were at war, you see. Bitter enemies who had no desire for peace in spite of the toll the constant battles took on both lands. How could they be anything but adversaries, when their very natures were so utterly contradictory?"

Lyssa nodded, intrigued and caught up in spite of herself. "How did they even meet?"

Finn smiled. "Ah, now we come to my favorite part of the story. The princess Ingrid was no ordinary woman for many reasons, her great power being but one. She was also possessed of a brilliant mind and a thirst for knowledge. As a young girl, the fire lords caught her attention. What were they fighting for? What made them so very different from her own people, aside from the obvious? She read everything she could get her hands on about them, studied them for years. She even tracked their battles. Then during a brief truce she begged her father to allow her to visit Ravenstone and observe them, incognito of course. As she had just turned seventeen years of age, her father, who had indulged her in every way since her birth, refused her. The danger, he said, was far too great."

"I take it things didn't end there."

Finn murmured his agreement. "Being a princess of the blood and unused to being denied, she disguised herself and left the castle. On the road to Ravenstone, she met a young man, Malcolm. Malcolm, being the chivalrous sort, pledged to protect her on her journey, as she flatly refused to return home. He guided her to

Woodhaven, the capital city of Ravenstone, all the while fighting their growing mutual attraction. It was then they discovered that they balanced each other out, being fire lord and snow queen. In any event, once they arrived in the city, he could no longer hide his attraction or his identity. He was no ordinary peasant; he was, in fact, the crown prince of Ravenstone."

"I would suspect Ingrid was more than a little peeved."

"That she was. She was so devastated that she took herself back to Halstad immediately and at speed."

When he paused, Lyssa prompted, "Well, what happened next?"

"Halfway along, Ingrid turned around. As soon as he discovered she was gone, Malcolm took off after her. They met once again out on the road. Malcolm vowed to be honest with her from that time forward and Ingrid promised no more running at the slightest problem. They professed their love, camped by the roadside and made love for the first time as the sun set, then again and again all night."

Trying to ignore the heat rushing over her cheeks and elsewhere, Lyssa commented, "Surely it could not have been that easy. What about their respective kingdoms? The war?"

"The two married in secret, but even so the ceremony was binding. Their countries had very little choice in the matter after that. Soon, however, it became clear that together they were stronger."

"The countries or Malcolm and Ingrid?"

Finn chuckled. "Both."

They sat for a few moments in silence, then Finn continued, "A lasting peace was finally forged and their joint kingdom became the strongest land the world had ever seen and the most content ever imagined. Their rule was a golden age for both peoples. Fire and ice, two opposite elements which unmitigated, create havoc in our world, but bring them together: balance. For centuries this intricate equilibrium remained intact."

"But…?"

"A terrible illness came. Chaos ruled again and eventually the kingdom split once more into two. The populations of Halstad and Ravenstone were decimated. Women with ice powers were affected most and even the royal family of Halstad was not spared. Halstad became a mere vassal country to Ravenstone when the queen and all the princesses of the blood were lost. All lost but one: your great-grandmother."

"Making me a queen without a country. Yet because I am a descendent of the royal family, you have come here to claim me as your wife." She was none too pleased by this realization. She would pick her own husband if and only if she wished, thank you.

"Not merely that," he hastened to assure her. "I want to restore the balance, not just for myself or you, but for my people and yours. It's my fate, it seems." He took a sip of water, reached out for her hand then drew back.

"And what of mine? My whole life has been about free choice. I longed for that and could only find it here, alone. Isn't this something you wish for as well?"

"Hmm, yes, it is. I have chosen. Fate carried me here, yes, but my own will has also brought me to you. Besides, if my fate is to join my life to that of a woman who is beautiful inside and out, who am I to argue?" He gave her an easy tempting smile and continued eating.

As an afterthought, he added, "Besides, you aren't alone. You are the snow queen, last of the royal blood line. There are none so powerful as you, but there are still some others with similar abilities."

"So there are others out there who escaped the plague?"

Finn nodded. "There are. Does that surprise you?"

"No, not at all. I've often wondered whether I was the only one."

When he let the talk turn to other more commonplace matters, Lyssa was grateful. Certainly, she had experienced quite enough upheaval for one day and any further revelations could wait. They spoke of the things, good and bad, which she did not know about the world because of her isolation. The rest of the meal passed most companionably and the remainder of the morning passed quickly.

****

Hours more elapsed before Lyssa again addressed the reason Finn had come to her. As they shared supper later that day in the dining hall, Lyssa studied the man sitting across from her and after some moments, she spoke. "How should we do this?"

He could have no doubt as to what she was referring to, but he chewed then swallowed a mouthful of buttered bread before replying. "I thought each day we hold hands longer and make note of any unpleasant effects, any problems. Then when we are reasonably confident it's entirely safe, we progress to more."

"Until when?"

At his blank look she clarified, "At what point do we stop?"

He shrugged. "We stop whenever you want to

stop."

When she laughed again, he smiled in response. "Gods, I think I'm addicted to the sound of your laugh."

She ignored that comment and concentrated on the subject at hand. "Those are the words of a man who will do his level best to seduce a woman and make quite certain she doesn't ever want to stop."

"Perhaps."

His smile had everything inside her going warm and liquid, a novel feeling she had yet to get used to. Saving that complicated issue for another time, she continued, "All that aside, there is another aspect of this we haven't considered."

"Oh?"

"You seem to have far more control over your powers than I. So I'd like you to teach me. I want to be in command of my powers, not the other way around."

He shook his head. "Control, mine in particular, is an illusion."

It was her turn to shake her head. "I disagree. You've already amply demonstrated that quality. And you're strong. You would never have made it here to me through my storm otherwise."

"True. Strength is not something either of us lacks. It is something you have in abundance."

"But not control. That is why…" Her voice trailed off.

"That's why you left Halstad. I know."

She looked into his eyes and felt he did. To be understood by another even that much was glorious. But it made her long for more. "If you could teach me how to rein it all in, to keep my power harnessed so I wouldn't hurt anyone, then perhaps I could live among people again, even rule."

"I can't teach you something I don't know."

Lyssa's heart sank then rose again just as swiftly when he continued speaking.

"Maybe we can learn from each other. I will say I already feel…steadier with you. When you are near I feel calmer."

"I feel the same," she admitted.

"There is one condition I must insist upon if we do this."

She waited, brow lifted.

"We must swear to do no harm. We must vow to never use our powers against one another or the innocent." He bent then grasped the concealed knife he carried in his boot, sliced his palm. "By my blood, I swear it. Will you do the same?" He offered the blade to her, hilt first.

Lyssa accepted it and slashed her own skin. "I swear."

As one, they clasped hands. A jolt shot through her and she wondered if it affected him as well. They both gazed in wonder as bright blue light came from where their blood and magic mixed. After an instant the light faded, but she didn't let go of his hand. She didn't want to, not yet. Finn gave her fingers a gentle squeeze then released her. With a slight wince, she grabbed the linen napkin near her plate to fashion a makeshift bandage for her wound. Finn did the same for himself then took a long sip of wine.

"Good. That's settled then. We'll begin tomorrow." He forked up a bite of beef and applied himself to finishing his meal.

****

Next morning she breakfasted alone as Finn did not make an appearance. Judging by the state of the table, however, it was easy to deduce he had not gone hungry and she wondered what might have had him up and about so very early. Surely not their decision to hone their skills? Yet she could think of nothing else which might motivate him.

When she stretched out with her senses, she discovered he was in what she liked to think of as her great hall. The rectangular room was vast, the largest in her castle. The roof arched up like a great cathedral, and all down the two longer walls were squares of thinner ice, which rose from floor to ceiling like windows. A settee or two and a few chairs placed strategically around the room completed the furnishings. The chamber stood ready for guests at a ball that would never take place. In the normal course of things, the place was quite empty apart from these few assorted odds and ends, but upon her arrival, she found it transformed into a training area.

Finn had assembled blankets to smother any fire or to put around himself if, conversely, he got a chill from her ice. Pails of melted snow were also lined up for safety. In addition, various items were laid out upon a table he'd managed to procure from somewhere.

"Good morning, Finn. You've been busy I see."

He turned from the table on which he was placing other objects and smiled. "So I have. Shall I show you what I've come up with?"

"Please."

He indicated an old piece of cloth, a bowl of water, and a hot water bottle all set in a line. "To begin, we'll see what you can do with these items. We'll determine what your limits are."

"My limits? Such as what? How quickly I can freeze something?" Or someone. She shivered inwardly at the thought.

He nodded. "That's just for a start. I also wondered, how far reaching is your power, a few feet or more? How long does it take for you to call up then use your power? How well can you direct it? When you freeze something, is it frozen solid or are there degrees? But most important, we want to determine what your triggers are."

He cast a contemplative glance at their surroundings. "What you've built here is indescribably beautiful and intricate, but while this palace makes it quite clear you have a certain amount of control over your power under specific conditions, that supremacy is not absolute. You've said so yourself, just as you said you would never have left home otherwise. Taking all that into account, the most important thing we want to determine is what situations act as a catalyst for this temporary loss of control. What is it that makes you lose authority over your gift? We answer that question, then we expose you to similar situations as much as possible and finally you work on keeping your powers entirely under your conscious direction."

"You make it sound so very easy."

"Not at all, but I believe it is possible for us both. But since we began this at your request, we'll start with you."

He lifted a finger. "First lesson: it's all about control. Accessing your power will be most easily done if you are calm and centered."

"Sometimes I can barely find my center. Do I even

have one? Oftentimes, it feels as though every bit of my soul is a swirling storm that engulfs me and everything else anywhere near. It won't be contained."

Finn digested this for a moment. "When you built this place, how did you feel? When your power rose up then, what was it like?"

"It was as though I was a conduit that had been closed for far too long, but no longer. Like a dam blocking a river had been released at last. For the first time, I didn't try to restrain it; instead, I used it to create all of this. When I did, oh gods, everything locked away inside of me was finally set free." For a moment she was back there, on that night so long ago, reliving that precious memory and all the feelings involved.

"And since then?"

"Since then it is the same so long as I am alone. But as soon as someone stumbles upon my lands, or gods forbid, comes here deliberately as you did, I feel that same storm rise up."

Finn sent her a glance which managed to be both rueful and triumphant at the same time, utterly charming her. "I can't say I'm sorry I took the risk."

He made his way to the table, took up a pitcher and poured a glass of water. "Let's start with something simple. Can you freeze this glass of water and nothing else?"

Lyssa stared doubtfully at the goblet. "I can try."

"Good." Finn joined her where she stood several feet away from the table. He placed himself behind her, lifted a hand to her shoulder. "Close your eyes." When she pulled a face at him, he insisted, "Close your eyes. Now imagine how you felt when you built this place. Then direct your power to the liquid in the glass."

Lyssa lowered her lids. To her surprise, her other senses sharpened and they were all, every last one, focused on him. She tried to call her wayward mind to order, but had very little success. She shivered once then with a burst of power, she froze one whole side of the room. She swore.

He gave her shoulder a light squeeze, offering what reassurance he could. "For a first try that was not bad."

She whirled. "Not bad? Do you see the other side of the room?"

"Of course I do. It's better than the whole room and a damn sight better than what I experienced while making my way here."

"I suppose so," she grumbled.

He was a little amused now, she could see, as he straightened lips which wanted to curve. "Try again," he suggested.

Setting that already firm chin, she did. It took time and effort, more than she expected, but they made progress. Soon she could direct her abilities with a greater degree of accuracy. If it was not as precise as she would wish, it was only their first day, she reasoned. Even so, exhaustion began to plague her until she at last called a halt.

Finn did not argue. Instead, he asked, "Do you have anything more suitable to wear? Like breeches?"

"No. I can't wear clothing made of ice, even I would be uncomfortable in such apparel, so I've only what I brought with me and things I've made since."

He studied her then nodded. "I've something I think will suit if we alter it a bit. I'll have it ready on the morrow."

One of Finn's talents, she was fast discovering,

was knowing exactly how far to push and just when to back off. This quality was a valuable one to be sure and she could appreciate it. Regardless, she was done for that day; that he knew it as well made things far easier than they might otherwise have been. With a small sigh, she retired to her chambers for some much needed rest.

****

Over the next few weeks the daily training sessions remained difficult. As soon as Lyssa mastered one aspect of her power, Finn would have her continue on to the next, forcing her to add new skills and hone those already grasped. Yet she began to look forward to them. Discovering her limits was a main goal, one she came closer to reaching every day.

Soon enough, they determined that she could freeze things solid or not, as she chose if she focused. Focused or not, she could call up her power quickly. It was more difficult for her to learn how not to call up her power inadvertently. Her full power reached for twenty miles in a perfect circle. Finn could attest to this since he had come through her storm. The closer in, the more she held sway and the more precise she could be.

It was this precision which was most difficult for her to learn. Any break in concentration or emotional upheaval and her powers went wild and all objects in the immediate vicinity were frozen solid. Much of their day was spent in practicing techniques to clear and calm her mind. This process was slow and painful, but each day she made progress. Even so, it was weeks before she could direct her power with any sort of accuracy or call it up only when she expressly wished.

But she was learning. Day by day Finn taught her to use her powers to deflect and defend and distract. By month's end, not only was her control over her powers increasing, but her physical strength was as well. He challenged her on every level and tested her in the best possible way.

That day's training session started off like any other. Using all of the feints, stratagems and ploys he had taught her, Lyssa was holding her own when Finn countered with an unfamiliar move then a blow to the abdomen which had her doubling over. An instant later, he had her restrained, caught between the wall and his powerful form. She tried to push him away, but only succeeded in getting pressed back even more firmly. Two large hands encircled both of her wrists then braced them beside her head, bringing his very hard well-muscled body mere inches from hers. Suddenly she could not catch her breath.

"Break my hold. Use your power."

The order was clear and his voice was as unyielding as the wall at her back. A part of her yearned to do exactly as he commanded, but...

"No. I can't. I might hurt you." *I'm also enjoying having you this close far too much,* she thought.

The frustration that filled him showed for an instant in his harsh expression. His distraction only lasted for a split second, but it was enough. She brought her knee up to deliver a blow to his groin. Since his reflexes were lightning fast he managed to step back in the nick of time, but it gave Lyssa the opening she needed. Elbowing Finn aside, she slipped past his guard and reversed their positions. Backed against the solid wall of ice with her dagger at his throat, Finn just looked at her while he caught his breath.

"Very good," he murmured, "but not quite good

enough."

Before she could register what he meant, a slim column of flame shot up and out from his hand to hers, grazing the tender underside of her wrist. Gasping in shock at the unfamiliar sensation, she loosened her grip on the knife just enough for him to disarm her.

He flipped the dagger to his dominant hand then put it to her throat. "You didn't win because you weren't willing to use all the tools at your disposal. Nor were you willing to do whatever it takes. Using all you are, that's the only way you'll survive."

Leading with the blade, Finn forced her back until he was able to step away from the wall. Then he grinned. "That bit of evasion at the start though, that was pretty damn good."

As she studied his arrogant smirk, her fury grew. An incoherent sound much too close to a shriek escaped her lips as she sent her ice flying in a graceful arch toward him. Again his finely honed reflexes came to his aid as he pivoted then blocked her ice.

"Finally."

He breathed the word so softly she almost didn't hear it. Or at least she could pretend she hadn't heard it.

"It's all right," he continued, his manner as calm as if he were walking in a quiet garden rather than being bombarded with large shards of ice. "Let all the frustration of all the lonely years out. I can take it."

The gentle words only incensed her further and she turned her power up another notch. Both palms outstretched, she sent a cascade of ice toward Finn. He stood firm and did not waver. Without fear, in fact with every appearance of eager exhilaration, he used his own power to counter hers.

When his fervor fully registered, her temper was sublimated slightly by shock. Just as quickly, however, her fury returned to the forefront twice as strong. She couldn't help but demand, "Have you lost your senses? Do you want me to kill you?"

Gaze locked to hers, he stood his ground. "No, I want you to be able to defend yourself using everything you have. I want you to have confidence and control."

With a bloodcurdling shout, she expended the last of her energy. When she collapsed with exhaustion, her power was extinguished in the same moment. The change was as abrupt as it was complete.

"Confidence and control." She closed her eyes, shook her head. "In case you hadn't noticed, I'm not feeling much of either right now." Forcing herself to open her eyes, she looked around at the carnage. A beautiful chandelier was shattered. The table where they kept weapons, tools and other training necessaries was overturned. Splinters and spikes of ice littered the floor.

"It may not seem like it now but this"—he gestured at the debris—"is an important step."

"Will it ever get easier?" She forced the words out from pursed lips. So many emotions churned within her, not the least of which was impatience with herself. Having embarked on this path, she wanted to see some clear progress. Control and confidence couldn't come fast enough for her. She was getting quite tired of waiting for them to make an appearance.

"It will. I promise. Have a little patience."

The words did little to reassure her, yet she clung to them anyhow. They were all she had to bolster her spirits and they were little enough.

"We are done for today." Finn offered her a hand, one she readily accepted, grateful for his assistance. Together they left the debris and destruction behind for her ice servants to deal with and adjourned to the dining hall to take some much-needed refreshment.

****

"We need a break," Finn announced a few evenings later. It was toward the end of another brutal training session which had been less productive than either of them had hoped and they were both exhausted. Since her "breakthrough" the week before, they had been working harder than ever and with greater will.

"A break?" She repeated the words as if they were in some foreign tongue she could not understand.

"Yes, Lyssa, a break. A respite from our efforts. A temporary release from care," he clarified. "We've been training every day for weeks. We need to relax. Tomorrow you'll show me around this castle of yours instead."

"I will?"

Finn smiled his most charming smile. "Yes, you will."

The abrupt realization that she was utterly incapable of resisting him when his lips curved in just that way was more than a little disturbing. Still, she agreed to do as he asked.

Next morning she found herself going over each chamber with him, arm tucked securely in his as she pointed out the unique features of individual rooms. His comments regarding various aspects of the construction of her stronghold were both complimentary and erudite. Not only well educated but highly intelligent, he appreciated the aesthetics of her personal citadel, as well as the structural achievement. In all, he was, she discovered, quite pleasant company and if she felt awkward and lacking in social grace after being so long alone, his own relaxed manner soon put her at ease.

As noon approached, she took him back to the entrance hall, thinking to show him the glorious light, which at that time of day bathed the room in a riot of color of every conceivable hue.

"It's like being inside of a rainbow," he said as, head tilted back, he took it in. "It's gorgeous."

For a long while he stood, admiring. "The ice acts as a prism, of course. I saw it that first day, but it was mid-morning and there was not so much of it. Now the entire chamber is filled with light and color."

She smiled. "It's near noon, the best time of day to see this room. The sun shines directly on my ice and creates this, as you see. The light travels down the south side until the sun sets. At dawn the same phenomenon occurs in reverse on the north side. Perhaps you might wish to return here at those times?"

"I would." He peered around once more then turned to her. "What you've built here is magnificent."

To have his eyes, which picked up every detail, see her work and appreciate, even admire it, meant a great deal to her. Quite conscious of the blush which rose and painted her cheeks, she dropped her gaze for a moment, but then she nodded and they walked on.

As they started down a short passageway leading to another massive room, Finn craned his neck to see the roof far above, then turned to Lyssa. "When I arrived here one of the first things I noted was that this place is vast. So much space for one tiny woman."

"Hmm, I suppose. Before I came here, I isolated

myself for a long time. The spaces that were safe for me got smaller and smaller. When I left my old life behind and built this place, I wanted light and air and the clean crisp cold of my power all about me."

"That seems a natural reaction. I myself often sought solitude. The freedom of it, just to be, with no restrictions and no fear was essential to me. There were many times I know I would have gone mad if I had not been able get away alone."

"I have often felt much the same. Strange, I don't feel much need for solitude when you are with me."

"Nor do I. Perhaps it's because for the first time, we can interact with another person without fear. Or maybe it's because we understand each other. It might be as simple as that."

Lyssa contemplated this for a moment. "Perhaps. We have only known each other for a short time, yet I feel we might come to understand each other one day." She grinned.

He bowed. "Your vote of confidence is overwhelming, my lady."

"Yes, well, come. There's more to see."

****

The remainder of the day flew by. Before Lyssa realized it, evening was falling and it was time to dine. They lingered over the meal talking of everything and nothing. They spoke of their lives before, of their experiences. It was surprisingly easy to find shared interests and fascinating to explore both common ground and unique perspectives. For the first time, they began to build a relationship based on more than mutual attraction, fate and a shared purpose. It was on that day they became friends. Or at least so it seemed to Lyssa.

In the evening, walking to her chamber once again on his arm, it did not surprise her when he expressed the feeling which had also taken hold of her.

"Thank you for a very pleasant day," he murmured.

"Believe me, the pleasure was mine. I've been alone so long that such exceptional company is a rare treat. It is I who should be thanking you."

He smiled. "Well, why don't we just say that the pleasure was mutual?"

She smiled, nodded. Such a sentiment had her wholehearted agreement.

At her door, he took her hand, bowed over it. "Good night, Lyssa."

"Shall we begin training at the usual time?"

"Yes. As lovely as this interlude has been, we should get back to work on the morrow. I'm sure we'll be all the better for having taken this bit of time for ourselves."

"Although I admit I was skeptical at first, now I tend to agree. You were right, we needed a break."

His expression remained quite solemn even though his lips twitched almost imperceptibly and his eyes danced. "I think you'll come to find I'm right about a great many things." Her hand was still warm in his and he gave it a gentle squeeze then let go. "Yes, well, I'll see you in the morning. Good night."

"Good night, Finn."

It was not until the door closed behind him and she was alone again that she realized an excellent opportunity for a kiss had gone by. Yet neither of them had taken advantage of it. Curiously unperturbed, she smiled and prepared for bed.

****

"I want to try something different," Finn announced as soon as she entered the training room some days later.

"Oh." She tried to hide her surprise and apprehension behind a neutral countenance, but had serious doubts about the effectiveness of her mask. While it was true her training had reached a plateau and her progress over the past week had been minimal, she was not certain how comfortable she was with a change in their routine. Still, he had been right before and she trusted him. Or at least she was starting to.

"Very well. What did you have in mind?"

"You've said on numerous occasions you are afraid that when under stress, when you're around people again, you'll lose control over your power and hurt someone. So let's test that theory."

"What? Finn, I'm not sure I'm ready to—" Her voice died away. He was suddenly there, invading her space. When he grasped her upper arm, his touch just this side of pain, the action shocked her to her core. Lyssa had to swallow several times before she could speak past the lump in her throat. "What are you doing?"

"Putting you under a bit of stress. You've got to stop trying to rein in your strength. Let your power run free again. Let yourself go."

"Finn, no."

"You can't hold it back all the time and you shouldn't. Damn it, Lyssa, that's how people get hurt."

His words had the exact opposite effect from what he'd intended. Instead of bolstering her courage, she remembered and feared her own power. She shook her head and tried to jerk her arm from his hold. "Finn, let me go."

"Not yet. Show me first."

"Show you what? You've seen my power before."

"But not your full power. Show me. All of it, as much as you like, as much as you have. You can't hurt me; you know that. You are safe here. Let your power do what it wants. Better still, do what *you* want."

Goaded beyond reason and tempted beyond bearing, wrapped in fear and anger and an unfamiliar excitement, she did as he asked. Her ice burst from her hands to the floor, creating a small frozen wall about a foot high which encircled them both.

"Good. That's a start anyway," he murmured. "But there are other ways. It's all right to touch me. It's what you want. I know it is."

Unable to resist his lure, she let sheer temptation rule her and stepped one inch closer. Close enough to touch.

****

Taking her movement toward him for the positive sign it unmistakably was, Finn leaned in until mere inches separated them. He pressed his lips to hers, and sensed an almost conversant jolt heightened by the more intimate contact until it was almost electric. His sharp intake of breath and her gasp were simultaneous and he pulled back. For several heartbeats they both stood still, eyes locked, absorbing the shock.

Then the desire for more rose up in him, sharp and clear, blocking out everything else until all he could see was her. He captured her lips once more then skimmed the tip of his tongue over their seam, begging entry. When she shivered then opened, a fierce sense of triumph filled him. Slowly be damned. Reveling in it, in her, he buried himself inside her mouth, surprised at its warmth. His tongue glided over hers, stroked evocatively, and tempted her to play.

As she responded, he moaned; he couldn't help it. The sound was muted, trapped inside her mouth, but audible. He began a rhythm of thrust and retreat and when she matched him, he moaned again, far more freely this time. Unfortunately, the sound startled Lyssa, and she shied away from him.

She broke the kiss and when she tensed in his hold, he let go, even though it was like twisting off a limb.

****

Her wits still reeling, Lyssa forced herself to focus on Finn's safety rather than on his wicked mouth or his glib tongue, which had caressed hers with such skill. She managed to corral her wayward faculties into some semblance of order though it took effort. That done, she looked him over for any sign of injury. "Oh, gods, what did I do? Did I hurt you? Are you all right?"

"I'm far better than all right. Don't stop." With that, he tugged her back to him and pressed his lips to hers for another incendiary kiss.

For the first time in so long she felt warmth bordering on heat. For an instant she was in free fall and when she landed it was on the surface of the sun. For a moment more, she indulged herself and him, so when his hands slid down her arms then grasped her hips, the heat which rolled all through her in waves seared her every nerve ending. The ensuing shock brought her back to reality. With power born of witch and woman, she disengaged from his embrace and knocked him back a full step.

"Fool!" She spat the word, almost literally, such

was her fury. "Do you have any idea how risky that was?"

"Yes. I don't give a damn."

The desire lighting his eyes was blinding and as he closed the distance between them again, his intent was unmistakable. Lyssa held up a hand then stumbled back a pace. "No, stay there. This is far too dangerous. In fact, this whole training idea was a terrible one after all. You should go." When he just gazed at her calmly, she added with far more vehemence, "Leave!"

"Lyssa—"

She shook her head. "Go. Just leave me alone." Then, without another word, she turned and fled.

****

What had she done? She had told him to go, that's what she'd done. It was what was best for him, for them both. But how would she live now?

Since his arrival her time had been so full. Days which had been empty for so long that she'd learned to prefer it that way, were now bursting. At least, she had preferred it until he'd come barging into her life to fill a void she hadn't even known existed.

Now the truth hit her full in the face. You can't turn back time, no matter how you might want to. As a consequence, her future, such as it was, looked bleak. Well, either way, the thing was done and despite the pain, she would not take it back even if she could. Matters between them were getting far too perilous, so it was better for him to leave now while no harm had been done, except to her heart.

Unable to deny that simple truth, she got no rest that night.

****

He gave her three days, days which were, for him, the worst kind of torture. He longed to bang on her chamber door and insist she stop being a stubborn idiot but whenever the impulse all but overwhelmed him, he reminded himself she acted not simply from mere pique or contrariness, but from a well-founded deep-seated fear. If he had only seen anger in her face after he kissed her, he could never have let her go, but terror was there as well. Not of him, but *for* him as well as herself. So he steered clear of her and gave her as much space as possible for three days and three nights. Other than slipping out to the kitchen to forage for his meals, he kept to his chamber. In spite of her orders, he stayed.

Leaving her to own devices indefinitely, however, was out of the question. So on the fourth morning, he joined her for breakfast.

Upon seeing him, she said nothing for a long moment. After a time, however, she sat down with him at table. "I told you to go. Why are you still here?"

He quirked a brow at her. "Not good at taking orders, as I'm sure you've discerned. Also, I wanted to give you time to process that, as you see, I am unharmed."

She sniffed. "That doesn't mean you will always be so lucky."

"Luck has nothing to do with it."

Ignoring that arrogant comment, she barreled on. "We agreed we would take things slowly. Then you..." Suddenly she ran out of words.

"Then I kissed you," he finished. "I. Kissed. You." he repeated the words more slowly, with pauses for emphasis. "Passionately. It was an impulse. One I don't regret. One I won't apologize for since you kissed me

39

back."

"Your rash impulses will get you killed. I won't be responsible for harming you."

He simply sighed. How long would it take for her to understand, to believe? "You won't harm me. You can't. Nor can I harm you. I think the last weeks have established that."

"In the realm of casual touching perhaps, but forgive me, Finn, I may be an innocent, but casual touching is absolutely not what we are discussing here."

"I am acutely aware of that, believe me." He shot her one heated glance then turned his attention back to his meal. "I swear to you, it is not possible for you to harm me. Let me prove it to you."

Though she was quite sure she shouldn't, she asked, "How?"

Finn set down his fork, scraped back his chair and rose. "Let me kiss you again. Let me show you no harm will come to either of us." As he had when they first met, he held out a hand to her. With infinite patience, he waited to see which path she would choose.

She wanted him to kiss her again; he could see it in her face. Since she couldn't deny it, he laid his lips on hers and she let him. The kiss was sweet and gentle this time. Somehow he found a way to imbue that simple meeting of mouths with all the promise of everything they could have together. It was a kiss explicitly designed to soothe, to tempt, to seduce then leave her yearning.

When their lips parted, he held her at arm's length to make sure that she didn't bolt as much as to see her face. "There now. No harm done, only pleasure." More than satisfied for the moment, he released her.

She *humphed* then sat down to eat.
Not another word was said about his going.

Chapter Three

As a storm poured down, half rain, half sleet, and very nasty, the kingdom of Ravenstone's council members gathered in the chamber, which had been theirs for generations. In the normal course of things, the king sat at the head of the room on a less-opulent version of his throne, with his prime advisor beside him. All the others sat in the low-backed chairs with curved sides placed in rows facing the king. Made up of thirty men and women, they met to discuss the most recent crisis in a land constantly plagued with them.

Lord Thomas Marbury was the first to arrive. He was young for the post, just twenty-six, but the king himself was only twenty-seven. The two friends were most unalike in looks and even somewhat so in temperament, but were as close as brothers for all that. Thomas's appearance was as light as Finn's was dark, his blond hair and fair skin standing out in a country where dark hair and medium complexion were the norm. He and the king were of a height, however, both a little over six feet tall. His eyes were a soft gray and well set in a very attractive face. His mouth was large and mobile with lips that could be soft and sensual one minute and thin and stern the next, depending on his mood. Right now, they were pressed into a grim line.

While he waited for the others to settle themselves, he thought back to a month ago to when the current crisis had begun.

After a preemptory knock, Thomas had entered the king's chambers as was his habit. He'd been sent for which was unusual and he had wondered what was afoot as well as what mood he might find his sovereign in. Of late, the king's mood had been foul for many and varied reasons; as his closest friend, Thomas ought to know. The fire glowed warm and bright in the chamber where he found Finn brooding into his wine. The king gestured for him to sit.

"The council feels it time. When they meet again, I am sure the matter will be put to a vote," Thomas informed his king.

Finn scoffed. "Obviously."

"So you agree?"

Finn considered as he poured the other man a glass of wine, refilled his own then nodded. "Yes. I had hoped for just a little more time. Time to try to locate then contact the snow queen rather than just paying her an expected visit but...yes, it seems I've run out of that precious commodity. I'll leave on the morrow without informing the council. No one must know that I am not only dealing with the curse, but that I might just come back with a bride who might possibly restore the balance. Once I am gone will be soon enough to give them the details. I will do this on my own terms."

Thomas stifled a sigh and said nothing. Finn would do this on his own terms and that was as it should be, but Thomas wished that he was not being left behind to deal with the council.

"Damn this curse," Finn muttered as he downed the last of his drink.

"There is no shame in this, brother. It happens to us

all as you well know. You have withstood the curse for far longer than most."

"Considering the strength of my power, the curse should have hit me harder and in some ways it did, but in others it did not. I had hoped the worst of it would pass me by altogether. I had hoped to be an exception."

Thomas snorted into his wine. "Of course you did. Get over it," he advised.

In spite of the gravity of the situation, Finn grinned.

"Sure you don't want me to come with you?"

Finn shook his head. "No, I need you here. I've spoken to my mother. I've named her as regent, of course, but her health is not what it once was. She will require your assistance. Look after my interests as best you can. Make sure I have a kingdom to come back to."

"As you command, majesty."

Setting aside his empty glass, Thomas had bowed and gone. The next day so had Finn.

For the past several weeks he and the Queen Mother Rowena had between them concealed the king's absence. But finally, it was time the council was told and the fact was made known.

There were few on the council he could count on to stand with him. One was Lady Joan Langston, distant cousin and ward of the queen mother, who had been at the king's side with him for almost as long as he could remember. As such, she was one of the few he could rely on. He was all the more grateful for her unfailing support since he would need all he could get once the council heard what he had to tell them.

As soon as all the members arrived, Thomas announced, "The king is gone."

"Gone? What do you mean, gone?" Senator Payne demanded in a curt tone.

"He left in order to deal with the curse as the council expected and indeed informally requested. As prime advisor, it falls to me to inform the council of this. I must also inform you that he means to find a more permanent solution and restore the balance for us all." In a few brief words, Thomas explained what Finn intended to do. Joan's gaze never left his face while he did although she said nothing.

"But—" Payne spluttered.

Mendelson managed to find his voice with little difficulty. "Yet he left without the council's express permission, without even telling us himself."

"No, he did not wait for your decree. He believed it would be best to seek the snow queen without delay." A sound like the buzzing of angry bees filled the room. Thomas wanted to sigh. "I fail to see the problem. You wanted him gone, as tradition dictates. Well, now he is."

After a stunned silence, Joan said, "That he had the temerity to do so with a modicum of his dignity intact when the council surely would have had it otherwise speaks volumes. What man, if he is fit to rule, would do otherwise?"

"Be that as it may, Finn has embarked on a fruitless quest. The snow queen will have nothing for him but death."

The man who spoke now was Lord Simon Fairfax and Thomas had never liked him. Always impeccably dressed, he never ever lost his temper. It made Thomas want to smash his face in just to get a reaction. He was very fit in his middle age, not yet past his prime at forty-five. Sandy brown hair, just beginning to be touched with silver, was pulled back at the nape of the neck and tied with a blue ribbon. His build was slim but muscled.

Years before, he had been the prime advisor to the former king, Finn's father, Seth. When Finn, who didn't much like Simon either, made Thomas his main advisor, Simon had not been pleased. From that time on, the man, who was still on the council, blocked everything the king attempted on principle.

As for Simon's feelings toward Thomas, Thomas knew beyond doubt that Simon hated him and everything he stood for even though the older man never did or said anything overt. He didn't need to. The sense of menace Thomas felt whenever he was near the man was enough.

As he spoke, Simon made his view on the present issue more than plain and it was shared by many of the other council members, if the murmurs of affirmation which reached Thomas's ears were anything to go by.

It was Mendelson who expressed the general consensus. "Let us pray it will not be so." His tone made it clear he did not hold out much hope.

Payne looked grave and ended with, "Amen."

"Until such time as he returns, he has named his mother, Rowena Hale, as regent." Thomas had a document to that effect and he handed it round for all to see.

Most glanced at the king's signature, made a quick perusal of the contents, then passed it to the next person. Some few did make a more careful study, however, Simon included. Once each member had seen it and it was back in his possession, Thomas placed it on a small table nearby. "Does anyone have any objections to Rowena Hale as regent?" Thomas held his breath. It was not unusual for a regent not to attend the council until approved, but if word of the severity of the queen mother's illness reached the ears of the council then some might wish her not to be named. As yet it was believed by most, even Simon, that it was a temporary indisposition only.

When no objections were made, Thomas breathed a sigh of relief, nodded his approval then stood. "Excellent. I suggest we continue as usual, bring any questions or problems to the new regent and reconvene in one month."

****

"How did the council take it?"

"As well as can be expected, majesty."

"Well, one could hardly imagine they would be pleased, what with the king gone and a frail queen mother such as myself left as regent." Rowena made a soft tutting sound. "It simply won't do."

It was afternoon and Thomas was in the new regent's chambers, giving her the news. The woman in the bed was frail, but still had that spark of life. Over the years, Rowena's auburn hair had become threaded with silver and it was now in a long braid down her back. Her green eyes, always her loveliest feature, were too large now in her thin face. A tiny woman to begin with, her recent illness left her shrunken, down to brittle bones. In deference to her state, she wore a clean linen chemise and a silk dressing gown which swallowed her. In spite of all of this, her mind was still as sharp as ever, thank the gods.

Thomas groaned, paced then groaned again. "What

right do they have to be displeased? It was their decision after all. His majesty left on his own terms and with a goal in mind, rather than to aimlessly wander as so many did before him, waiting for the curse to loosen its hold so he can return."

"On his own terms. Precisely. That is something the council won't forgive."

Knowing the utter truth of her statement, and what it could mean to them all, made Thomas's belly churn. "Damn it, Rowena, I need your help here."

"Don't worry, boy. My body may be disintegrating, but my mind is altogether intact. I'll do all I can."

"I know you will, but will all we can do be enough? Simon has always been dangerous but now, with Finn gone? I'm not sure any of us has the strength to stand against him."

"Keep talking like that and we most assuredly won't."

"Well, I don't intend to give up without a fight, that I can promise you. Your son charged us with maintaining the welfare and protection of the realm. That is exactly what we are going to do."

"That's the spirit." She grinned and patted his hand.

****

Alone in his chambers, Simon could no longer contain his elation. At last it had happened. Finn Hale, king of Ravenstone, was gone. At least for a time, his royal highness would not be underfoot, making a nuisance of himself. Time enough for him to put all of his carefully laid plans into action. Thomas would, of course, put up a fuss, but he would be easily dealt with, as would the dowager queen. Usually formidable, her recent illness was a gift from the gods meant expressly for him. She was expected to recover any day, but for the moment she was frail, far too frail to gainsay him. He must put all of this good fortune to use without delay. All was in place, had been for ages; it only waited on his word. That being so, he took the initial steps.

His first act was to write to his most ardent supporter, Queen Adriane Wentworth of Minden. Adriane and her people had long detested the Hale dynasty as it was the only one to challenge Minden's supremacy. The troops and goods Minden would bring to an alliance were essential to Ravenstone. Ravenstone's fertile lands would in turn benefit Adriane and her people. A mutually profitable relationship would form. One Simon would turn to his advantage at the first opportunity.

That needn't be a concern now, of course. Other steps must be taken one by one first, including but not limited to putting Minden's troops in play as soon as possible. With this in mind, he constructed a communiqué meant for the queen.

My Queen Adriane,

At last the time approaches. Hold your people in readiness, and as you love me, have them here within a fortnight after you receive this missive. I look forward to putting our careful plans into action. I long for all to come to fruition, just as I long to look upon your face at last.

Your most obedient servant,
Simon

He labored over the wording for some time before

settling on its current form. Even so, he perused the sheet one last time before sealing it. Calling a trusted messenger, he handed the man the letter. "Deliver this to the hand of Queen Adriane and no one else. On pain of death."

"As you command, my lord."

The messenger bowed and departed, leaving Simon alone to put the rest of his plans in motion.

****

"Who shall call this meeting to order in the absence of our regent?" Simon demanded.

"The queen mother has given me leave to call this meeting of the council to order and act as her proxy."

The month which had passed since last the council had met had not seen Rowena's health improve. With no other choice, Thomas agreed to act in her stead. He could only hope the council would accept this state of affairs rather than throw him out on his ear.

"Unacceptable. Already we are ruled by a regent. It is imperative she be present," Simon insisted.

"I assure you, she would be here if she could. Her illness prevents her—"

"If her illness prevents her then clearly—"

"Clearly, this meeting must be postponed until her health returns," Thomas interrupted.

"I hear her illness is serious and any postponement would have to be indefinite. I'm afraid the business of the country will not wait so long," Payne stated.

"That it will not," Simon agreed. "Let us adjourn for a week. It is our hope the queen mother's health will improve within this allotted time. If not, other options will need to be considered."

Unable to refute this very sensible argument and

with little choice in the matter, Thomas acquiesced. *Round one to you, Simon,* he conceded with a strange mix of bitterness and admiration.

****

Thomas pounded his fist on the door to Rowena's rooms. "I must see her," Thomas began without preamble when the maid appeared at the entrance.

The girl looked harried, if her red sweaty face and the few stray curls which escaped from under her cap were any indication. "I'm sorry, my lord, but the dowager is far too ill to see anyone."

"It is vital to the safety of the realm. I must see her." He started to jostle her aside, but to his surprise, the girl was strong and she managed to keep him on the other side of the door.

"Meg, isn't it? I'm sure you are doing your duty as you see it, but I swear if you do not get out of the way in the next five seconds, I will move you myself. My request is not a capricious or fickle one and you had best heed it."

Something in his face must have convinced the girl of his sincerity. She cast him a baleful glance but said, "Very well. Wait here and I will see if her majesty will receive you."

A weak querulous voice questioned the plump little maid and Thomas caught the brisk tone of the girl's answer, but not the words. Another voice, male this time, joined in and a short argument ensued. Moments later, however, the maid reappeared and gestured him forward. As usual, the dowager had won. That made Thomas smile.

He entered and the change in her shocked him. A month ago she had been fading, but since then she had suffered a severe decline. She had lost two stone or more, weight she could ill afford to lose, and her complexion was deathly pale. Her hair, while clean, was lank. The room also held the stench of sweat, vomit and blood common to most sick rooms. Dismayed, he came forward, his steps slow and halting.

Her eyes were closed but she said, "Well, say what you've come for, boy. It was obviously important enough."

Somewhat reassured by her matter-of-fact tone, he stepped closer. "It's over," he began without preamble.

"What's over, Thomas? You'll have to be a bit more specific. I'm a frail old woman who's dealing with quite a lot just now."

"Simon insisted we postpone the council meeting until next week. Unless you can manage to attend, he is going to make a motion to remove you as regent and put himself in your place. If this vote occurs, the motion will carry in his favor."

Weariness settled over her, face as well as body, all but smothering her. Her already damaged form shrank even more, collapsed in on itself under the weight. "This disease-ridden body of mine will not allow that. In another month or two perhaps, the physicians tell me, but a week? No. I'm so sorry, Thomas. I've let you and my only son down. What's worse, I've let the kingdom down. How long will it be safe in that fanatic's hands?" She let her heavy head fall into her hands and muttered, "Gods, I am sorry."

"That is not true, majesty. Without you and your intervention, we never would have lasted as long as we have."

"Thank you, you are very kind." She patted his

hand. "Be that as it may, what do we do now? You and I have done all in our power to block such a vote. Now you say we cannot prevent it and the outcome is all but certain. I'm fresh out of ideas."

Thomas narrowed his eyes, considering. "We can still try to block the vote although I don't hold out much hope. I suggest we focus on minimizing the damage."

"How?"

"By protecting the king's supporters and getting them out if necessary."

"That," she decided, "is an excellent notion."

Getting into the spirit of the thing despite her weakened condition, Rowena added, "We could set up provisions for a government in exile. Gather then supply loyal troops so that when my son returns he can retake the castle."

"Just so."

"Very well. I'll work on that. You try your best to either stop the vote or at least postpone it. Failing that, insure it goes in our favor."

Thomas nodded then rose. "I will do my utmost. You focus on regaining your health."

"For the good of the realm?" she asked, half-joking.

Thomas shook his head. "For mine. I can't afford to lose my greatest ally. Still less can I afford to lose the woman who has been like a mother to me."

"I'll do my best, dear boy."

He kissed her pale cheek and took his leave, ready to face the challenge before him.

****

"My fellow council members, forgive the

impertinence, but I would be remiss in my duty if I did not ask the question. How long will we allow this to go on? Our country is in a state little better than anarchy and it is time we take action." Simon demanded this of the room at large.

One week later and it had finally come to this. The council chamber was again full and there was nothing more Thomas could do to block a vote; Simon had made sure of that. Yet still, the younger man tried.

"A gross exaggeration," Thomas began.

"Is it? I think not. Unrest abounds at our northern border. There is rioting in Lees, a port city of great importance, and general discontent throughout the kingdom. Discontent which stems directly from the lack of strong leadership."

"Rumors. The kingdom is as content as it has ever been, as content as I have ever seen it. The king will soon return and these vicious lies will be disproved," Thomas insisted.

It was clear to Simon that even in the face of Thomas's best efforts, the man was losing.

"We cannot afford to wait forever. The problem is here and now and must be handled without delay."

Before Thomas could respond, another council member jumped in. "What do you suggest?" Payne directed the question to Simon in particular.

Simon could barely contain the triumph coursing through his veins at the words. His elation was overwhelming. How long had he waited to hear that question? Years. He took just one moment to savor the fact that the wait was over then rose to address the room at large.

"The time for change has come. I will, with the

council's full and free consent, be its instrument."

"In acting as that instrument, what do you intend? Be specific."

"Make me regent and I will restore order."

A disturbed murmur rose up. "But the queen mother is regent, as has always been the case in such circumstances," Thomas insisted.

"As we are all aware, the queen mother is unwell and unable to be present at this gathering. It is clear she cannot fulfill her duties as regent at this time. Let me take up this burden."

"What exactly do you have in mind?"

Again, Simon experienced that thrill, but he remained calm. "I have contacts which I can call on. As I said, I intend to restore order. That is all you need to know at present." He locked gazes with each man and woman in turn. "Do I have your consent to act as I see fit?"

"I move that we make Simon interim regent with all the rights and powers thereto." Payne held up a hand. "Who will second the motion?"

"I second it."

"All those in favor?" Hands were raised and more than half of the council voted in the affirmative.

"All those opposed?"

Again, hands lifted, far less this time, but Simon took note of each one. Some of his opponents were already known to him, chief among these was, of course, Thomas. Others surprised him. There were some few who were hesitant to, in essence, hand over the kingdom to him, but the majority were ready and willing to follow wherever he might lead.

"Motion carried," Payne announced.

Keeping his face cool and expressionless had never been more of a challenge. The light of success glowed within him and he wanted, gods, he wanted to let it shine. Yet his control, always superb, held. On rock-steady legs, he rose. Taking a careful breath, he searched each face. "I humbly thank the council for its support. I trust you will never have cause to regret it. My first act as regent shall be to adjourn this session. We will reconvene at eight o'clock tomorrow morning."

As the meeting broke up, Thomas approached Simon as he gathered the last of his things. "It isn't over, you know. I won't give up. You may be regent, but this kingdom belongs to his majesty, never to you."

"Really? In name perhaps, but in fact...well that is another matter."

Quick as thought, Thomas had his hand on the hilt of his sword. Seeing this, Simon went still. Then his hand gripped the hilt of his own steel. "Try it. Please. Give me a reason."

Thomas loosened his weapon in his scabbard, but then Joan, who had been monitoring the tenor of the conversation from a cautious distance for some moments, stepped in. She placed a hand on Thomas's shoulder. "Now is not the time," she murmured in his ear.

"Very well." He took his hand from the hilt of his sword, met her gaze. "I trust you and your judgment."

When Thomas spoke again, his words were for Simon alone. "The time will come. Count on it."

Simon acknowledged this with a nod to Thomas's retreating back. "I look forward to it."

Chapter Four

Although it seemed like an age to Simon since he had sent for her, not a mere month, at last Adriane Wentworth entered his kingdom, her arrival perfectly timed. A well-sprung luxurious carriage with the ornate design of her family coat of arms etched in gold on the side rolled into the drive. Simon waited with growing impatience as the contraption rocked to a stop and her footmen helped her to alight.

When she stood before him at last, he bowed low over her royal highness's hand, considering her as she curtseyed. "Queen Adriane, I am honored to make your acquaintance at last."

She acknowledged this pleasantry with a small smile, but said little beyond the basic civilities. Intrigued, he sped the proprieties along and as soon as possible, he escorted her to a reception room where they might speak without interruption or an audience or indeed any fear of being overheard.

While she took a quick turn about the room, he took the opportunity to study her at length. Like all of her people, she was tall and willowy. Her hair was the color of rich brown caramel and her eyes were of the same shade. Her skin was the color of good porcelain and he would venture to guess it would be as soft to the touch as rose petals. Her bearing, her delicate features, everything about her suggested a feral grace covered with a thin veneer of elegance. The combination fascinated him.

To intensify the impression of the foreign and the fascinating, the gown she wore was a different style from the usual cotehardie which was the current fashion and what most Ravenstone women wore. Instead, she was dressed in a surcoat of dark red damask over white silk, which laced up both sides. Her unruly locks were not confined in a snood, but pulled back by a head band with sheer white silk attached to its back to cascade over her hair. The slippers on her feet were the same sort he'd seen a thousand times before, only far fancier with tiny rubies decorating the flap of the shoe.

Having looked his fill, he broke the silence. "It is a great honor to meet you face to face at last, majesty."

As she turned back toward him, she gave him her full attention. "A sentiment I share. Yet I am also curious. Why am I here? Or to be more precise, why now?"

"You are here now because the moment has come."

In a few brief words, he described the current situation and his plans to use it to his advantage, with her help.

"You said as much in your note. You know in all these years, I've never asked you why. Why commit such treason?"

"Like most of us, I don't remember a time before the chaos." In his mind's eye he could see that time, could feel the turmoil and it was more real to him than the present. "Long before I was born, it all went to hell. After the plague, it took years to bring order back, but we did. That's the world I grew up in, a world struggling to return to civilization and succeeding a little more every day. Now it's all slipping away again. I want that orderly world, the one of my childhood, back. It is unfortunate, but things can never be precisely as they were. I know that better than most. Balance is not a thing bestowed on us by magic. It is a thing of the past unless we make it for ourselves. I will go to great lengths to achieve this goal. I believe I am the only one who can accomplish it."

"Perhaps you are right. It certainly looks that way with Finn gone." She smiled, all predatory charm. "That being true, my warriors await."

He raised a brow. "Do they?"

Adriane inclined her head. "I can call them with a word. You did say discretion was imperative."

"So I did." He turned to pour wine for both of them from a decanter on the table top. "My lady, may I say your intellect is surpassed only by your beauty. I am fortunate to have so valuable an associate, and more, I am pleased to find a true partner at last."

Gracious as ever, Adriane inclined her head. "It is I who am fortunate. You are as influential as you said and you are also far more attractive than I dreamed."

He lifted an eyebrow. "I am…gratified by the compliment." He grimaced. "How did you picture me?"

She tilted her head, studied him. "I envisioned someone older, bordering on distinguished. Instead I find a handsome powerful man in his prime. Would you like to go to bed with me?"

Simon blinked, looked over her svelte form from head to foot and then let just a fraction of his desire show. It was as unexpected as it was welcome. "Are you always so blunt, not to mention so eager?"

"I am. In truth, most men find such plain speaking

a refreshing change, at least in my experience."

Simon scoffed. "Adriane, there is nothing plain about you." He set down his empty glass then took hers from her hand. "I would very much like to go to bed with you."

She smiled, cat-like, then offered him her hand. Already hot and hard, he accepted.

****

The sun shone brighter than any diamond when Simon called the council together again the following morning.

Once the opening formalities were complete, he began with new business as was the custom. "Fellow council members, I wish to introduce a new ally to you, the queen of Minden, Adriane Wentworth."

"And what is a stranger from a foreign land doing in the midst of this governing body as if she were one of us?" Thomas demanded.

"She wishes to form an alliance with us. She believes as I do that we are far stronger together than we are apart," Simon asserted.

"Are we? What can she offer us, and most important, what does she want in return?"

"We need fresh troops to defend our borders and quell the growing unrest throughout our land. I believe all of you are more than aware of this. Minden can offer a solution."

Before Thomas could express any objection, everyone began to speak at once and he was not heard in the resulting hubbub.

"How many troops are we talking about?" an older councilwoman asked in a voice which carried over the noise.

"Five battalions, one in each direction of the compass and one housed here in the palace."

"This is the most secure stronghold in the world. Why would we need a battalion of foreign troops to defend it?" Thomas pointed out.

"The unrest on our borders in every direction makes it necessary. Ever since the plague, ever since the balance was lost, this world has been on a knife's edge between chaos and order. If, gods forbid, such turmoil ever engulfs the very palace itself, we must be prepared."

"This unrest you speak of has been wildly exaggerated," Thomas countered hotly. "Even if it had not been, I have no doubt our own troops would be better suited to this task."

Another councilman piped up. "All of our current troops are already being utilized. We could conscript more, but the number of able-bodied young men of military age is still low. The plague killed so many," he finished, his air mournful.

Simon spoke with the natural authority developed over years of being second in command to the most powerful ruler in the world. "I will not allow this country to return to what it was after the plague. I will give my life if need be to prevent that. Right now, I can best serve this country by providing it with troops. Adriane has, gracious queen that she is, agreed to aid in this."

"Again I must ask, what does she want in return?"

Simon opened his mouth to respond to Thomas's question, but Adriane stopped him with one small gesture. "I think I can answer that best. Ravenstone is as well known for its unique culture and its rich farmland as for its instability. I can provide the troops needed to restore the land to its former strength. That is what my kingdom can provide. As for what we wish in return, we would require access to the food produced. What good are troops if you cannot feed them? What good is an abundance of food if it is left to rot or worse, taken from you?"

"You want us to feed your troops?"

"Not just our troops, but our people. Minden is a far less fertile land and with the drought last year, we are struggling. The simple fact of the matter is we require more food while you require more troops. I see no reason why we cannot negotiate a mutually beneficial relationship."

No one had an answer and Simon discerned then that the tide was turning his way. For a moment, he did not speak, worried he might upset the delicate balance. At length, he stated, "I suggest we put the matter to vote."

"I beg of you, do not do this. Not so very long ago Minden was a sworn enemy of our nation." Thomas was reduced to abject pleading much to Simon's abject delight.

"All those in favor of an alliance with Minden?" Hands went up and far more than half of the council was in favor. Since his entreaties fell on deaf ears, Thomas said no more.

"All those in favor of remaining as we are?" Again, hands rose.

"Motion carried," Payne announced.

Victory, admitted Simon, could really give a person a charge. One he could get very used to. "Very good. On to new business. The trade routes to…"

****

Finn practiced alone. Unwilling to advertise her presence and still less to disturb him, Lyssa watched in awe as he executed a complicated fencing maneuver. The very audible gasp she couldn't stop had him whirling toward the sound, however.

When he spun in her direction, the look on his face all but took her breath away. Strength, determination and a passionate intensity came off him in waves. For a moment, all she could do was appreciate him. Then her mind clicked back on and she realized her eagerness must be clear for him to see. She schooled her expression to what she hoped was polite interest, or at most professional admiration, cleared her throat and began. "That was excellent. You are more than good with a sword."

"Thank you."

He lowered then sheathed the blade and strode to the end of the table where a pitcher sat with several goblets alongside. He filled one to the brim with water then drank it down without pausing for breath.

"I didn't see you use your fire, though."

"No. A man ought to have more than one weapon at his disposal, yes?"

Lyssa inclined her head in response. When it became clear this was all the answer she was likely to get from him, she decided to pursue the matter further. "Perhaps it's time we focused on you, on your training."

"Not today."

"Whyever not? We can't always focus on me."

"For now, we can. Besides, I've trained my entire life. You on the other hand have not."

"So? That doesn't mean we should allow you to get out of practice." She grinned then shrugged. "Besides, I want to see what you can do. No holding back."

With a little shake of his head, he unbuckled his sword belt and strode to the center of the room. When she made to follow him, he lifted a hand and gestured for her to stay where she was.

"You said no holding back. If you truly mean that then stand well clear."

She held her hands up in surrender, tipped her head in acquiescence and slid a few feet away.

They faced each other across the spacious room. His gaze, at first fixed on her, soon turned inward and unfocused. Even from a distance she could see his pupils shimmer then go burnt orange in color, something she had not been aware of during earlier training sessions. Finn held out both hands, palms up, raised them to shoulder level. There was a sudden whooshing noise and flame burst to life in his palms, forming a swirling column twenty feet high and five feet wide by Lyssa's guess. Since the roof was perhaps thirty feet above them she was not unduly concerned. He lifted his hands and the fire rose with them, straight up until it almost touched her ceiling of ice. It grew in size and whirled like a cyclone in the wind she now recognized as part and parcel of his power.

What was more appealing after all than an attractive powerful man? Which was more fascinating, his flame, or the sight of him conjuring it? Lyssa could not decide, nor in truth did she want to. For long moments she did no more than observe, captivated by both. The entire chamber filled with light and warmth and still, she stared in awe. It was only when she perceived her ice beginning to melt that her senses returned.

"Finn, you must stop now."

No response, not one word or sound, nor even the flicker of an eyelash.

"Finn, stop!" Panic shot through her now. Unable to reach him, she did the one thing she could think of; she sent an ice storm upward to counteract his fire, even though she had no hope of extinguishing it. This was of course only a stopgap, a purely temporary measure, and so she tried again. "Finn, please."

The sound of her entreaty snapped Finn back to reality. His eyes, though still opaque, cleared somewhat, sense returned to them and he hastened to reassure her. "It's all right. I'm fine now."

He did not quench his flame all at once, but by degrees. When it was done, she could see the sheen of perspiration on his forehead, whether from the heat or the exertion she could not be sure. The silence stretched to the point of awkward until she ventured, "That was most impressive. Are you sure you are all right?"

He nodded as he sat down on a rough bench against the far wall. "Using that much of my power after so long was quite a rush."

"So I see." Clear as day, she thought. He trembled all over. Sweat still glistened on his skin and his breath came in deep pants; all visible signs of his recent efforts. "You're not in pain?"

His color rose a little, but he laughed. "Gods no, just the opposite in fact. I feel better than I have in a very long time. I'd forgotten it's almost as good as—" He stopped speaking abruptly and cleared his throat. "Never mind."

"No, tell me."

He pursed his lips in the way she knew he did when he was trying to make a decision. "Come now, you can tell me," she insisted. "Whatever it is you're thinking it can't possibly be so wicked that you can't tell me."

"It's almost as good as lying with a woman."

"Oh, well." Lyssa could think of nothing to say to that. All she could do was stand there as heat crept into her own face. "Yes, ahem."

He looked about, as if searching for a way to change the subject, and she suddenly understood he was almost as uncomfortable with the topic as she.

He cleared his throat and continued, "As you can see when I use that much, I am not in complete control."

"You seemed quite in control to me."

"So I was, until it came time to stop. That's always been the way of it for me."

"But you did stop."

He continued as if he hadn't heard her. "Eighteen was a very difficult time for me. Twice I almost caused permanent damage. It is only by the grace of the gods that what happened then was temporary."

"What exactly happened? If you don't want to talk about it I understand…but perhaps if you shared your past with all its hopes and fears, it might help."

He did not speak for a long time, but in the end conceded she might be right, that it was a least worth a try. "I was in love with a beautiful girl named Celestine. Things reached a certain point. I took her to bed and almost killed her. We both lost our virginity, but it nearly cost her life. She was scarred, not badly but even that little was enough. I couldn't take the chance of ever hurting her or any other woman again, so I told her our understanding was at an end. All this made me even more determined to control my power. Such things come with age and practice and time, but I was stubborn. As a result I almost burned down the castle a few months later."

"I see."

"Do you? It was two years before I attempted to use my powers again at all. And I've never touched another woman. Not even Celestine," he stated, tone flat. "She waited even after I told her it was over, but then she fell madly in love with another much less dangerous man. A few years after our estrangement, she married him and I let her go with a full heart. She's quite happy with a kind husband and three beautiful children. But you see even now, I have difficulty with control." He took a deep breath. "If you hadn't been here, who knows what might have happened. You, your very presence, did steady me. I didn't even have to touch you."

"Almost carries no weight. The fact is you did stop. It seems to me you could use a bit more practice though."

Her tone was light, almost teasing and he answered in the same vein. "Quite. Not today, though. Today, I could use a drink. Do you have any rum about?"

****

They went in quest of rum and after some searching, she found one crate in a room she used for storage. When leaving her home, she had taken certain basic supplies. Other things, including the rum, were given to her by men who wished to gain her favor.

Since she'd never had a fondness for the drink, it was still there.

"Are you quite certain you want to drink that? I'm not sure the liquor is still good after so long and it was never all that tasty to begin with in my opinion." She gave the bottle a dubious glance.

"Oh, liquor like this will keep for half a century. Have a drink with me." He poured them both a generous glass.

"Oh no, my head might explode."

He chuckled. "It won't if you drink only one glass."

She took the glass he handed her, drained it in one then coughed violently as fire shot down her throat, into her esophagus, ending in her stomach. "God's teeth, that is truly awful stuff." Laughing, she held up her goblet for another.

Finn raised his eyebrows, but tipped more of the so-called awful stuff into her glass. He then took a healthy swallow of his own drink.

"Can I ask you a question?"

"Of course. Ask away."

She took a deep breath and her courage in her hands then asked the question she had longed to since the moment they met. "You said we could stop whenever I want, but what do you want?" She figured from the look of him he was just drunk enough to give her an honest answer.

"What do I want? I want you. More with every breath I take. Every time I touch you, it gets harder to stop. Well, this should come as no surprise to you, since as I said, any man who doesn't wish to bed you is a man I'd like to meet. Given our recent interaction, my opinion on this has not altered. But I will continue to defer to your wishes in this matter. If your own change, you need only tell me. I've made mine more than clear."

"So if I want you then…"

"I am yours to command. Any time you like, in any way you want, for as long as you wish."

The mere thought made her tremble. At last she managed to murmur, "That's…lovely to know."

For just one moment, she lost herself in his eyes, in all the promises, then she tore herself away. "I'm not quite sure yet what I wish."

"Decide soon, I beseech you, my lady. Until then…" He took her hand, kissed her knuckles then left her.

****

She had let fear rule her for far too long. No more, she decided. If she wanted Finn Hale, then why not tell him so? She also was tired of being alone and by all the gods she did not mean to be so tonight. Since their conversation over that glass or two of rum, she had been considering the situation quite seriously. Coming to a decision had, in the end, been easy. She was finding acting on that decision much harder. Perhaps the wine she drank would give her some form of bravery. Liquid courage, wasn't that the expression? Lyssa giggled over this as she proceeded down the hall to Finn's chamber.

Stumbling a bit, she reached his door then pounded on it without hesitation. "Open up, Finn, darling," she called.

There was a brief pause then the sound of footsteps nearing. An instant later the door opened half-way with a creak and Finn peered out. "Are you all right?"

She smiled rather blearily at him. "'Course I am."

"No you aren't. You are drunk," he stated, his tone flat.

Lyssa grasped he wasn't sure whether to be amused or disapproving. Either way mattered little to her. She pushed a bit on the door and he stepped back just as she hoped. Path cleared, she weaved her way into the room. "I had a drink or two," she conceded. "I'm not a child. I'm allowed. I don't want to be alone tonight either. So here I am," she finished cheerily as she half-perched, half-flung herself onto the bed.

"Lyssa, this really isn't wise."

"Whyever not?"

"I think you know."

He offered her his hand. "Come, you need to sleep this off. Let me help you back to your chambers."

"I don't want to go back to my chambers." She sulked. "I told you, I want to be with you tonight." Reasoning that surprise was her one clear advantage, she grabbed hold of his hand, and instead of rising, pulled.

Off balance, he managed, just, to keep from landing fully atop her. As it was, he caught himself with his left hand. He looked down at her, shook his head. "You, beautiful, are in no shape to—"

Just as she hoped, the rest of what he had been about to say was forgotten when she put her hand to his cheek. "I am ready to embrace my fate at last."

For just a moment he closed his eyes, pressed his hand over the one framing his face. But then his jaw firmed and he spoke through gritted teeth. "No, what you are is completely soused. You are in no shape to make any major decisions. Not tonight."

"You said...I thought..." Lyssa's voice faded. She was far too embarrassed to say what she had thought. Her face flamed and she could no longer meet his gaze. Her only goal was to get away, to be alone with her humiliation, but when she tried to shove him aside, he held her fast.

"You thought I wanted you? I do, more than anything. But Lyssa, it is obvious you have had more than a little wine and I would not want there to be any regret come morning."

"There wouldn't be," she protested, surprised by the very idea.

His finger at her lips kept her from saying any more. "Perhaps not, but presently your wits are a bit clouded. When I take you I want every moment to be crystal clear. Every kiss. Every touch. Every caress."

Her eyes widened and her mouth formed a little oh of realization. She swallowed hard against a parched throat, then said, "Those are good reasons I suppose. Still..."

Tentatively, she placed a hand in the center of his bare chest. "Are you quite certain you don't want to just...?"

The muscles in his throat worked as he too swallowed heavily. "Believe me, I would love nothing better than to 'just' but here and now is not quite the proper time. You should go to your chamber. Alone," he emphasized when her face lit up. "Go."

She formed her lips into a pout which she hoped would be irresistible, but he stood his ground.

"Go," he ordered. With a put-upon, slightly drunken sigh and a soft smile, she left.

Chapter Five

On the west side of the large bedchamber, doors opened straight out onto a terrace. But at that hour, light streamed in from the large uncurtained windows on the east side of the room. That as well as a head pounding fit to burst woke her. Amidst vows of never over-indulging again, Lyssa dragged herself out of the massive four poster bed. Aside from the floor and walls being made of ice, there was a lovely chair set before the window with a small occasional table beside it. On the north wall, water poured from an icy spout in the wall itself. A basin of ice grew out of the floor to catch then drain the liquid. She had spelled it so the water would gradually melt and thus fresh water was always available.

After drinking about a gallon of water then cleaning her teeth, she struggled out of her crushed gown then into a fresher one. Once her tangled hair was brushed, she deemed herself as presentable as she would get and she made her way down to breakfast.

Not that she could eat. Her stomach rebelled when the smells she normally found delicious wafted through the doorway of the dining hall.

When she entered, Finn made no mention of her less-than-stellar state. Instead he handed her a glass of some vile-looking concoction. "Drink this," he ordered.

Lyssa accepted the cup filled with some

unidentifiable green liquid, sniffed, and gagged. "Oh, that smells as awful as it looks."

"Hold your nose and drink it," he advised. "You'll feel much better if you do."

With reluctance uppermost, but desperate enough to try anything, Lyssa did as he bid her. She pulled a face, pinched her nostrils together then took a long swallow. The brew tasted tart, but it was warm and as soon as it hit her battered stomach, she felt much improved.

"Better?"

"Much. Thank you."

"Good. I'd like to talk about last night, if you feel up to it."

Lyssa focused on a piece of buttered toast, the one food she might be able to keep down. "I'd rather not discuss last night if you don't mind."

Rather than argue with her about it, Finn stated, "I won't hold back from you anymore. Not as I have been. I doubt I could after last night. Still we should take things step-by-step."

Her attention was well and truly caught at the mention of steps, which logic suggested would bring her closer to him, so she raised her eyebrows in question. When Finn did not elaborate but instead shoveled in more ham, she asked, "What's involved? How many steps are there?"

"There are not so very many but there are some few between kissing and going to bed together."

She giggled a bit at that. "Going to bed. It sounds as though we'll sleep when even I know that's the last thing we'll be doing."

"I'll be happy to educate you. In detail."

The heated look in his eyes curled her toes. She wanted to be brazen and demand he commence her education right away. Since she wasn't exactly at her best, however, she concluded such a statement would have to wait. She contented herself with giving him a heated look of her own then attending to her meager breakfast.

"Oh, and Lyssa, if I have my way, we won't sleep until dawn once I do share your bed."

The intensity and the passion of his words, not to mention his tone, was unmistakable and she thought it wise to leave the subject there, at least for the present.

****

"What are you doing?" Despite her best efforts to steady it, Lyssa's voice trembled as she asked the question. The inquiry was a purely rhetorical one, as she knew quite well he was kissing his way down her neck. Since the interlude in his bedchamber a week ago, he had kissed her again, more than once and had made free to touch her far more often, though in a casual way. This, on the other hand, was something quite different.

"I said I would not hold back from you anymore, not as I have been. I meant that."

"But what does that mean precisely? How far do you intend to go?"

He must have perceived the slight trace of panic in her voice, for he stopped and looked her dead in the eye. "Only as far as you and fate will allow me."

"But what if—"

"Lyssa, there are a thousand 'what ifs' in this world. Stop to consider them all and a person would never even get out of bed in the morning. Although, in my present frame of mind, I am not inclined to consider that such a bad thing."

"What if something goes terribly wrong?" Her voice was barely above a whisper.

"I believe it won't, but if I hurt you even a bit, tell me and I'll stop."

"And if I hurt *you* even a bit, tell *me* and I'll stop." When he hesitated, she continued, "It must work both ways. Swear it."

"I swear it." The simple statement, made with utter assurance, left her close to speechless.

"How can you be so confident?"

"Because there is no other choice for me. No other viable option exists. Not just because of our powers, in fact, that's the least of it. But because even if I could have anyone, the only woman I will ever want now is you."

She let him lead her to the settee but before he could kiss her again, she confessed, "I-I'm still nervous. I have never done any of this before. I've only ever been kissed."

"I know. Shh." He soothed her then whispered into her ear. "There's a time to rein it all in and a time to let go. Just let go, Lyssa."

She allowed him to kiss her and to touch her as he would, as he willed. When he encouraged her to do the same, she did.

She divested him of his shirt and was pleased when he reveled in her touch for long moments. Marveling at his warmth, she sent her hands exploring, coasting over his beautiful sculpted chest. When her fingers skated over his flat nipple and he gasped, she wondered if he would enjoy her mouth on him there. When she suited thought to action, he drew in a sharp breath and arched to meet her lips. Thrilled, triumphant she did it again. An instant later, she found their positions reversed, with her flat on her back, sinking into the soft cushions.

She opened her mouth to ask what was wrong then she saw the look on his face. It was so fervent, his touch so ardent, that all her questions died away. The naked longing in him met and matched her own and it was almost more than she could bear. To know she was the recipient of all this emotion left her shaken to her core.

His hand journeyed up her leg from ankle to thigh, lingered there. Capturing her gaze, he asked her consent without saying a word.

"Don't stop," she whispered.

In response, his warm palm traveled over her inner thighs and she parted them. At last, he touched her at the apex where all her nerve endings centered. Everything inside of her went hot and liquid and she moaned. Deliberately, he entered her with one long finger, slid in then slowly out.

"Sweet gods," was as much as she could manage.

Never taking his eyes off her face he added a second digit to join the other. With a moan of his own, he pressed his palm to her center. The utter pleasure of that sent her reeling and still he gave her more. Stroking and caressing with such skill, she soon hovered near the edge of some sensual precipice. Rather than question, she raced headlong toward it and was rewarded when he let her fly. Waves of pure glorious sensation suffused every inch of her and she shuddered with unfettered delight.

As the shock waves subsided and her wits gradually returned, she became aware of the tension still filling Finn's body. The release she experienced had not been shared she realized. So a burning question formed in her mind. One she had to voice. "What about you?"

Eyes shut against temptation, he swallowed audibly but shook his head. "Truly, I am most grateful for the offer, but I am focused on you tonight, on your pleasure. My turn will come later."

"Soon?"

He chuckled though the sound was more than a little strained. "Yes, soon if the gods are good. Now, rest another moment then it's to bed for you. Alone."

****

Leaving her each night was becoming a form of torture, still he did. Despite this, his days were more fulfilling than any he'd ever known.

She'd been less talkative than usual that evening and he wondered what might be simmering in that beautiful mind of hers. He waited for her to tell him, but when their meal was concluded she had not. As she pushed back her chair and rose, he assumed he would have to possess his soul in patience and wait a bit longer.

At the door she hesitated. Quite familiar with her by now, he could see she was gathering her courage. She did not leave him in suspense for long after all.

"Finn, when you said I had only to make my wishes known, did you mean it?"

His whole world slowed then skittered to a halt. "Absolutely." It took considerable effort for him to get the word out, but she didn't seem to mind.

Her voice trembled when she murmured, "Stay with me tonight then." When he said nothing, she added, "I meant what I said the night I drank too much.

Now more than ever, I am ready to embrace my fate, to embrace you. Will you stay?"

Her words left him trembling. "Tonight and for as long as you wish." He held out his hand to her, she placed hers in his and she led him to her bed.

Everything had to happen slowly, excruciatingly slowly, for a myriad of reasons, Finn constantly reminded himself. First, their powers, second, fate's influence, third her virginity. He kept listing these in his head like a mantra. Step-by-step was something else he kept repeating. None of it helped. All he wanted was to follow his body's dictates and bury himself inside her and it was getting harder and harder to deny himself. Yet he would, for her. To make this night as perfect as possible for them both he would hang on to his control for just a bit longer.

He was desperate to let her feel his love for her, wanted her to experience it with every shred of her being. So he did all he could to bring that about. With every stroke of his body, with every instant lost in her clear blue eyes, he let her know without a doubt that he was hers and vice-versa, thanks be to all the gods.

This possessiveness, this part of the man he was deep down, was put on flagrant display for her alone. It was time, long past time, to drop all of his shields and let her see the man he was: wild, passionate and untamed. Yet above all he was fully and freely hers.

****

He would make love to her at last. Lyssa could hardly believe it was actually going to happen, yet here she was, hand in his, as they headed to her chambers. This dream-like state persisted even as they made their way to her door then stepped inside.

His touch was slow and steady as he kissed her. He began to undress her with confident yet worshipful hands. When this was half accomplished, strong fingers clasped her aching breasts, kneaded and when his fingers found her nipples and played with them, her spinning head fell back. Somehow the rest of her clothes were gone and she was in her bed, yet still she felt no fear or even anything close to an attack of maidenly modesty.

He seemed to know her every thought, her every desire and his unerring instincts told him when she was ready for the next embrace, the next caress. When his hand skimmed between her legs, she opened them without hesitation. The first climax took her like a storm and went on and on, yet he didn't join her. Had he claimed he lacked control? By all the gods, not from her vantage point, she thought as her own shuddered and broke.

Deep within her pleasure-soaked mind, she wondered why, when her longing for him was clear, he would deny her this final step, as he had called it. Then she understood. He loved her and his love was a tangible force. One that grew stronger with every moment until at last he was poised at her entrance. Everything stilled and the whole world seemed to pause for breath. Then, with one inexorable stroke, he entered her.

For a time, he did no more than hold her, his face buried in her hair. Soon enough, however, he lifted his head to trap her gaze with his. So he was cognizant of the precise instant the pain faded. A heartbeat later, he withdrew from her only to return home in one slow controlled thrust.

"Finn," she murmured. Then she arched up to meet him.

As her feelings for him swamped her, his feelings for her surrounded her. She couldn't fail to note it, couldn't fail to see. Not when every thrust of him, hot and hard inside her, made her aware of him to her very bones. He was her most willing servant and yet he was her master too. Perhaps this was what it was like to be utterly in love with a strong man. This give and take was, perchance, a natural consequence. If so, she could learn to revel in it. He was naked before her in every sense of the word, surrendering, yielding every iota of himself. To see him so emotionally vulnerable was a shock, a sight which shook her very soul. Not least because she understood the price of his surrender was hers.

She paid it gladly, because whether he knew it or not, the force prompting his every action this night was love. It was clear in his beautiful eyes and reverent touch. With all of his heart, he freely offered her his very self. With such feelings so eloquently expressed, so beautifully, pleasurably, actively displayed, who needed words? Not she, at least not tonight. Not when she was safe and free and above all desired.

When he was so deep inside of her heart, her mind and her body that all she could see or hear or feel or know was him, he gave her the words as well. "My love, be my wife."

Every part of her responded to his entreaty. "Yes, oh yes."

****

Her words released something in him, something held in check since the moment he had come into his power. He took her hand in his, kissed it gently then placed it near her head on the pillow. Holding tight, fingers laced with hers, he at last let himself go. The feeling of her soft skin against his, her warm flesh enclosing him, made him wild, until all he wanted was her. He rode her and she was with him every step of the way.

When he could hold back no longer, it was she who gave him that last thrust over the edge into ecstasy. Inner muscles caressed him, inside and out and he came. The hot inevitable rush of his climax was increased a thousand fold when hers began a heartbeat later. They reached the peak, the pinnacle of sensation, simultaneously with their hearts, minds, and bodies in utter sync.

****

When his wits fell back into place and he could speak again, he managed, "Are you all right?"

She took stock. Since she was currently lying in his arms, head on his chest, relaxed in every limb and happier than she'd ever been in her life she supposed that yes, she was all right. "More than. This was beyond all of my expectations."

"Worth waiting for?"

"Hmm. Yes, but now that I know what sharing your bed is like, I'm sorry we waited so long. I mean we could have been doing this for weeks."

"True, but neither of us was ready."

She conceded the point with a small nod. "I suppose we needed time to be sure we wouldn't hurt each other with our powers and that we actually meshed, that this wasn't something driven solely by fate."

"Mmmm hmmm."

The sound was low, almost a purr, like that of a very large, very satisfied cat, and hearing it, she smiled. In truth, she couldn't help but feel very contented herself. It was obvious their shared intimacy had been as rewarding for him as it had been for her. Considering his history, his skill in this arena and his particular personal attributes, this was quite gratifying.

For her, the experience had been eye opening in so many ways. The sheer relief of knowing she could at last function like any other being in this sphere was tremendous. Added to it, she had always supposed, when she contemplated such matters at all, that sharing a bed with a man must, for a woman, be more often a duty than a pleasure. She was delighted to find the exact opposite to be the case. In fact, she began to wonder how soon they might repeat the experience.

"Lyssa, I can hear you thinking," he murmured. "What is it?"

"Oh, it's nothing."

"Nothing." He tilted up her chin, searched her eyes a moment, then shook his head. "I don't think so. What is it? Surely there isn't anything we can't say to each other now."

Heat rose in her cheeks and she stared at the curve of his neck rather than meet his eyes any longer. "I only wondered how soon...if you might wish to...again," she finished a trifle lamely.

He did not hesitate, but replied, "I do wish to. As to how soon, that would depend."

Heart fluttering like mad in her chest, she got the words out, barely. "Depend on what?"

"On how sore you are. On how much I want you."

"I'm not sore at all," she assured him. When he narrowed his eyes at her, she admitted, "Not very."

Accepting her second answer as a bit closer to the truth, he kissed her hand and kept hold of it. "In that case…"

An instant later he reversed their positions. She wasn't quite sure how, but she wasn't complaining. He touched gently between her parted legs and checked to see if she was ready for him. Apparently she was; she certainly felt so. With great care, he removed his fingers then increment by infinitesimal increment, he entered her willing body, setting a gradual but inexorable pace as inevitable as the tide. Unable to wait a moment longer, she arched and drew him in that last glorious inch. He hauled in a huge shuddering breath, and she savored the heat of him inside her, utterly surrounding her, for just a fraction of an instant, then he withdrew.

She half-expected the same pain as the first time, but there was none. There was only the same voluptuous pleasure which spun out to encompass her body and soul.

****

Once they started, they couldn't seem to stop indulging themselves and that was just fine with Finn. Hours turned into days. Days turned into weeks, most of them spent in her bed. They still trained, but they did the bare minimum now, too wrapped up in each other to care for much else.

Perhaps it was partially due to the fact that he had never touched or been touched, not in all of his adult life. That he could touch her without fear of hurting her and vice-versa was a constant miracle to him, one he embraced with alacrity. For the first time he felt free and uninhibited. He never wanted it to end.

Experience had taught him long ago that the one constant in life was change and so he made the best of this stolen season while he could. He treasured each moment, every memory he already had of her, of them together, and every new one they would make. As the weeks passed, he became certain that, while he might not be able to hold on to this brief perfect interlude forever, he could and would hold on to her.

****

Even with their decreased practice schedule, they still improved. Each day they gained more control over their powers until they became like two fine-tuned instruments working in tandem, in perfect harmony.

During one session they went through a possible attack scenario, full of wraiths spelled to threaten them, something they had done many times before but with countless variations. They fought back to back as they so often did, her blasts of ice going one way, his of fire the other. When the last wraith they had conjured attacked her from the right, she blasted it with ice right through the heart. It was dead in seconds and disappeared in a puff of smoke.

Finn counterattacked another with fire and it met its demise in the same manner. They both stood at the ready, looking about for any further threat. When there wasn't one, they took in the damage. Aside from one small scorch mark and one frozen goblet, the training area was altogether intact. It was only when they realized that that the truth began to sink in. They had beaten their own attack scenario.

"Finn," Lyssa said, surprised at how calm her voice

sounded, "I think we've done it. We have complete expertise." Triumph raced through her and could not be contained. She hugged Finn hard, giggled then released him.

"We've yet to go up against any true opponent and that is no small thing," he temporized. "But otherwise...we have," Finn conceded. "We both have full control of our powers. All that can be done has been done. We are both ready at last."

"So, now what?" She hated even to voice the question, feared the answer, but it had to be asked.

"Now, we celebrate."

"And after that?"

"After that, who cares?"

She was inclined to agree.

He took her mouth in a hot passionate kiss then carried her across and out of the training area into the entrance hall, up the stairs and to his chamber. Once there, he began to make love to her in the plush velvet chair near the hearth in front of the fire he conjured. The chair seemed specifically designed for the purpose. The feel of the velvet against her body, especially when compared with the sensation of Finn's naked skin brushing over her own was a novel one, tantalizing, fresh and downright glorious. His skin was just as soft but warmer and the combination left her exquisitely sensitized anywhere and everywhere they touched.

They took each other with exuberance and a joy of spirit rarely experienced before. Lyssa reveled in all of it, in her new confidence and proficiency, in her power and most of all, in him. For one unforgettable shining moment her existence was a vision come to life, a dream made flesh and it was glorious.

****

For the first time since Lyssa initially used her power, spring came in her domain. Weak, slow and reluctant though it was, it arrived. When the weather began to turn, somehow their thoughts turned with it, back to the wider world. She recognized he would have to return home. When he asked, she would have to let him go. But until then, she vowed, she would not think of it. She would focus on him, on the moment.

Yet the knowledge of it was there within them both. She could sense it in the unmitigated passion of his lovemaking which was now edged with just a touch of desperation. Each hour which passed was a treasure to her, in spite of or perhaps because it would end, one way or another. So she indulged herself to the hilt, took and gave as much pleasure as she could hold to fight back the dark.

Yet nothing lasts forever, and one cool spring evening, he told her what she already knew.

"I want to stay with you. We both know I can't. It doesn't stop the wanting."

The words were a dark soft murmur from above her. She didn't respond with words of her own. Instead, she took him into her arms, let him into her body. And she tried not to dwell on all that could take him from her.

****

Later that night, in between waking and sleep, she reached for him and found he was no longer beside her. For one terrible instant, she feared he was gone but then a gentle breeze flowed through the room and she turned to see the terrace doors ajar. His feet were planted firmly on the flagstones and he leaned on the banister to watch the sunrise. She rose, donned a silk robe then joined him.

Before she could speak, he did. "I have to go back to my country, to my people, and soon." Turning to face her, he continued, "Just because we are lovers that fact hasn't changed."

She backed away, hurt, but before she could even process it, before she could even feel it, he continued.

"What I said before also still holds. You are my one true love. In my heart we are already married. You are my wife in all but name. Come with me. Rule at my side."

He took her breath away. She had never expected him to desire such a thing, much less to ask for it, yet he was asking now. When she could speak again, she tried to find the right words but could only manage a few all but incoherent ones. "Finn, I…"

He took her hand, kissed it. "Don't answer now. Just think on it."

He said nothing more as they enjoyed the sunrise together.

Chapter Six

With each day more perilous than the last, Thomas could not stand the constant and perpetually rising tension. His every waking moment was spent trying to counter each move Simon made with little success. For weeks it had been so, and unable to cope with the steadily ratcheting pressure, he had to be alone. At last in his own chambers, he felt a touch safer.

He sensed her before he saw her. Joan. Familiar with her every move, her every gesture, he didn't need to actually see her to know she was there. She was as close to him as family. As such, she was one of the few who would dare to invade his privacy by showing up unannounced. This was probably because she knew she could do so with impunity.

He studied the girl a moment as she sat, quite at home. Possessed of hair rich and golden brown as honey, many said it was her one beauty, though he tended to think of it as her most obvious, not her only attribute. That glorious hair of hers, which had it belonged to another woman would have been dressed in the latest style, was almost always braided for practicality's sake. She was fond of remarking when asked, that it got in her way otherwise. Her face was an attractive heart shape while her eyes were as green as the forest she loved.

Raised alongside Finn and Thomas, she had

insisted on sharing all of their pursuits and thanks to an indulgent foster father and mother, she had. This gave her a well-muscled athleticism most females lacked. Her body was slender and coltish, all long limbs and spirited energy. She wore a simple kirtle with its less obtrusive sleeves and its front lacing rather than the more formal cotehardie gown with its long row of buttons down the front. Her life was so active; she would have it no other way. More in touch with her physicality than the majority of women, she was anything but the fragile ethereal ideal of womanhood.

"What news?" she demanded from her place on his settee.

"I might ask you the same question." When she raised her eyebrows and said nothing, he added, "It's you who's waiting for me."

"I've nothing to report; nothing good anyway. Adriane's men have made themselves quite at home. There are rumors that Simon will be placing some of them amongst the palace guards soon."

"Perfect," he muttered. "Nothing good to report indeed." He poured them both a cold beaker of ale and joined her. "Things grow more dangerous by the hour. Have a care."

"I can look after myself." She took a long sip of her drink then waited.

"Even so, have a care," he repeated. "For my sake. I won't have your death on my conscience, especially since it is totally unnecessary for you to risk yourself."

"It's unnecessary for me to risk myself? Well, now I'm insulted. I am no weak female, despite what you think. I've just as much love for this country and my king as you and have just as much right to guard both.

I've been trained to do precisely that just as you have been. When I became a shield maiden of Ravenstone, I swore to protect and defend this land with my very life. That is what I intend to do." She set down her mug on a side table with an ill-tempered little snap and made to rise.

He stopped her with a hand on her arm. "I know how loyal and how noble you are and I'm much obliged to you. I never meant to sound ungrateful, particularly not to you, the one person I can trust in this world gone mad. I am sorry. I don't know what I would have done without you these last weeks."

Somewhat mollified, she replied, "I am glad to be of service. Truly, I would do anything to help you. All you need do is ask."

The offer, perhaps the most sincere he'd ever had, was one he cherished. He had her to rely on even as the rest of creation fell apart, thank the gods. "I know and I'm grateful, from the bottom of my heart."

For a moment, his gaze held hers, and he lost himself in the lovely green of her eyes. Then she looked down and the ephemeral spell was broken. He shook his head to clear it, bowed and showed her out.

****

Ravenstone Castle
April 1st

Sire,

I regret to inform you that the situation here has become untenable. Simon was far better prepared than we ever suspected. As soon as you departed, he put plans into action. He has taken your mother's place as regent and this is only his first step, I believe. I did all I could, but without your royal authority, my hands are tied. Your presence here is desperately needed. Return as soon as may be or I fear you will have no kingdom to come back to.

I will remain for as long as possible, but if and when I feel I have no other option but to leave, you can find me in Brighton Forest.

You left your kingdom in my hands, to protect and serve in your absence. To my shame, I have failed you in this. I hope someday you can find it in your heart to forgive me. Until then, I remain

Your most devoted servant,
Lord Thomas Marbury

The messenger arrived against all odds. Like everyone else in Ravenstone, he knew where the snow queen was now purported to be and he traveled there without delay. After many false starts and no little searching, luck was with him at last and he picked up his king's trail. From that point it was just a matter of following it through miles of hostile territory then crossing the frozen wasteland. No trouble at all.

"I'm to wait for your answer." The poor man gasped as he collapsed on a nearby bench in the snow queen's entrance hall.

Finn scanned the missive then scrawled his reply.

Thomas,

I will return with all speed. Rest assured I will take back what is mine. There is no failure. In fact your loyalty will be rewarded. Have a care for yourself until then.

Finn

"Wait." Finn stayed long enough to spit out that one curt word then he clattered upstairs.

"Lyssa," he began without preamble. "I need you

to provide a messenger with safe passage."

Startled, she looked up from a book she was reading. "Safe passage? For a messenger? For what purpose?"

"I've received a communication from Thomas. I wish to send his messenger with my answer. Also, I…have to go back as soon as possible."

"Very well."

Her voice was cold and distant, but he had no time to worry about that. His entire focus was on getting the messenger on his way as soon as possible.

He took the stairs down two at a time. "I've spoken with the snow queen and your way should be far easier this time. Go north until you come upon the Dimsis River, then southeast. Deliver this to Lord Thomas Marbury's hand and no one else's, by order of your king, on pain of death. If you do not find him at the castle, he will be somewhere in Brighton Forest. You will find him and deliver it to him there."

The messenger blinked but he had been given stranger directives before. The man bowed low. "Yes, sire," he murmured and without further comment, he was gone.

****

"What precisely is the current situation in Ravenstone?" Lyssa posed the question over a hasty supper a half hour later.

"According to Thomas's message it is very grave. When I came to seek you I left a kingdom on the brink of turmoil, but now…the storm has broken and unrest has engulfed it. I named my mother as regent, but she has been deposed by a political opponent of mine, a man called Simon. Because she is ill and because he is far more powerful than I suspected, he has been able to set himself up as regent in my mother's stead." Black fury roiled through him at the mere thought.

"And you intend to rid your kingdom of him, I take it?"

"Oh yes."

Her brow furrowed, a sure sign of worry, so he sought to reassure her. "I'm not without allies, you know. I am the rightful king after all. Thomas is working tirelessly on my behalf even as we speak. He will do all he can to gather my supporters. The queen, my mother, may be unwell, but I assure you her mind is quite unaffected. She will do all she can. My people are also well aware I only did what other rulers before me have done."

"Which was?"

"I have walked the earth to diminish the curse which comes along with my power. I've done better than that even. I'm bringing back a bride and not just any bride, one who will restore the balance."

"But what if we're wrong? What if we, if I, can't restore the balance? How will your people react then?"

He was silent a moment as he considered how much to tell her. Deciding full truth was best, he began, "I have thought of it, planned for it, but as a contingency only, and an unlikely one. I believe in who we are and what we're doing. It's fate. I've felt it just as you have. The gods, or the fates, or destiny itself, call it what you will, is behind us. I place my faith in them, but even more in you and myself. Either way, I will not let Simon's treason stand. I will take back my kingdom and all shall be as it was."

"When you say it, I believe it."

"Good. That will comfort me when I return home and am apart from you."

"Apart from me? Why?"

"You are to stay here."

"What do you mean, I'm to stay here? Just days ago you said you wanted me by your side. You all but begged me to accompany you and now you say I'm to stay here? I don't understand. What's changed?" Lyssa demanded.

"Everything. The entire situation has fundamentally altered. I won't be bringing my betrothed triumphantly home. I'll be entering hostile territory, territory which I will have to re-conquer."

"None of that matters to me. I won't leave you."

"And I won't lose you. I can't," Finn countered.

"You won't."

Oh how he wanted to believe her but… "You can't promise me that. Lyssa, you have no idea what my world is like. It is brutal, it is violent and it is merciless at the best of times. This is not the best of times and I don't want you anywhere near any of it."

Her lips tightened, her jaw hardened and her eyes narrowed in an obstinate expression he was growing to know far too well. "And what about what I want? I will not allow you to go into danger alone."

He narrowed his own eyes at her and his whole being turned cold as ice. "I could make certain you stay."

"Could you? I could make certain you never leave."

Stalemate, he supposed and for one mad instant he had the desire to sweep her away somewhere so he could bask in her, in her power, her confidence, her sensuality and the glorious challenge of her. But with an enormous effort of will, he managed to do no more than look at her. For a while, he was able to match her stare for stare.

"Lyssa, I am going, no matter the danger," he stated flatly.

For a long time she said nothing and he began to think she wouldn't answer at all. Then her soft voice floated to him on the evening air. "When you first asked me to come with you I was flabbergasted. I didn't know what to say. That does not mean I meant to refuse."

"I know, but I've told you, things have changed. If you come with me now the danger would be substantial. I would never have suggested it if I had known how drastically things had worsened."

Lyssa laughed then and it was a reckless, roguish, downright daring sound he'd never heard from her before. "Danger?" She shook her head, nonplussed. "You talk of danger when I am far more hazardous than anything else the world could ever conjure. What else have the past weeks been about if not that simple fact?"

"Lyssa, please—"

"Besides," she continued, rolling right over him, "you could use an ally, right?"

This was an undeniable truth. A war, entirely internal, brief but intense, took place within him. His desire to be with her, to have her beside him through everything, won out over his protective instincts. Little else would have been strong enough to counter-act the impulse to keep her safe.

"I'd urge you to reconsider." He studied her face with its implacable expression then sighed. "Since I know you won't, I'll no longer waste my breath. Pack your things. We'll leave at first light."

He was careful not to mention the smile, small but triumphant, which curved her lips.

****

Simon spent the next days consolidating his position and his nights with Adriane. When at last the time was right, the wait was over and once night fell he could begin. Arrests would be made. His opponents would be dispatched and by the end of the evening, his rule would be firmly established. It would begin with an emergency meeting of the council. All would be ordered to attend. Those who did not would be sought out and taken into custody. As regent of Ravenstone, Simon would make the most important arrests personally. Among them would be Councilman Balthazar, leader of the political opposition; he would come first. After that, the queen mother's ward, Lady Joan Langston, would be taken. As a longtime companion of both Thomas and the king, she could be used as leverage if necessary.

He would, of course, save the best for last, Thomas. The man had been a thorn in his side for years, as much if not more than the king himself had been. Soon that would all be over, he comforted himself. Throwing Lord Thomas Marbury into a cell and turning the key with his own hands would be very satisfactory. It would be almost as satisfactory as torturing him for his traitorous actions and his bone-deep loyalty to the king. His blood sang with the anticipation of pleasure long denied but now about to be tasted at last. It was all more exciting than he had ever dreamed. Considering he had dreamed of this moment for decades, that was saying something.

Adriane caught Simon's attention as she chose jewelry at her dressing table. "Are you ready?" he asked her.

She chuckled. "More than. You and I have prepared for this moment for years, so if we are not wholly ready by now, the fault is our own."

She rose, the epitome of lethal elegance. "All awaits your command. Come."

Reveling in the eagerness quivering in his belly, he offered her his arm and they headed to the council chamber.

****

The council chamber held about three-quarters of its members, as Simon predicted. As he entered, the discontented murmuring filling the room cut off and an abrupt silence fell.

Without preamble, he began, "Gentlemen, ladies, I called this emergency meeting tonight as a test of loyalty. Those of you here have passed. Loyalty is a quality I value above all things," he continued. "Another trait I value is strength in times of adversity. It is that loyalty and that strength I demand of you now. The king is dead."

Everyone in the room went deathly still; no movement, not one sound heard.

"The king is dead," he repeated. "I am regent, as you are all aware. Since the king has died without issue, I propose to rule in his majesty's stead for the foreseeable future."

Tension filled the air, crackled and transferred like some electric current from person to person, as the council members glanced at one another in shock and horror. One other reaction seemed to fill at least some members of the group: suspicion.

Yet only one man, Senator Neville, dared to ask the question they all wished to know the answer to. "Is he? Produce his majesty's body then and let us bury him."

"There is no body to bury. The snow queen he so eagerly sought killed him. There is nothing left of him save shards of ice."

"If this is so, in what way did you learn of his death?"

"I sent some of my own men to find him. They returned with this."

With what he considered an admirable balance between restraint and showmanship, he produced a signet ring belonging to their ruler. Adriane's eyes widened, all but bulged, and she gasped. She rose with great rapidity from her seat and all but sprinted to him. She clasped her hand about his and brought it and the ring closer, so she might examine it in all its fine detail. After a moment, she concluded it was what she first believed. His Majesty Finn Hale's signet ring was in Simon's hands.

No one spoke as the jewel passed from hand to hand so each might examine it. Every person present was well aware no king, least of all Finn, would voluntarily give up such a thing or lose it by some accident. Therefore, it was taken from him. Passed down from monarch to monarch for generations, each new royal to ascend the throne received this unique ring at his or her coronation. Once accepted, it was not removed until death. For decades it had been a great sign of the office. At least, this had been the case until now.

"It is true then. The king is gone."

Simon inclined his head in agreement. Someone gasped. Someone else sobbed, soft and low.

After one heartbeat of respectful silence, Simon stated, "The people are free to choose a new king. I humbly put myself forward."

"And if we refuse? If, as I believe, you yourself are implicated in the king's demise, why would we ever allow you on our sacred throne?" Senator Neville demanded.

"For that matter, how do we know the king is truly dead? I for one require more definitive proof than this that my sovereign is dead and gone," Senator de Courtney stated with a firm shake of his head.

In one smooth motion, Simon rose. "You doubt me? I swear upon my life, his majesty was killed by his own foolish arrogance. He assumed he could ensnare the snow queen; instead she destroyed him, like all the others who came before, just as I predicted. Did I not advise him against such an action? All of you were present when I gave him every rational reason to not do as he did. In his pride, he refused to listen and now he's left his kingdom without a leader."

"None of this means that you are the proper person to rule. Such things are ordained by the gods," de Courtney stated with a somewhat stuffy air.

"Have I not run this kingdom well in the last months? Have I not always been the most loyal subject of his majesty? No, I cannot offer you his body as proof. But I ask you, if he is dead then who will rule this country?"

The entire room was silent. No one could deny all Simon said was true. Nor could anyone deny that he was the most able and qualified to govern among them. At the side of King Finn and his father before him, he had been a close advisor for years. No one understood the inner workings of the kingdom better.

Yet it was just as clear that even some of his supporters wanted to balk at such decisive action. Choosing a new ruler right away made them nervous. It was obvious from the expressions on some of the faces that they had not considered he, Simon, would ever go so far as to put himself forward for the job. He wanted to slap a few of them silly for such stupidity and their almost criminal lack of foresight. What had they thought, he wondered? What had they supposed would happen once the queen mother was deposed as regent? Even now some looked shocked.

Fools, he dubbed them, but displayed nothing of his assessment on his face. It wouldn't do to show all of his cards at once. He would need his meek mask for only a few minutes longer then he could and would be anyone he wished, he promised himself. He was so close to victory he could taste it.

"As you are already regent, you are suggesting we let you continue to be so until a new ruler can be chosen and crowned? Seems reasonable to me." Payne began.

Simon laughed, but there was no humor in it and the other man's words died in his throat. "No, I suggest you name me as ruler. I am already king in fact if not name. All I am suggesting is that we make it official."

"You have no royal blood. There are several distant cousins of the king with far better claims," de Courtney protested.

"Are there? Where are they? Produce them." When no one spoke, he continued, "You cannot. These distant cousins are untrained and have no desire to take Finn's place. There is no one with more skill or more power in this kingdom than I at this point. This is something I beg all of you to accept."

"Accept?" de Courtney scoffed at the idea. "You are not king here. Not yet."

"Exactly. Not yet. Up until now, I have treated you all with the utmost courtesy and graciousness. This will end if you challenge me now."

"So you are saying we have no choice in this? That it is a *fait de accompli*?"

Simon shook his head. "You always have a choice. Those who sought to challenge me are even now being arrested. You can support me or throw your lot in with the rest. Imprisonment or even death awaits anyone who opposes me. Or you can join me in this new realm I will create."

Adriane, having gotten over her shock, was the first to offer her support. "Minden is your ally. This I swear."

One by one they pledged their fealty to Simon.

****

"I can't believe they all swore fealty to you. It's finally happened." Adriane beamed and her glee was clear, but she did not care. Soon, however, her smile faded a bit. "I can't believe the king is dead. Why didn't you tell me? This is definitely something I ought to have known before going in there. And why don't you look happier?"

"No it isn't, since he isn't."

"Who isn't what?" Adriane asked with an irritable twitch of her skirts.

"Finn isn't dead," Simon stated. With a movement

steady and sure, he closed the door to his private chamber to ensure they remained alone and uninterrupted.

"Not dead? Well then what the hell was that performance all about?" When he did not answer, but instead poured himself a drink, she continued with more vehemence. "What is this, Simon? What is going on?" She prided herself on being an excellent judge of character, so much so that it was rare for her to have no idea about a person's next move, but in this case she hadn't a clue. It was alarming to say the least.

"Well, I finally received this." With a flourish and a gleam in his eye, he produced a ring made of pure gold. It was set with a gorgeous burnished orange stone with a flame etched in the amber.

Adriane tore her gaze from the royal signet to look at Simon. "How did you get this if the king is not dead? What dark magic is this?" She found she shared his excitement. Her breath came faster and she trembled.

Simon smiled a little then stated, "I regret to inform you that the king still lives, at least so far as I know."

"Then how?" Adriane gestured at the ring.

He leaned close, whispered in her ear. "It's a fake."

Her mouth slackened and her eyes widened. "You are jesting. This ring, more than any other in the world, is unique. There is no other like it. It can't possibly be…"

Her voice trailed off as he shook his head and grinned.

"A fake." She narrowed her eyes. "Let me see."

He put the ring into her palm and Adriane turned it over in her hands, looking for any tell-tale sign or flaw.

Finding none, she handed it back to him. "It's very good. I could not tell the difference and I am no poor judge of such things. How did you get it?"

"I commissioned it some weeks ago. I got the best jewel maker in Ravenstone to fashion it."

"What if he talks? What if it is discovered he made it and committed this fraud, this…" she sputtered, unable, for once, to find the right words.

"This elegant bit of treason?" Simon supplied. "Trust me, he won't talk. Artisan Mark Bromwell met with a terrible accident the very day he completed this for me. Tragic."

Impressed, Adriane took in this bit of information. Lost in her thoughts for some moments, contemplating the many implications of this, she finally spoke in a far different tone. "You have already convinced the council, you even had me convinced, that he was gone. I take it you will use this trinket to convince the populace their king is dead then take the throne?"

Simon nodded, poured them both a celebratory glass of wine. "I already have the regency in my grasp. Soon enough the council will crown me. As you yourself observed, they have already recognized me as their sovereign, if unofficially."

"They did. How did you manage that?"

"Because, my dear, I'm just that good. They will offer the crown to me and after some hesitation, I will accept."

Adriane laughed in genuine delight. "You know, Simon, I think you're right. You might be just that good."

"Oh, I am," he assured her.

An eager, predatory smile curved her lips. "When

do we start?"

****

The rest of the night was organized chaos, exactly as Simon had planned. The element of surprise was key, so his troops began arresting detractors in the dead of night just as the council meeting began. Once he completed that grand gesture and filled in Adriane, Simon joined them.

"General Clay, you sweep the west wing," he instructed the older man by his side. "General Powell, you take the east. Adriane, you cover the south and my men and I will take the north. Offer each a choice, swear their allegiance to me, their new king, or be sentenced to death."

"If they resist?" Clay asked.

"Kill them." He gave the order so easily it surprised him. His people acknowledged his command then left him, eager to do his bidding.

Sending out his guards along with Adriane's soldiers in a coordinated effort to arrest as many as possible as quickly as possible was no accident. Blood would be spilled and he expected many would die, but once word got round that he was serious in his claim and more than prepared to back it up, resistance would decrease. The shouts and screams would also be many, but would, he was certain, eventually be silenced.

Foremost on his own personal agenda, he wanted Thomas. The primary reason for taking the north wing himself was that this area held Thomas's quarters. Thomas would be the first and most important man he would arrest personally. Unlike the others, Thomas would be given no choice. For his crimes against the realm, his life was forfeit, one way or another. If the man offered anything other than abject surrender, Simon would kill him outright with his own hands. As he and those he'd handpicked to join him pounded down the corridor, he hoped Thomas would prove to be stubborn.

****

He had no idea what woke him, but as soon as his brain clicked on Thomas understood he was not alone. It could only be someone coming to kill him. On the thought, instinct took over. In one smooth motion, his sword, which had been propped beside him, was in his hand and he rose from the bed.

Its point came to rest in the dark space where all his senses told him the intruder bided.

The interloper stumbled back a pace and something about the movement seemed familiar. The entirely feminine gasp he heard next was far more than familiar. He was well acquainted with the woman who possessed that voice. "Joan! What the bloody hell are you doing? I almost ran you through!"

"I've come to warn you. Simon means to arrest you. Even now, his guards are on their way. You must flee."

"I am going nowhere. I swore to the prince I would—"

"Bollocks to that! Senator Neville woke me not a quarter of an hour ago to tell me that Simon held a council meeting, one you and I were not informed of, and during this meeting he said…he said the king was dead."

For an instant, sorrow stabbed through Thomas's heart then sense reasserted itself. "What? That can't be. Where is his body? I want to see it."

"That's just it, you can't. There is no body. Simon produced Finn's signet ring as proof. He claims that the snow queen destroyed Finn and that there's nothing left of our king but fragments of ice. I don't believe it for a second."

In spite of her assertion, distress was written all over her face. Seeing it, he reached for her hand, took it in a firm grip. "Nor do I. And I won't until I am standing over his corpse."

"There's more." The misery in her voice was clear and so he braced himself.

"Go on."

"He got himself named king. He did it using threats and promises and deception, but he is now king."

Thomas stared at her for a long moment then vowed, "I won't ever kneel to that man."

"Nor will I, but Simon has won for the moment. You tried your best, no one would have or could have done more than you, but there it is. It's time for you to leave."

He shook his head. "I also promised the rightful king I would not leave. I swore an oath—"

She interrupted him again. "He has won for the moment," she repeated. "You are all which remains between us and tyranny. If you leave now, you can live to fight another day. You can be there to aid the king when he comes to take back what is his." He tried to speak again, but she stopped him. "This is not flight. It is strategic retreat which you will no longer be able to effect if you don't get moving."

After rummaging around for a moment, she tossed a pair of wool trousers in his direction, pointedly not looking at the vast expanse of muscled chest on display as he yanked the pants on over his linen drawers in tacit agreement then fumbled for a shirt. He lit a candle, then turned to her. "You've probably saved my life. I don't know how I can ever repay you."

He watched with intense fascination as Joan's cheeks grew pink, but she spoke in her usual matter-of-fact way. "There's nothing to repay."

He hadn't time to argue the point, but privately he decided they would see about that.

Minutes, as few as he could manage, passed as he gathered his things.

After a time, Joan muttered, "Oh gods, they must be close. I think I can hear them. They have to be nearly here. You've got to go. I'll distract them."

"What? No, you are coming with me. I couldn't possibly leave you here to face Simon's men, or the gods forbid, Simon himself. Not alone."

"Don't be ridiculous. If they find you, they will arrest you or worse. They don't dare touch me, at least not yet. I'm not going anywhere." When he started to protest, she held up a hand. "You still need someone on the inside, someone who can gather as much information as possible. We have to know what else Simon intends to do. Added to that, someone has to stay and help get the queen mother out, not to mention all the others who will want to leave. You must go and organize the troops, the supplies. You must protect all those who have fled. Aside from all of that, if Simon finds you, he will kill you. We both know it. I won't have your death on my hands."

"Joan, what about you? If you don't think he won't kill you at the first opportunity, you are wrong."

"I still have the queen mother's protection and I am

a shield-maiden in my own right besides. I'll be safe enough for now."

"Safe? No one is safe. Joan, please come with me."

She shook her head. "I can't. Not yet."

"Then I will stay as well. I won't leave you."

"Do you want to die, you stubborn fool? You will go or I'll gut you myself before Simon has the chance."

He knew her well enough to know that she was more than capable of attempting it. The fact that she just might succeed and that he had no desire to be gutted by anyone decided him. What was more, she was right. Since Simon did not intend for him to survive this, he had little choice.

The sound of boots and clanking metal told them their time was nearly up.

"I'll distract them," she repeated.

"Distract them? What on earth will you say, Joan? What reason could you give for being in my rooms at this time of night?"

"The usual." When he merely looked at her blankly, she continued, "Why do you ordinarily have a woman here, Thomas?"

As realization dawned he came perilously close to blushing for the first time in his adult life. Taking firm hold of himself, he managed to respond, "Ahh, well, I take your meaning. Are you sure about this?"

"I'm sure. I'll be fine. All I have to do is pretend I've just left your bed."

As her words registered, his mind provided a most unhelpful vision, a vivid image of her in his bed, over him, under him, surrounding him in every possible way. It was just a flash, but it was enough to get him to reach for her. "We'd best make sure you're convincing then."

The gasp which issued from her mouth left her soft lips conveniently parted. He placed a hot open-mouthed kiss on those lips then plunged in. It was an impulse, one which on one level made him question his very sanity, but on another made him wonder why on earth he'd waited so long. Why had he waited to indulge her and himself until it was almost too late?

****

Joan only had a moment to prepare herself before his lips met hers. The first brush was like a shock, a jolt of pure desire to her system, one which she barely had time to absorb. When his tongue slid in then over hers, she shuddered and surrendered to him, her own need rising and making itself known.

As he stroked her tongue and the sensitized, soft inner skin of her mouth, she struggled to find her mental feet amidst glorious sensation. She'd wanted this for years and for years it had been denied her. Now here he was, lavishing pleasure on her as if he would never stop. Tentatively, she responded by gliding her tongue over his. And she was rewarded almost instantly when he drew her to him. They had been close, perhaps a mere inch apart, but now her body was flush with his from shoulder to knee. He set a fascinating rhythm of advance and retreat and she followed, making his cadence her own.

****

For protracted minutes, he stopped thinking while he lost himself in the kiss. Never had a simple meeting of lips been so satisfying, yet the experience brought him nowhere close to satiation. The caress was complete in and of itself, yet it left him longing. As he played, as he claimed her mouth, he could not deny wanting to claim so much more. Nor could he deny that this was not the time or the place. As gently, as skillfully, but as quickly as he could, he ended the kiss. Dropping the arms that had wrapped around her seemingly of their own accord, he put just a little distance between them.

Once he could feel his own wits steadying and sense hers were stabilizing as well, he caught her gaze. "Come with me."

"I can't. We've already discussed this. Who'll distract the guards? Who'll help the queen mother get out? I'll follow as soon as possible. I promise."

More than a little reluctant, he acquiesced and set her aside. "I'll head to Brighton Forest. I'll give you three days. If you haven't joined me by then, I'll come back for you." Taking up the saddlebag he'd filled with basic necessities, he started for the window then turned back. "Thank you for saving my life." He stepped up, stepped out and was gone.

Chapter Seven

Joan stared after Thomas until she could no longer see him, telling herself she only watched to make certain he made it safely at least as far as the stables. Then she raced over to the looking glass in his dressing room. After a fascinated study of herself, she concluded that while she looked as though she'd been thoroughly kissed, she didn't quite look ravished. Perhaps a bit less clothing, she mused. Shedding the leather jerkin she wore over her day gown first, she then wiggled out of the garment with haste. In only her chemise, she felt a bit too exposed so she donned Thomas's dressing gown then proceeded to unbraid then muss her hair. And as she did she couldn't help but imagine Thomas's fingers running through it while he kissed her and more. Deeming herself as disheveled as she was going to get, she headed back into the sitting room.

None too soon either. A distant crash followed by the sound of numerous stomping boots warned her of the imminent approach of Simon's guards. They all but blew the chamber door off its hinges when they approached. Joan positioned herself in what she hoped was a natural way on the settee when they burst in without so much as a by-your-leave. One man pointed his sword at her, another tried to take her by the arms. Tried and failed. To all appearances, she was unarmed, but looks could be deceiving, as she had cause to know.

Before they arrived she took the precaution of placing her knife on the side table near her and so she had a weapon to hand. The man got a pretty severe slash on his forearm for his trouble and was just about to retaliate when Simon appeared.

"Enough!" The authority in his voice had all of the men going still. One gesture of his hand and the guards closing in on her stepped back.

"Joan, I'm surprised to find you here. I had not supposed you of all women would succumb to Thomas's dubious charms."

"What I have or have not succumbed to is none of your concern, Simon. What do you want?" The slight blush which rushed into her cheeks came as naturally to her as the haughty tone. She could only hope it would be enough to convince him she'd spent the night in Thomas's arms.

"Thomas, of course. But he isn't here, at least not any longer, is he?"

She sent him a grin that was only a touch short of brash. "I'm afraid you just missed him. He said he wanted to check the library for some book or other which might hold the key to stopping you. Try there," she told him with an airy wave of her hand.

She turned away, but Simon grabbed her arm and dragged her roughly back. "Lying to me is not very wise. Where did he go?"

Joan jerked from his hold. "Even supposing I knew, why on earth would I tell you? You're obviously here to arrest and imprison him or worse."

Simon studied her face for a moment then grimaced, clenching his jaw hard enough Joan wondered it didn't break.

"He's gone," he informed his guard. "He's not in the castle. Search the grounds. Damn it! Find him. His capture is vital to our success. I won't have him walking around free to wreak havoc. I want his head or I'll make do with one of yours," he threatened. They scurried to do his bidding and he turned back to Joan.

"You will never find him you know." Joan straightened her disarranged chemise then caught Simon's gaze. "You're right, he's long gone. No one knows this land better than he does, except me. Since I am the queen mother's ward, you can't force me to do anything against my will. You can't touch me, so…" Joan laughed. "Find him? Not a chance."

Without warning, Simon yanked her up by both arms. Strong fingers tightened enough to bruise but she remained calm and met his vicious glare with as much confidence as she could manage.

In a low dangerous voice, he stated, "When I'm done with him, I'll come for you. Once this kingdom is mine, you will do anything and everything I command. Count on it."

He released her none-too-gently and she stumbled back a pace. And for the first time, for just a moment, she knew true fear.

****

It was quite some time before Thomas deemed it safe enough to slow his horse from the mad gallop he'd been compelled to indulge in since his departure.

He'd never considered Joan as anything more than his king's cousin, not until tonight. Now, he couldn't seem to stop. He couldn't get that bloody kiss out of his head. A good thing, he supposed, as it kept his attention at least somewhat off the mess he left behind. And the even more disturbing fact that he had been forced to leave her.

He'd been obliged to abandon her in the face of serious danger and he liked it not one bit. Considering that she was the queen mother's ward, his friend, and a woman he considered practically family, leaving her to fend for herself was bad enough. But now, after that kiss…everything, even saving himself, became entirely secondary to protecting her. If there was only his own life to consider it wouldn't have been a question. He would have stayed with her or taken her with him. Either way he would never have left her. Yet there was far more at stake and they were both conscious of it. The fate of the entire kingdom hung in the balance.

That being so, he had to find Finn and bring him home. He could not accomplish this if he were captured and put into Simon's hands. He could only pray to all the gods that Joan would be all right. All he could do was hope things would fall out as she had said.

****

Frustrated beyond bearing, Simon headed to intercept the next name on his list. Thwarted in the most essential part of his plan, cheated out of executing Thomas on the spot and forced to leave Joan to her own devices, he was in a distinctly murderous frame of mind. He burned to hunt down Thomas himself. In his entire life, there was little he could remember wanting more, and he wanted so much, so often, but for now he had to deny himself that pleasure and leave the task to others. Other plans were in motion and he could not afford to lose sight of the big picture in favor of personal vengeance, no matter how sweet it would be.

"Who's next?" he barked as he and his men

pounded down the hall once more.

"Conrad Mercer and his family," the soldier beside him said.

Another soldier pounded on the door. "Open in the name of the king!"

The demand was at first met with silence then firm footsteps and muttering could be heard. At last, the door opened a bare inch.

"What the hell are you doing rousing decent citizens from their beds at this ungodly hour, Simon?" Conrad demanded. His hair stood up in tufts and he was a bit groggy as if he had indeed been asleep, but Simon could see the man was gaining clarity by the second. This being the case, he didn't waste any time, but pushed through the door along with his men.

"You neglected to attend the council meeting tonight. So, you are being given a second chance."

"A second chance to what? Betray my true king? No thank you," he snorted.

Without another word or any warning whatsoever, Simon punched Conrad in the face. Blood poured from the man's nose and he grunted in pain while he tried to staunch the bleeding.

"That was for your impertinence," he told Conrad coldly. "Now, you have a choice, you can swear fealty to me or you can die here and now."

"Do it then. I'm more than prepared to die. I would rather see my life over now than ever swear an oath to the likes of you."

An angry uncontrollable flush spread over Simon's face. "You may be willing to throw away your own life, but what about your family?"

"You leave my family out of this, you coward."

Conrad spoke with strength and vehemence, but Simon was pleased to see panic now filled his eyes.

"Lieutenant, wake them and bring them to me."

Conrad's wife, an attractive woman of perhaps thirty-five was dragged in along with a boy of twelve and a little girl of no more than seven.

"Hold him, the woman and the girl fast. I want no interference. Then bring me the boy."

The boy struggled, but he was no match for two grown men and they dragged him before Simon with ease.

Simon grabbed the boy by the hair then grasped him by his throat.

"Will you swear the oath now?" he asked Conrad, his voice calm and cool.

"Unhand him! He's just a boy," Conrad's wife shrieked.

The child struggled valiantly, fighting his own terror as well as the strength of a much larger adult man but it was clear he would lose.

"Margery, be quiet!" Conrad ordered his wife. "Leave him be, you scoundrel," Conrad commanded Simon.

"I suppose I have my answer then." Simon shrugged and with one wrenching twist, he broke the boy's neck.

"Danny!" Margery cried. With superhuman strength, she broke free from the men holding her and rushed to where her boy lay crumpled on the ground. Nothing coherent issued from her, only the disjointed sound of utter grief.

Conrad roared then did his best to free himself from the four men restraining him. Hard as he tried, he

116

was not able to break free, much less kill Simon. Strength spent, he fell to his knees, two men still holding him.

"I'll take the oath," he agreed, voice no more than a shattered whisper.

Simon smiled, but there was no humor or joy in it. "Good." He clapped Conrad heartily on the back, as if they were the best of friends.

Then he turned to his men. "Kill the woman. I'll take the girl. Jane isn't it?"

Conrad's bowed head shot up as he looked into Simon's face. When Simon started toward Jane, Conrad renewed his desperate attempts to free himself. It took six men to hold him this time. In the end, he could do no more than look on, helpless.

Margery made a sound like something from out of the depths of the earth and fought like a wildcat while they restrained her. Jane screamed and sobbed while both parents tried everything to get free and protect their daughter until Simon himself ran the child through.

Margery's primal scream rang in everyone's ears. It was too much for her to take in and her entire body went limp. She was conscious but no longer aware of the world around her.

Tears, silent and unrelenting, fell down Conrad's face as Simon turned his attention to Margery. Having discarded his sword, stained with his young victim's blood, Simon grasped his knife and slit the unresisting Margery's throat.

This time, when Conrad struggled, Simon raised a hand to indicate he should be let go. There was nothing more to be done and no one left to save after all.

Conrad crumpled to the floor and cradled the lifeless body of his little girl in his arms and wept. He stroked and kissed his daughter's pretty hair but from time to time he looked about him at the rest of his family lying dead. Simon looked on Conrad in his grief and felt nothing. He crouched down beside the now broken man. "Now perhaps you'll remember to do as you're told in the future."

With great gentleness, Conrad laid Jane's body aside and rose. He trapped Simon's gaze with his. "You will pay for this. Just because it can't happen here and now doesn't mean I won't spend the rest of my life making sure of it. And if somehow I fail, then know that one day there will be a reckoning, even if it comes when you are dead and at the mouth of hell."

Simon stood, shrugged. "So, no loyalty oath from you then."

Conrad spat on the floor in response.

"Very well. Take him to the dungeon and lock him up. We will execute him at our leisure. One day there may indeed be a reckoning. Who can say? As for hell, such a place will probably be my end, but I'll see you there first." Since there was little more left to say, Simon turned on his heel and walked out.

****

It was not until dawn that Simon considered the night's bloody work done, if not done quite properly. It had been years in the planning. He used every tool at his disposal, from bribery to intimidation to violence and it all fell into place, except the most essential piece.

As if in direct opposition to his own assessment, Adriane commented, "In all, I would say we've done well."

Simon ran a fingertip down Adriane's neck. "Well? I disagree. The three worst threats to my power are still viable, Thomas, the so-called snow queen, and worst of all, his majesty. If Finn returns with the snow queen and if, as I suspect, there are others like her, it could change the balance of power irrevocably."

She was silent a moment, as was her way when she was searching for a solution to a difficult problem, then she sighed. "What's to be done then?"

"I've been considering that very question. I think we need assassins."

Adriane lifted an eyebrow. "Whatever for? Finn and Thomas have fled. Who knows if this snow queen is even real?"

He grimaced. "She's real all right."

"Very well, say she is real, then judging from all the stories, Finn is probably long dead just as his subjects believe."

"Perhaps, but I won't be satisfied until I stand over his bones, along with the snow queen's and Thomas's for good measure. She, Thomas and his majesty are the only true threats to my kingdom now. They must be found."

"So, assassins then."

"Yes, one for Thomas, one for the snow queen, and one for Finn."

"Hmmm. Let me take care of it. There are several men I can easily assign to the task."

"Your best?"

"Of course." She smiled and lethal intent was clear in her dark eyes.

Simon smiled right back. "Lovely."

"Do you think you might now be in the mood to

celebrate our victory?" she asked as she began to unlace her gown.

"Hmm, perhaps we could look forward to our future success?" His gaze traveled from her gorgeous face to the expanse of firm, white flesh slowly revealed.

She inclined her head, eyes glinting in the firelight. "Most assuredly."

He took her face in his hands and they said nothing more for a long while.

Chapter Eight

As planned, they were ready to depart at first light. Once she mounted her favorite mare, Lyssa could not resist turning back for one final look at the solitary fortress she had created. The harsh beauty she had made for herself alone still struck her. It still called to her. She studied the walls, the towers and turrets, trying her best to commit them to memory.

For so long this place had been both refuge and prison, but it had been hers. It had been her home and had encompassed her entire world. Now she was about to leave it and only the gods knew when she would see it again. The wind stung her eyes. They watered and she hoped it might disguise the tears she could not keep from falling.

Seeing her hesitation, Finn, already astride his stallion, drew up alongside her. As if he read her thoughts, he made her a promise. "You will see it again, I swear it. I can't say when, but you will."

Sniffing, she wiped the back of her hand across her eyes before she turned to him and said, "For years this has been the only home I've known. I won't say I've been happy here, but I have been content and safe. It's more difficult than I expected to leave it behind, that's all."

Nodding, he stretched out a hand, took hers in his own. "Not to mention the fact that you are leaving to go into uncertainty and danger. I'm sorry for it. If there were any other way…"

"But there isn't and I'm not sorry because I am needed and I am ready."

"You are. So for now, let go of the past. The present and the future have desperate need of our attention."

Determined, Lyssa set her chin and nodded. With one final glance, they took their leave.

****

In the beginning, the places they rode through were ones Lyssa recalled. The forest and roads were part of her recollection of the night she fled. For a time, she occupied herself with comparing present facts to memories. Soon enough, however, one question dominated her every thought and would no longer be ignored.

"Do you have a plan?" Lyssa demanded.

"Do I have a plan for infiltrating my own capital city?" Finn shrugged. "Surely. I know the city well enough and I know the castle, my castle, better than anyone. I'll meet with what supporters are to be found and we'll enter secretly. The fatal blow will come before Simon even thinks to put out a hand to stop it."

"Well, I will help in any way I can with whatever strategy you come up with. I only hope it works."

He grinned. "Oh, believe me, it'll work."

"And just where do I come in? What exactly is my role in all this?"

"I want you at my side. Since you won't let me protect you by leaving you behind, I want you fighting with me of course."

"Using my powers?" Sheer panic raced through

her. The all-too-familiar terror was back in spite of her recent training and of her new-found confidence. "Finn, I can't. I swore I would never use what I am to harm ever again."

"My love, I would never ask such a thing of you. I want your help to protect and defend. Not to attack. Or in truth, to attack only in the gravest necessity."

"But what if I can't control it?"

He slowed his horse, placed a hand over the one she had clenched on her reins. "You can. So can I. These past weeks have proved that. Trust yourself. If you can't trust yourself, then trust me."

"I trust you, with my life." Gazing into his beautiful eyes, the tight knot of tension in her belly loosened just a bit.

Knowing she trusted him down to her bones made her feel somewhat better, but trusting herself was another matter entirely. She looked back over the weeks, over how far she'd come and hoped it would be enough.

****

When they made camp that night, Lyssa all but collapsed from exhaustion. Spending an entire day on horseback was not something she was used to and her muscles protested, violently. To rest them, she sat, back against a tree and reveled in the lack of motion. Shock then dismay filled her when she saw Finn remove his sword and begin preparations for a training session.

"You want to train? You must be joking, Finn. I can barely stand."

He grunted but did not stop making his arrangements. "Which is why it's important we do this now. Do you think the enemy will care if you are exhausted when we go into battle? Added to it," he continued, "this is a less controlled environment. This is exactly the sort of thing you need to cope with if you will be fighting at my side. I won't have you dying out there, certainly not from lack of training, not if I can help it." He made a "come ahead" gesture with his hand. When she didn't rise, only continued to stare up at him, he kicked her booted foot. "You wanted this. You insisted on coming with me. Did you think it would all be fun and games? You assumed it would consist of days meandering down a pretty road and nights in my bed?"

Her reply was not delivered in words. Instead she rose, and quick as a flash, pivoted and sent her ice directly at him. When he cursed and scrambled out of its path, she grinned. Her smile was wiped away a heartbeat later when he took her down with a kick that swept her legs out from under her. Doing some cursing of her own, she rolled then got back on her feet. Panting a little, she lunged forward. His smile was fierce, all teeth, and soon there was an answering one on her own lips.

For a few fraught minutes they struggled and thrashed, dodged and weaved. Lyssa used every move, every technique Finn had ever taught her and for a while she held her own. Her pride was short-lived, however. She began to tire and this lessened her coordination. There came a time when she zigged when she ought to have zagged and he used brute strength to knock her to the ground. Using his weight he held her entirely immobile in spite of all her efforts to break free. When she tried to elbow him then nearly scratched his pretty face, he took both her wrists in his hands and drew them up beside her head.

Well and truly pinned, she lay beneath him and tried to catch her breath. Two types of tension merged and as their gazes locked, the more passionate sort got the upper hand. Letting go of one of her hands for an instant, he immediately locked both her wrists in his left hand. With his right, he caressed her body from arm to waist and back again then lingered on her breast.

Heated and wanting him, she arched against his seeking hand offering herself. He responded by unlacing the bodice of her traveling gown with his teeth. The feel of his palm, warm and strong and rough with calluses, touching her smooth bare skin made her tremble. His touch was more…commanding than it had ever been before. As if she were his to do with as he would. As if tonight he would take her and do as he liked with her. One word from her, and he would release her, but she didn't want him to. In fact, she didn't want him to ever stop.

When he put a hand beneath her skirts to touch her even more intimately, she thought she might faint, but prayed she would stay conscious because she did not want to miss a moment. At last he freed her hands while he rose above her to loosen his pants. For one magnificent moment, she was allowed to touch him, to run her hands over his chest, to place her hand over his heart and feel its rapid beat. Then he bore her back to the ground and covered her. When he entered her, she wondered for just a moment whether she might die. Instead, she came in a glorious seemingly endless rush.

****

He clung to her as she climaxed. To her and a rigid control which seemed to invest him completely tonight.

He longed to join her, knew she was sure he would, but he didn't. Not yet, he told himself. He wanted more. So he held tight and when the last shuddering contraction eased, he set about taking her up a second time. Not quite biting back a moan, he rocked into her, brushed against her still sensitized skin and she gasped.

Her eyes widened as she realized he was still hot and hard and deep inside her.

"Again," he breathed the word against her lips. "Go up again."

When he pulled out almost completely, her eyes opened even wider then went blind as he thrust firmly back. His own vision clouded as he drew back once more then plunged into her warm wet heat. He set a rhythm as inexorable as the tide, as unyielding as he felt. He would have the sensual surrender from her he'd longed for and then, he vowed, he would give her his. For minutes or hours, he wasn't sure which, he indulged in joining their bodies over and over. Her hands roamed freely now and he reveled in that as well. The force of his own culmination rushed up to meet him. It built until it could not be denied. As in sync with her as he was, he immediately discerned she was on the brink as well.

"Come with me now." The command came from somewhere deep inside of him, from a place made up of sensation, pure and primal and unadorned. His words touched her very core, judging by the emotions that flared in her eyes.

She gripped his hand tightly and gave herself to him with complete abandon. The next roll of his hips caressed her inside and out and she climaxed. With one final, solid, firm thrust, an instant later he followed her into sensual oblivion, into a world made up only of sensation.

****

For some time they lay there, dumbstruck, too stunned to do anything more. Where had that come from, he wondered? Not that he was of a mind to complain, but still... He tried to come to some conclusions, but found his mind was too pleasantly relaxed to come up with anything much.

Soul searching be damned, he decided. Lyssa was probably most uncomfortable in the here and now. "I don't want to crush you, but I'm not sure I can get my limbs to function properly yet," Finn commented.

"Oh that's just fine. Stay." To ensure he did, she lifted her limp and heavy arms, and wrapped them around him.

For just an instant more he let himself enjoy the feel of her embrace and her hands in his hair then he sighed and rolled to his side, taking her with him.

"By all the gods, that felt good." Finn stretched then gave her rear-end a friendly pat. "You did well enough tonight, by the way, once you decided to get off of your excellent bottom."

"Well enough to knock you onto your even more excellent one," she shot back.

He rolled them both, reversed their positions so she was beneath him once more. "I wasn't just talking about the training session, you know."

She chuckled. "Nor was I." She kissed him with lips still curved and they enjoyed each other, indulged each other all over again.

****

As they rode out the next morning, Lyssa

determined that although she could have passed the time perusing the vast unfamiliar landscape, this interval would be better spent getting to know the man beside her. It struck her that aside from the necessary facts, she knew almost nothing about his history. He spoke little of his life before. She intended to rectify that omission starting now.

"What is your family like?" she began. It was as good a place to start as any. He sent an inquiring glance her way so Lyssa elaborated. "You never speak of them. I just wondered."

"My mother, the dowager queen, is the only family I have left. I was an only child."

"What is your mother like then?" She tried to keep the wistfulness out of her voice, but was not at all sure she managed it. Her mother had died of the plague when she was a child of ten so the memories she had of her were few and greatly cherished. She missed her every day.

His smile was swift and sweet with uncomplicated affection. "She is amazing. Strong-willed and stubborn as the day is long. But her heart, now that is as big as the sea and as warm as the glowing sand. She misses my father every day, but she manages to soldier on. Her illness these past months worries me more than a little, however. I don't know that I can stand to lose her."

"You won't lose her anytime soon if the gods are good."

They rode on for a few moments then she chanced another question. "Is there no one else you are close to?"

"There is Thomas and Joan. Lord Thomas Marbury is of noble birth and a cousin on my father's side. Lady

Joan Langston is a distant kinswoman on my mother's. When Joan's parents died she became my mother's ward and Thomas was fostered with us. The three of us grew up together, as close as any siblings ever were." Now his whole manner grew nostalgic. "We got up to all sorts of trouble. There is no one I trust more. I asked Thomas to do his best to look after my mother and the kingdom while I was away. Where Thomas goes, Joan follows, so I am sure they did the best they could, but Simon has been planning this takeover for a long time. Let's just say I need to get back there, soon."

"Important matters must be attended to. I understand. I'm so glad I'm with you."

He gave her a look. "When I said this would be difficult and dangerous, I meant it. I wonder that you are so eager."

She shrugged. "Not for difficulty or danger, but to share life with you." She extended a hand, grasped his. "All of life, the good as well as the bad. I've been alone so long, I cherish every experience. Every moment is an adventure I want to have, with you."

"You are a constant fascination to me," he murmured and kissed their joined hands. "I feel much the same. Here's to adventure."

He spurred his horse on and with a whoop, urged his stallion into a gallop down the road. With a little whoop of her own, Lyssa followed.

****

As they journeyed on, Lyssa continued her campaign to get to know Finn as well as possible. Broaching one vital topic was as good a way as any to ignore her aching muscles, she concluded. "How do you view marriage?"

The abrupt question had him raising his eyebrows, but he only asked, "I'm sorry?"

"How do you view marriage? How do you view a wife and how do you intend to interact with her…err…me?"

He rubbed his chin in what she now recognized as a contemplative gesture then met her gaze. "In much the same way as I do now, I suppose, as friends, lovers, allies. You are my wife in all but name."

"Yes, but I am also a queen in my own right. I won't be ruled by anyone, certainly not by any husband. Not even by you. I need you to accept me as your equal. Few men would be able to handle that. Can you?"

He flashed that charming grin of his at her. "I keep telling you, I'm not most men. You want to be seen as an equal. That's good. I would expect nothing less. I want no weak, frivolous girl on the throne beside me. Lyssa, as far as I am concerned, we are partners in every sense."

She measured his words for a moment then nodded. "I thank you for that. Please know I feel same." They rode in silence a while then she added, "I do believe you mean what you say. What is more, your actions thus far bear that out. Still, I am not in the habit of placing faith in anyone. Not even you. It will take time for me to trust you fully. Forgive me."

"There's nothing to forgive. I too trust little. You and I will simply have to do our best to change that."

His proposal sounded promising but… "How do you suggest we go about it?"

He shrugged. "There's not much to do really. Mostly, it just takes time as you said. And honesty. We must be honest with each other always."

"I'll do my best if you will."

His charming smile made an appearance once more. "Agreed."

Feeling rather pleased with herself as well as him, Lyssa rode on.

Chapter Nine

The two housemaids entered and began to build up the fire, strip the bed then cover it in fresh linen and do all the other duties such girls commonly did. Joan was in her dressing room and could hear them chattering like magpies. She let the talk roll over, paying little attention as she completed her morning ablutions.

"When does the king return?" Edith asked.

Sal, a year or two older and more experienced, sniffed and Joan could well imagine her pert nose lifted in the air. "He doesn't. Haven't you heard? It all happened so fast, I suppose you haven't. The king is dead, killed by the snow queen. Lord Fairfax has set himself up as regent, king in all but name. A few days ago there were arrests made. Those what weren't detained or killed bolted. It doesn't do to be askin' too many questions about the king or the disbanded council." Joan thought she just about managed to sound nonchalant rather than afraid.

Edith made a little sound of distress. When she spoke again, her tone was more serious than Joan had ever known it to be. "Dead. Oh, no." Voice shaking, she added, "That's terrible. To die in such a way and without an heir."

"For now Lord Fairfax is regent, until he can be crowned, I expect."

"Will there be a war do you think? I've heard my

132

brothers talkin' and they say there will be. I paid 'em no attention 'til now but…"

"I don't know, but you and your brothers might want to be careful and think seriously about getting out. Come, we'd best see to the dowager's rooms."

The two girls left, but shock held Joan immobile. Surely this was not correct. The council disbanded? Within two days? All of the king's supporters imprisoned, murdered or fled save herself and the dowager queen? Simon had had a busy few days indeed, she mused. Her own time had consisted of keeping her head down and helping as many people as possible to get out.

As the morning sun streamed through her window, she resolved this day would be her last in the castle. She would follow Thomas. It was time. She would gather a few essentials and set off. Perhaps she could convince the dowager queen to join her. It would be easy enough to pick up any stragglers on the way. She just hoped she hadn't left it too late. Hastily, she began to collect her things and pack.

****

"You wished to see me? I dislike being ordered about, especially into your presence. What do you want, Simon?" Joan demanded. She also detested being interrupted when she was trying to plot a secret escape, but of course, she would not tell him that. Never would she let her fear show either. That this might just be it, that already aware of her plans, he would kill her on the spot was her greatest fear. Yet she stood before him in the main audience chamber, demeanor impassive, and waited to see what would happen next.

"The other night you said I couldn't touch you.

That's true, but things are changing. I am king now and there are others. Innocents I know you would like to keep from harm. If you do not want their blood on your hands, you will do exactly as I say."

"Will I? I think not. Don't threaten me."

"It's not a threat. You've a younger sister do you not? Born mere months before your mother's death then fostered in Sutton village. It would be a very simple matter to send someone to violate her chaste young body then slit her throat."

Cold fear and hot anger melded into a mix so vile it nearly clogged her throat. "My sister is thirteen. You will leave her alone, you scum."

"Will I? You might also consider what I will do to Thomas once I catch him. Execution will be the least of it. Mutilation and torture, until he is a shell of the man he once was. If you cooperate, I might be lenient and give him a quick merciful death. Try my patience, however, and…" He shrugged, the picture of nonchalance.

She understood that at least for the moment, she was beaten. There was no doubt in her mind that Simon would do precisely as he described unless she capitulated. Vowing this wasn't over, she accepted her current situation and bowed her head in defeat though even this small, temporary concession sickened her. "As you say. What do you want?"

The smug expression on Simon's face made her want to do him a serious injury, but she held herself under strict control.

"For now, all I want is your tacit agreement. Your acquiescence, if you will. Do not obstruct me in any way. When I need more from you, I'll let you know."

When he said nothing further, she asked, "Are you done with me now?"

He studied her for a long moment, looking for any trace of defiance, she supposed. "For now. You may go."

****

A quarter of an hour later, Joan was at the dowager queen's door. Her every instinct was warning her to get away and not alone. It was vital Rowena escape with her, yet she was certain deep in her gut Rowena would never leave. Even knowing full well that arguing with the older woman was futile once her mind was made up, she did it anyway.

"I know you are very ill, but you must see you can't stay here."

"I see nothing of the kind." The stubborn set of the dowager's chin was so like her son's it would have made Joan smile at any other time. As it was, she gritted her teeth and tried not to imagine giving the queen mother a firm shake.

"Argh!" The inarticulate sound of frustration was not enough to relieve her feelings.

"Sit down, Joan." When she continued to pace, the dowager repeated, far more sharply this time, "Sit down. Listen to me, I am not leaving. I can be of more use here, getting people out. What is more, right now the journey would probably kill me."

Joan closed her eyes to shut away the knowledge. She could not block out Rowena's voice, however.

"You and I both know this is true."

Neither woman spoke for a time, then Rowena explained her reasoning as best she could. "At this point I am not high on Simon's list. He has other more pressing matters to deal with before he turns his attention to me. So why don't we make use of that time? People are frightened. Many are ready and willing to leave in secret but have no idea how to do so. I have been and I will continue to help them."

"And I should just leave you here?" Joan's tone matched the new bleak shape of her world.

"Yes." Rowena inclined her head in a decisive a manner. "I am still the queen mother after all. It is my duty to stay and it is yours to obey me and go."

"Abandon you to Simon who wants you dead? No, that I will not do. You are the king's mother. What is more, you are the only mother I have ever known—I—" She choked on those last words, surprised to discover tears running down her cheeks before she was even aware of having shed them.

"And you are so very dear to me, daughter." Weak though she was, Rowena managed to frame Joan's face with her hands. "So strong, so beautiful," she crooned. An instant later her voice hardened. "But that is why you must go. We each have a part to play. Mine is to spirit others away, not to fight myself. That is your role."

"My role is to leave you behind? Never."

In an abrupt move, Rowena gripped Joan's hand, desperation lending her a temporary strength. "You must. My son must have every good warrior beside him if he is to win. That includes you, my daughter. I'm stronger than you think and I can and will take care of myself. I will be here waiting when you return with my son and an army at your back. Until that day have no concern for me."

Joan opened her mouth to protest once more, but

Rowena held up a hand to forestall her. "This is my command as your true regent and former queen."

With little choice in the matter, Joan curtseyed low and took her leave.

****

Her plan, such as it was, was simple enough. She would walk right out. Often part of the daily hunting party whenever she had a mind to be, today Joan would join them as if everything was normal. Such an occurrence would cause little or no comment and it would get her past the gates now guarded by Simon's men. Once out, she would separate from the group, never to rejoin them. Easy.

Of course, she banked on the fact that Simon would not want to cause a public scene, at least not yet, by arresting and/or executing her on the spot. It was a risk she would have to take. Staying was no longer an option since a death wish was not something she possessed. If she remained, her death was inevitable. Sooner or later, Simon would find a way to be rid of her. To hang about waiting for that day would drive her mad. Suffice it to say that such an alternative did not bear thinking about.

Her mood was decidedly grim as she checked one last time that all she needed was in her saddle bag.

****

So far, her plan was working. When she informed the head huntsman she would be joining them, he grunted in reply and did not even look up from the horse he was saddling. Joan prepared her own mount without further comment and counted herself lucky. To avoid unwanted questions, she stuck to her usual routine with one slight variation. Her saddle bag contained far more than it normally would have, but she was careful to pack so it did not look that way. It was only if someone lifted her bags that he would notice the far heavier weight of them.

Her head shot up at the clatter of footsteps. Her mare, picking up on her tension, whinnied and backed up a step. Pretending to stoop for something she dropped, Joan ducked her head. Hidden in the corner of the stall, she listened.

"Prepare his majesty's horse. He wishes to join the hunt."

She recognized the voice of a guard she knew slightly. This was the worst possible news and she wanted very much to groan aloud. It was rare for Simon to join the hunt; she could count the number of times he had done so in the last five years on her two hands, yet here he was accompanying them today. Did he suspect something? Did he suspect her?

Her heart picked up its beat until it was frenetic and she worried she might faint from its palpitations. Knowing full well this would be the most terrible thing that could happen, she tried her best to calm down and think. She reviewed her plan and concluded Simon's presence changed little if anything, at least in so far as this was still the best plan she had. Of course, with him there it became a hundred times riskier, but she had little choice. Unable to deny that truth, she pulled herself together and finished saddling her horse.

A few minutes later, she joined the others in the forecourt. Simon (she swore she would never call him king) was already mounted and ready. She nodded in greeting in a brisk if not quite civil way. He could hardly expect more from her given the circumstances.

"Good morrow, my lady."

"Good morrow. I was not aware you intended to join us. We are honored." There was a slight edge to her voice, but if there hadn't been the lack would have been cause for curiosity as well, so she made no effort to hide it.

Ignoring the hostile undercurrent coming off her in waves, Simon replied in a genial way, "It has been some time since I joined in a hunt. The weather is still cool but fine. It is the perfect time to introduce Adriane to the pleasures of hunting on the king's grounds. She'll join us in a moment."

The situation just got worse and worse, she concluded. Now she had to contend with not one but both of them. Joan had a terrible vision of Simon and Adriane hunting, but instead of stalking deer, she was their prey. In her mind's eye she raced through the woods to elude capture with them mere steps behind. She quelled a shiver and sent up a fervent prayer to the gods that this would never come to pass.

Banishing the terrible images from her brain, she made the right polite noises then subsided to wait for Adriane to appear. As promised, Adriane arrived five minutes later and the entire party set out toward the forest.

The game on the king's land was plentiful, she knew from experience. Deer, rabbit, wild boar, pheasant, and duck all abounded. It was more than enough to provide for the court, the castle servants and the surrounding city.

As she was the best shot with a bow in the kingdom, missing a clear target would cause comment, possibly even suspicion she was desperate to avoid.

This was a pity since it would have been best if she could have slipped away to retrieve an arrow on her own. By the time anyone noticed she had not caught up with the main party, she would be long gone. Since this was not a possibility, she would have to hope for something small to shoot, such as a rabbit, which it would be feasible for her to recover without assistance. At least that had been her original plan. With Simon and Adriane joining the group, however, she was taking a terrible gamble. Simon did not take his gaze off her for even a moment and she suspected if she did leave, even for some ostensibly legitimate reason, the pretender would know in an instant and perhaps even send one or more of his minions after her.

Well, she would have to be as watchful and stealthy as she had ever been. It was vital she choose her moment carefully and make the most of it. A quick getaway during some brief moment of distraction was now her best, if not her only, option. She had half a mind to create a diversion of her own, but that carried its own peril. No, best to take advantage of whatever the day might hold.

****

After hours on horseback alternately bored and tense, Joan was more than ready to make her escape, if the right opportunity would just present itself.

As if the gods heard her prayer, several things happened in very quick succession. One man's horse threw a shoe and backed into Adriane's mare. The mare, not liking this one bit, reared. Simon's entire focus was on calming Adriane's horse as well as his own and Joan realized there would never be a better time. In the ensuing chaos, she slipped into the woods.

The gods were with her as there was a fallen log covering a slight indent in the ground. Since it was large enough for her to crawl beneath it, she wasted not a second and did just that. With a few piled leaves and underbrush hastily gathered to block the open side, she would be concealed. As she rolled, drawing leaves and branches after her, she cursed explicitly but silently.

Mere seconds later, Simon demanded, "Where is Lady Joan?"

The disruption had been momentary, but served its purpose and she was already settled. At the sound of her enemy's voice, she froze, however. Locked in place and trying her best to not even breathe, she tried to calm her racing heart. Through a minute gap in the leaves, she could see and hear her erstwhile companions.

"I'm not sure, majesty. She was here a moment ago," that sycophant Payne replied after a moment.

It only took one glance to see her horse was now sans rider while Joan herself was nowhere to be seen. Now it was Simon's turn to curse and his oaths were creative and not at all silent. "Find her," he spat.

The guards, who were always with him now night or day, split off, one in each direction, without question or comment.

"You don't think she would try to run do you? Right here and now, under our very noses?" Adriane asked.

"I think that's exactly what she has done. It's bold, audacious and unexpected."

"Well, she can't have gotten far. We'll find her."

Joan had to stifle a snort when she heard that. She was not twenty feet from them and they had no idea she was there.

Simon shook his head. "She knows this forest better than anyone. We will never find her if she doesn't want to be found."

For the second time that day, she prayed to the gods it would be so. The only other thing she could do was wait.

"Bring in the dogs," Simon ordered after an hour of fruitless searching.

In the normal course of things, with any other person, panic would ensue. But she had trained those dogs herself and they listened to her above anyone else. Easy enough to issue her own counter-command to the dogs once they picked up her scent and tracked down her hiding place. She patted each canine head in turn then signaled them that the hunt was over and they were welcome to run. By the time Simon's minions caught up, the dogs were headed in the opposite direction, barking with great enthusiasm.

After that, it was only a matter of more waiting. Simon and his men, with little help from the hounds, combed the forest for hours and found nothing.

At last, as the sun was setting, one of Simon's men approached the new king. "Sire, we've looked everywhere with no luck. Even the dogs can't find her. With dark coming on, I suggest we resume come morning."

"No, it's a waste of time. She's long gone from here. Gather the men and return to the castle."

The young man looked relieved for an instant then he winced. "Err…Sire, what should we do about her horse? The hell-creature won't let anyone get near it."

Simon shrugged. "Leave it for tonight. She'll come home when she gets hungry and cold enough. If she doesn't, send a groom out here to fetch the mare tomorrow."

The guard bowed in acquiescence and was soon gone. Simon took one last measuring look around then twitched, as if unable to throw off some weight. It was almost as though he sensed her presence, but was frustrated in his attempts to pinpoint where she might be. Joan's abused muscles wanted to spasm and the impulse to confront him and end her torment once and for all was strong, but she held both in check. At last he shrugged and turned his mount toward home.

To be on the safe side, Joan waited another hour until full dark before she moved even one stiff aching muscle. She rose and stretched then grinned. She was free and clear but for one last thing. Putting two fingers to her lips, she whistled two short sharp notes. Her loyal mare trotted forward, as eager to be gone as she.

****

Having accomplished her daring escape, she headed deep into Brighton Forest. The rest of her journey was an uneventful one, at least until she arrived at her destination. Joan heard the noise from a quarter mile away. Once on the high ground to the south, she found a spot which offered both concealment and a view of the people below. What she saw made her smile.

Several large white pavilions were set up along with countless smaller tents for the personal use of the soldiers. But best of all, her king's standard was in full view. That, along with the horses, the mostly male voices and all of the clatter, clamor and general racket which made up the sounds of a large encampment, filled her with pride. All these were her king's supporters and it was the man she loved who had organized them all.

Even so, she sobered as she drew closer and approached with caution. It wouldn't do at all to be taken for an enemy. "Hello the camp." She called the standard greeting as she rode into clear view.

Two young men, guards by the look of them, signaled her to stop and she reined in. As an extra precaution, she raised both hands to appear unthreatening.

"State your business."

The curt greeting did not bother her and she answered readily enough. "I am the dowager queen's ward, Lady Joan Langston. Is Lord Thomas Marbury here? I would speak with him."

The two men glanced at each other. The blond one shrugged and the dark-haired one sighed. "A moment, miss." The dark-haired one left his post in search of Thomas.

A few minutes wait in the saddle and he appeared. He exited from a medium-sized tent some distance away then walked with long purposeful strides in her direction.

She took the rare opportunity to study him unobserved. He looked in need of a bath, but otherwise none the worse for wear, praise be. In fact, the slightly disheveled look suited him. A day's growth of stubble, a simple open-necked linen shirt and an old pair of trousers which fit him like a glove, made him seem a bit dangerous and infinitely sexy. She carefully studied his gorgeous form, checking for injuries. Finding none in evidence, she breathed a sigh of relief.

At last he reached her. "Joan!" He quickened his

pace, a huge smile on his lips.

Her lips quirked into a smile of their own as he all but raced toward her. While he closed the distance between them she raised a hand in greeting.

When his strong hands seized her hips, hauling her from the saddle and straight into his arms, she gasped.

"Joan, thank the gods you are safe."

He held onto her for a long time, almost as if he would never let her go. With his warm breath fluttering her hair, his strong arms wrapped around her and his steady heartbeat resonating with hers, she could have stayed that way forever. He smelled like the forest, horses and his own unique scent. Just one deep breath, she promised herself, closing her eyes. Just one more moment in his arms then she would tear herself away.

Too soon he drew back just far enough to see her face. "I hated leaving you. I would never have forgiven myself if—" He stopped speaking abruptly and began checking her for injuries. "You aren't hurt? You're all right?"

"Of course I'm all right. I'm right as rain. You?"

"Better now you are here." Another hard hug, then he put an arm around her shoulder. "Come, you must be hungry and thirsty. You'll have a meal and tell us your news."

"Yes. I fear it's nothing good."

He offered her a wry smile. "As is so often the case."

She joined him and in spite of the tenuous situation, she already felt safe and at home.

****

The quiet of the forest at dawn was undisturbed except by the sound of their passing. The swish of fallen leaves round horses' hooves on a path of hard-packed earth, and the clink of the bridles were the only sounds. Then the solid *thunk* of an arrow into a tree five feet ahead made Finn still. When another arrow slid past his ear, he grinned, not at all alarmed. Only one man of his acquaintance could shoot with that level of accuracy. His call drowned out Lyssa's soft gasp. "Come on out, you lucky bastard."

Moving on silent feet, Thomas stepped into the open. "It's about time you made your way here, your grace."

Finn chuckled. After a moment, he dismounted. "Well, I've been a bit busy."

Thomas grinned. "So I see. Well, that is as may be, if you hadn't shown your face today, I would have sent someone to fetch you."

"I worried I would need to send someone to fetch *you* when I was informed about the new regent." Finn's face darkened for moment when he thought of Simon, but focusing again on Thomas, it lightened. "I'm happy to see you alive and in one piece."

"The same to you, majesty. I knew he was a liar."

"Who was? Simon?"

Thomas nodded. "He said you were dead."

Total silence fell as Finn and Lyssa absorbed the shock of this revelation.

Thomas flushed. "I myself am alive, but I shouldn't be. I don't deserve to be. I failed you most unforgivably, sire. I could not prevent it."

Finn shook his head. "There's nothing to forgive, my friend. You did the best you could, better than most. Simon played us all." He gave Thomas a reassuring clap on the shoulder then turned to lift Lyssa from the saddle. "What of my mother? Is she here?"

Thomas winced. "No, she is not. As the situation became more and more untenable, I begged her to go, as did Joan, but she would not. She was determined to remain and do what she could to stop Simon."

"And as she is the queen mother you could not order her. Stubborn woman," he muttered.

"As you say, majesty." Thomas's lips twitched, but he manfully straightened them. He glanced at the beautiful woman still on horseback, then at his king. "This is her I take it?"

In answer, Finn helped Lyssa dismount. Once her feet were planted on the ground again, Finn took her hand. "Lyssa Jennings, Queen of Halstad, may I present Lord Thomas Marbury."

Thomas bowed low over Lyssa's hand then she curtseyed. The formalities thus observed, Thomas studied her a moment. "I hear you will restore balance to this land and usher in a new age of peace and prosperity," he stated.

"I hear you are a paragon of virtue and you will be instrumental in bringing this new age about," she countered.

"I suppose we both have our work cut out for us then, don't we?"

Her lips quirked, but she straightened them before taking his offered arm. "Indeed we do."

"Allow me to escort you both to the camp." Thomas bowed then helped her back onto her mare.

"Lead the way. We could do with a hot meal." Finn settled himself astride his own animal. Since the path was not wide enough for them to ride abreast, Thomas went first, Lyssa fell in behind him and Finn brought up the rear.

As they rode through the woods, Thomas drew Finn aside. "There is something I'd like to show you, if you'll ride ahead just a bit with me. I assure you Lyssa will be safe here alone for a few moments."

A vision of Lyssa as she knocked him off his feet flashed through his mind. Inwardly amused, he said only, "I'm sure she will be. Let's go."

A touch of the hand and a murmured instruction to Lyssa to remain, and they were off.

Thomas directed him to a narrow path heading west. Although it looked recently created, the hard-packed earth and numerous tracks were evidence it had been much travelled since, Finn noted.

"I hope what you are about to see pleases you, majesty. I pray you will look at this as a silver lining if you will."

Finn raised his eyebrows. His friend's tone was casual but excitement underlay it. When Thomas said nothing more, Finn's curiosity at last got the better of him and he demanded, "Well?"

"It's best if I show you."

For five minutes more they continued on, Thomas filling the silence by giving a brief account of his adventures since Finn's absence. He told of all he did to try to prevent the coup, the sorry state of the country in spite of his best efforts, his reluctant escape, and concluded with Joan's part in it all.

For some time Finn had detected a murmur, as if the forest was not empty. He wondered at it, but said nothing. Until a man's voice reached them, as clearly as if he had been at their side. Putting a hand out for his sword, he gripped the hilt and searched to find the source of the noise. It seemed to come from all about them, however, and he could not pinpoint its direction, so he turned back to his companion. "Who or what is that?" he demanded.

Thomas grinned. "Look." The younger man brushed back bushes to reveal a large clearing below them. Some distance away was a bustling encampment.

Jaw slack, Finn watched the people go about their business for a moment. "Who are they?" he managed at last.

"Your army, sire."

Slowly, Finn turned to meet Thomas's gaze. Words, so many of them, crowded his brain, but he could latch on to none. A thousand different emotions roiled within him too but he could not hold on to any one long enough to say which was uppermost.

A little uneasy now, Thomas shifted in the saddle, hesitating before he spoke again. "When Simon usurped your throne, many fled. When I admitted at last that I would have to leave as well or die, I traveled here and found some had already gathered. Joan joined me soon after and she and I organized them and have tried to prepare them. Your mother has sent as many as possible from your army along with whatever supplies she could manage. Your supporters and the enemies of Simon are ready for you to lead them. Well, what do you think? I know allowing the kingdom to fall into Simon's hands is unpardonable, but perhaps with this I might begin to atone."

Finn found his voice at last. "All of these people are ready to fight and die, for me?"

"For you and what you stand for, yes."

"By all the gods." This soft murmur was all he

could manage. It was clear that it wasn't only soldiers, but farmers, tradespeople, even aristocrats who made up his new army. The coup had been a severe blow to his ego. He realized he had had no real idea of the depth and breadth of his support. So many from every walk of life believed in him and stood ready to give their lives for the cause of freedom. Wonder filled him at the sight.

Thomas studied Finn's expression for a moment. "I know. It is awe inspiring."

For some time they stood watching the activity, observing the comings and goings, all the little daily activities of a military camp.

At length, however, Thomas caught Finn's attention. "We should get back to your betrothed and ride in. If we hurry, we will be right on time for dinner."

Knowing his friend's appetite was legend, Finn guffawed. "By all means let us try to get back in time for dinner."

****

As evening fell, Joan galloped into camp carrying her portion of the day's game, a plump pheasant, but the sight of Thomas and a woman of incomparable beauty walking arm-in-arm brought her up short. And behind them, praise the gods, was the king. A fact which she would have registered right away if she had not been so distracted, she chided herself.

Thomas was preoccupied as well. Perhaps since they had yet to notice her, it might be best to slip away, greet them all once she had the chance to splash cool water on her hot face, perhaps change to fresh clothes. Such good fortune was not destined to be hers, however. The king himself hailed her and her joy at his arrival swelled in spite of her embarrassment at her disheveled appearance.

"Joan, well met. Please, join us. Welcome me home."

She grimaced, yet had little choice but to obey; the command came from her monarch after all. With a hasty gesture, she surreptitiously wiped her sweaty countenance on her sleeve then faced the entire party. Hastily, she fumbled through a clumsy curtsey. As always when she was in the presence of fine ladies, she felt dreadfully awkward but she did her best to project confidence.

Finn made the introductions and as the beauty responded with a curtsey of her own, Joan evaluated the other woman's appearance. Tall, ethereal, slender and with a face more than pleasing was her initial assessment. How could Thomas, or anyone for that matter, see her with Lyssa, the snow queen, nearby?

"Lyssa, this is my cousin, Lady Joan Langston. She is my mother's ward and along with Thomas, is responsible for all this." Finn gestured to encompass the men, horses and tents that made up their not-so-small community.

"His majesty is too kind. Truly, it is his people's loyalty to him which makes all of this possible," Thomas added.

Finn shook his head. "But it is the two of you who have taken on the task of organizing all of this. I am impressed and you have my thanks."

Thomas bowed and Joan curtseyed, but as he straightened, Thomas grinned. "You, my king, are safe. More, you were successful. Still more, you have returned and are willing to bear my company again. That is more than enough."

Finn beamed back. "You did mention supper, did you not? Well, lead on, I'm starved."

Glad to have a justifiable pretext with which to excuse herself, Joan did not waste the opportunity. "If you'll forgive me, your majesty, I am in no fit state to dine in company. I beg your leave to make myself presentable before I join you for a meal."

Finn took in her ruffled appearance for the first time. "You know I never stand on ceremony, but very well. Try not to be long." He kissed her forehead with great affection and no apparent hesitation.

Grateful, Joan curtseyed once again then turned on her heel in the direction of her own tent while the rest went in search of sustenance.

****

After enjoying an excellent meal together where they talked of nothing of any importance, Finn, Lyssa, Thomas and Joan regrouped in Thomas's tent. Finn was still shocked at the news of his supposed death but he began to feel the beginnings of real anger.

Lyssa looked as wrathful as he felt. "How did this happen?" she fumed. "How did this Simon convince anyone that you were dead, let alone everyone, with no more proof than a ring?"

"I don't know, but by all the gods, I'm going to find out." Taking a deep steadying breath, Finn tried to get his thoughts in order and to form some cohesive plan. "Joan, send your best people back into the city to get more information," he directed. "I want as much detail as possible. I want to know the situation as it is now. We need as much current information as we can get. Once we have that, I will decide how long I need to stay dead."

"Stay dead? Are you serious?" Joan burst out.

"If Simon has people believing I'm dead, I'm less of a threat to him. As long as I stay quiet, anyway. When I do let my people know I am alive, I need it to happen quickly and with maximum effect. I want it to cause the most potential harm to Simon and the least potential harm to me that can be managed." He gave his friends a moment to digest all this then continued, "In the meantime, let's talk about the most likely ways to accomplish this."

"I think the first question we need to ask ourselves is why. Why would Simon take such a huge risk, one that could so easily backfire? Why put it about you are dead when he isn't sure if you are?" Thomas wondered.

"Because he's impatient and determined. He wants what he believes is his and he wants it now, no matter the risk. He's determined to make the best of this opportunity. I hadn't realized how power-hungry he was until now. I never should have gone. My leaving and then putting myself into danger played right into his hands." Finn clenched his fist at the realization, angry at himself.

"There's one more reason for him to say you are dead," Lyssa stated quietly. Everyone turned their full attention to her. "He intends to make this rumor a reality as soon as possible."

Stunned silence reigned for a full thirty seconds then Thomas exchanged a look with Finn. "She's right."

"I agree." Finn made a concerted effort not to so much as glance at his betrothed's pale face. He couldn't afford to, not now. "He will not succeed," he assured them in a calm tone. "So, the next question we need to answer is how."

"But that's a question we can't answer. We can't know how or when or where Simon will strike." Joan's voice vibrated with tension and sounded tight.

"True," Thomas agreed, "but we can start to theorize. We can gather more facts. Once we've done that we can be prepared for more possibilities."

"We'll send people as I suggested. Meanwhile, all of you think about what you know of Simon. Given his personality, what is he most likely to do?"

"That's just it; I never would have expected him to do any of this. Take over the kingdom and be utterly ruthless about it or put it about that you are dead? These are the kinds of risks I never believed he would take." Thomas shook his head at the idea.

Lyssa spoke again. "Judging by what the three of you say, his behavior seems to be changing. I say seems to be because in life-altering situations like this, a person doesn't change, not really, they just get fined down to who they really are. Believe me I know."

"So we should think about who he really is underneath." Finn considered this then nodded. "I agree. Very good point, Lyssa." He looked around at each of them in turn. "All of you keep thinking about what we've discussed. Otherwise, we continue to prepare as best we can and we wait."

The expression on each face was mirrored by the three others. None of them liked the idea of inaction. "I know. I promise it won't be for much longer. Things are coming to a head; I can feel it. When they do, we'll strike."

On this somewhat more optimistic note, Finn, Joan and Lyssa took their leave.

Chapter Ten

As they broke their fast, Finn and Thomas discussed their plans for the day, which included scouting around the outskirts of the camp.

Before Joan could express her wish to join them, Lyssa said, "Perhaps Joan might show me around while you do that? Finn has told me so much about you and it would please me if we could know each other better. The forest and meadows hereabouts are lovely and I would like to see them up close. We would stay within the perimeter, of course."

The snow queen's smile was encouraging and friendly, and really, what else could she do but acquiesce? So, an hour later she found herself walking about the encampment. In a stiff tone, she began to point out the various areas and sights of the place. "If you go left, you will see the river Trill—"

Lyssa placed a hand on Joan's arm and the rest of her words died in her throat. "Actually, while I am interested in the area, the beauty of the river and the woods and so forth, we'll get to that later. But first, well, my real motive was to talk to you."

Joan tensed. What on earth could Lyssa have to talk to her about? On so short an acquaintance and with so little in common, she couldn't imagine what the other woman might have to say.

"I am in love with Finn."

The statement was blunt and to the point and Joan couldn't help but admire it. Lyssa went up in her estimation.

But the queen was not finished. "I think I fell for him the moment I saw him. I'm a very fortunate woman because, well, he loves me too. In fact, he loves me so much he's asked me to marry him."

Joan took a moment to gather her wits enough to speak, but she managed to get her tongue working at last. "I wish you every happiness."

The queen inclined her head, and the gesture was so regal Joan wished she possessed a little of the other woman's poise.

"There are several reasons I am telling you this," she continued. "The first is that I want you to understand that there is no one else for me but Finn. I will do my utmost to be a loving and loyal wife to him. I have no interest in any other, certainly not Thomas."

Joan's cheeks burned. Apparently she had not hidden her feelings for Thomas as well as she supposed if the queen was aware of them.

"Secondly, as a result of knowing true joy for the first time, I want everyone else to know the same. Perhaps it's presumptuous of me to mention it, but I've seen the way you look at Lord Thomas and the way he looks at you."

Joan longed to deny it. For the queen to see not only that she was smitten, to all intents and purposes besotted with Thomas, was beyond humiliating. But even worse, she had to believe that Lyssa was mistaken about Thomas's desire for her. It was not the same for him.

Since her arrival in camp, their interactions had

been the same as they always had. He treated her no differently. Not one mention of the kiss they shared had crossed his lips nor was there any other hint he felt the least bit attracted to her. Whenever she thought to broach the subject with him herself, her courage failed her. It was best, she decided, that no one know anything of her deepening feelings, especially Thomas. Unfortunately, she had not succeeded. Realizing this, all she wanted at that moment was to crawl away somewhere quiet and be alone, but she told herself to have more grit and tried her best to keep her expression neutral.

"I know I'm overstepping," Lyssa continued. "But it's lovely to see. He loves you and he doesn't even know it yet. I am so happy for you."

For a long moment, Joan was speechless with shock. Thomas in love with her? For a heartbeat she considered the notion then tossed it aside. What utter rot. The man viewed her as a sister, comrade-in-arms and friend, nothing more. To believe anything else was to invite anguish. Anger heated her cheeks. Who was this woman to say any such thing? Barely even acquainted with any of them, yet she was so sure of everyone. Presumptuous wasn't the half of it. "I beg your pardon, my lady, but you are quite mistaken. To Lord Thomas I am family, nothing more or less. He has no idea of courting me."

"Perhaps not yet, but—"

Impatient with the entire discussion, Joan interrupted. "You've been here all of twelve hours; whatever makes you think he is in love with me?"

Lyssa shrugged. "I'm not sure exactly. Perhaps it's that he only has eyes for you. It could be the way he smiles at you. It might be the concern he shows for your welfare." She smiled then paused. "Has he truly never made any advance?"

"No, never!" She had not ever been a good liar, but it was close enough to the truth and none of the other woman's business in any case. Would her cheeks never cool?

Lyssa merely lifted an eyebrow.

Joan gave up, threw up her hands in surrender. "Oh all right, he kissed me. Once," she clarified.

Lyssa gave a small rather un-queen-like sound, somewhere between a squeal and a giggle.

"It didn't mean anything."

"I'll be the judge of that." Lyssa took Joan's hand. "Oh, I know we don't know each other well but I have the distinct feeling I will really like you. I hope you'll soon grow to like me. It's been so long since I've been around people, since I've been gifted with any stories other than my own. Please tell me."

Joan studied her companion's face: pretty, trusting and unjudgmental. She'd never had a female friend of her own age. The queen had already shown her great kindness and in truth, it would be a downright relief to speak of it. In addition, since Lyssa had already all but guessed, what harm could there be in speaking of it? Perhaps talking the matter over with someone would shed some light on her own confused feelings. So, Joan gave Lyssa a brief history of her own childhood, much of it spent playing alongside Finn and Thomas, then continued all the way up to and including the rescue and the kiss.

"So he kissed you. Did you like it?"

Before she stopped to think, Joan blurted, "It felt

wonderful. Better than anything that has ever happened to me."

"What of his reaction? Did he seem to enjoy it?"

Again, Joan's cheeks flushed. "I've little experience in these matters, but yes, he seemed to."

Lyssa's lips twitched, but she straightened them before the smile could form. "Well then, there you have it."

Joan shook her head. "But I told you, he only kissed me because Simon was closing in and we had to make it seem like I was…that we were…"

"Lovers. You said." Lyssa nodded then appeared to choose her words with care. "Joan, a man might kiss a woman in such a situation but he won't necessarily be fully engaged. From everything you say, he was."

"So you think he desires me?"

"Only you can say that for certain, but I would say chances are good."

While the two women continued to walk along the riverbank, Joan's mind was only half engaged in her conversation with Lyssa. The other half was contemplating what it would mean if Thomas actually wanted her. The possibilities were as intriguing as they were daunting. If her feelings were unrequited, then speaking of those feelings could do nothing but harm to them both. He would feel awkward. She would be humiliated. Never able to look him in the face again, much less remain his friend, she would lose him. The most important man in her life would be lost to her forever. Was she willing to take such a risk?

Yet that thought brought her around to the other possibility. What if she was wrong? If she was mistaken and he did have feelings for her beyond friendship, how amazing that would be. A man of flesh and blood could take the place of her fantasies. As a general rule, she was not given to romantic notions and she had no mistaken idea of Thomas's perfection. How could she when she had known him all her life? Still, she had to ask herself what such a huge restructuring of their relationship might mean. At last she would have all she longed for, but she was not such a fool as to believe that true joy would necessarily follow. Such a thing was by no means assured. This frightened her above all. To have all she could desire and then lose it would devastate her more than anything.

As they returned to the dining tent for the midday meal, Joan told herself to put it out of her mind. It was a complicated question which must wait to be addressed at a more opportune time, when they were not in the middle of a rebellion perhaps. Try as she might, she met with little success.

Considering whether to take the risk remained foremost in her mind, her best efforts notwithstanding. Her thoughts circled round and round, repeatedly hitting on the same key points until she wanted to scream. Was he worthy? Yes, in every way. Could she bear to lose him if he did not feel the same way about her, or worse, if he became her lover then his feelings changed? Unclear, but brutal pain of a kind she'd never known would certainly be the result. And the most important question of all: if she chose to do nothing, was she willing to give up all she might gain? His love, his body, his particular regard, and his constant companionship might all be hers for the asking or just as easily might not. Either way, she was most unwilling to give up the possibility.

More and more often she found herself longing for him, craving him like some drug long denied her and each time she did, she came closer to letting him know it. She seemed to find fewer and fewer reasons not to. Sighing, she accepted she would, in the end, simply have to act or not. But for now, as nothing immediate could be done, she must slow the merry-go-round of her thoughts. So, she gave herself a stern mental shake and forced her attention back to the present and her companions.

****

After dinner the next night, Finn ordered Thomas to collect the troops so he could talk to them. It was early evening and while the sun had set, the moon had yet to rise. The troops had gathered in front of the royal pavilion and it was time he addressed them.

"Everyone is assembled as you commanded," Thomas informed Finn. "They are honored that you will speak to them."

In spite of those words of encouragement, Finn had no idea what to say. The firm hand of his closest friend on his shoulder helped somewhat, yet he could not steady his nerves. For eight long years, he had ruled as their king. For nine years before that, he had received instruction on the same from his mother the regent, the council and a plethora of independent advisors and experts. None of this changed the fact that he had never lead men into battle before. Well, he would just have to buck up.

A moment's reflection brought his father to mind. "But what if I can't, Father?" His eleven-year-old self had demanded when it was time to embrace his birthright and create fire out of nothing.

"You can." Seth Hale assured him. "If not the first time, then the second or the third or the twenty-third. Besides, you will never know unless you try." The king had given his shoulder a reassuring pat then had left him to it.

His father, still healthy and whole and with him, had been right. He had created a flame, warm, fragrant and perfect, the very first time he tried. At home in the massive hearth in the library, he conjured a blazing fire that heated the entire room. The memory of the older man's firm hand upon his shoulder and the pride in his sire's eyes as his son called up flame for the first time had touched Finn's heart. With great clarity he recalled the thrill and pleasure of coming into his own, of embracing his heritage at last.

His training, his instincts and his father's confidence in him had come to his aid and he had succeeded. From that time on, he had never looked back. His father had been right then and would be right now. His father's faith in him had not been misplaced and never would be.

When he raised a hand, the murmurs quieted and everyone looked at him with great expectation. He took a deep breath and addressed his people. "I gaze out among you and I am humbled. So many of you have come, I am nearly speechless, though not quite." Light laughter greeted this remark and his lips quirked up the tiniest bit in response. "Now more than ever, I am determined to show myself worthy of your loyalty in these troubled times. Simon, a once trusted member of my council, has overreached and turned traitor. He has his supporters, as you know. His treason cannot—no, *will not*—be allowed to stand. I intend to take back what is mine, no matter the cost to myself.

"As a first step, I will negotiate with him. To avoid the shedding of blood on both sides, I will humble myself and go to him." A rumble from the crowd like distant thunder, a clear sound of discontent rose. He lifted a hand again and quieted them. "Have no fear, I will never bend the knee. Instead I will offer him a choice: a chance to escape the horror of war. If he steps aside and surrenders to me, he and all his army, I will pardon those who wish it and allow those who prefer exile to go, never to return. He and those closest to him, the ones most responsible for this state of affairs, shall be imprisoned for the rest of their natural lives."

"If he refuses?" The question came from some anonymous person in the crowd.

Finn could not tell whether the speaker was a man or woman, much less pick him or her out. But he answered nevertheless. "If he refuses then we will have no choice but to fight."

A cheer went up, but after the initial enthusiasm subsided, the people closest watched him. Finn could sense their utter fascination with him and his face set like stone. Seeing this, they quieted once more.

"Make no mistake, my friends. This outcome is not to be desired. It is to be avoided at all costs. War is no romantic tragedy. It is long and painful. It is a gruesome and bloody business and it breaks my heart to burden you with it. For all our sakes, we must exhaust every other option before turning to it.

"Yet we will not give up without a fight. I will protect you and your freedom to the last drop of my blood. I will preserve this kingdom with all I have. I will preserve it for you, for your children and my own."

Another cheer sounded, a louder one this time, and Finn did not try to silence it.

As the noise diminished, he turned and held out a hand to Lyssa. When she stepped forward and put her palm in his, he went on. "This is my betrothed, Lyssa Jennings, Queen of Halstad. She is one of the mythical snow queens and royal blood. Our union, with the blessing of the gods, will restore the ancient balance so long lost to us."

An almost reverent silence fell. With great dignity, a man close to the king genuflected in pledge of his fealty. In little more than the space of a heartbeat others adopted a similar posture until the whole of the assembly knelt.

Then the one who had been first to kneel spoke in a strong clear voice, which carried to all. "Long live the king. Long live the queen."

By the third repetition the entire company took up the chant. With a myriad of emotions swirling inside him, Finn held his and Lyssa's joined hands aloft and prayed he would be worthy of their devotion.

Chapter Eleven

Warwick recognized right away that he was too late. The castle was magnificent, but it was also deserted. As he was the best assassin and the most gifted tracker in Minden, he'd had little trouble following Finn's trail to this point and right to his target, the snow queen. It was unfortunate that he missed them. By his estimation, they had left no more than a day or two before. Though it was a pointless exercise, he cursed his fate. After a bit of this self-indulgent behavior, he resolved he would not give up. He would find them. He would bring King Finn Hale's head to her majesty on a platter if she so desired. Anything less and his queen and lover Adriane would flay him alive.

With great care, he entered the palace, checking for any signs of life. His instincts told him no one was there nor had been for days, but he must see it for himself. How else could he give a full report to his queen? Searching for any clue as to their whereabouts or even their general direction was also paramount. Yet every room he entered, from the magnificent great hall to the smallest broom cupboard, was as empty as the last. There was nothing which might give him any starting point, nothing to enlighten him. In disgust, he went out again, none the wiser.

Mounting up once more, he scouted around the

entire castle looking for their tracks. At last fate, that fickle wench he'd so recently cursed, smiled on him. One set of hoof prints was all it took. Two days old, in his estimation, the tracks confirmed what he already knew. The snow queen had left before he had even arrived at the border.

Of even greater interest, she hadn't left alone. In a secluded glen perhaps half a mile from the palace, he picked up two sets of tracks, not one. The new tracks were larger and etched deeper into the soft earth. The original tracks were from a smaller horse carrying less weight. It was also clear, at least to him, that while some effort had been made to cover their tracks, it had not been enough. Branches and leaves had been used to erase them and to cover what could not be erased, yet tell-tale signs were still visible. A broken twig here, another half-concealed hoof print there and in less than an hour, he was well on his way and on their trail.

****

Drake approached the ice palace with great caution. All signs were that Finn's trail ended here at the home of the snow queen. By all appearances, the place was deserted and yet altogether there were three sets of tracks leading from the place. Two sets some days old and one fresh all headed in the same direction. With no other leads and little choice, he followed them.

As he approached a bend in the road, a knife flew past his cheek, so close the wind of it stirred his hair. Cursing, he spurred his horse forward and flattened himself against its neck to present less of a target. He rode as though the devil were after him for perhaps five minutes. Then, just as he reached the curve in the road, he came within a hairsbreadth of crashing straight into a rider who galloped across the path and halted directly in front of him. He pulled hard on the reins and slid to a standstill mere inches from the other man.

"Move even one muscle and I'll have this knife in you before you can get five feet. You know I don't have to miss, Drake. It is good to see you by the way."

"Warwick. What the devil are you doing here?"

"Same as you I expect. Who's your target?"

Drake scoffed. "It's more than my life is worth to tell you. You know that as well as I do."

Warwick shrugged. "Have it your own way. I just thought perhaps we could help each other." The man turned his horse in the direction he had come and made to leave.

Drake resisted for all of ten seconds. "How could you possibly help me and why would you want to?"

"I think your target and mine are together. Why track them separately?"

Again, Drake could not help but scoff. "Maybe because you threw a knife at my head not five minutes past and I'm no fool?"

Warwick threw back his head and laughed. "That was business. I had to get your attention. Like I said, I don't have to miss."

Still more than a little skeptical, Drake decided he might as well find out more. "And how do I know I won't end up with a knife in my back one night once we find them?"

The other man's wide grin was a harsh contrast to the cold look in his eyes and Drake's blood ran even colder. "You don't."

Drake considered his options for a long moment. The man was one of the best hunters in the kingdom, second only to himself. Finding his target would be quicker and easier with Warwick around. It also might be better to keep Warwick close rather than have to be worried that the man would ambush him again. Or come upon then take both targets.

"All right. So long as your target and mine are together then I suppose we could pursue them together."

"Excellent." Warwick cocked his head. "Aren't you going to demand my word not to double cross you, kill you in your sleep or capture both targets for my very own?"

"Why would I bother when you aren't exactly a man of your word?"

Again Warwick threw back his head and laughed. "You aren't as stupid as you look," he commented once he could draw breath enough to speak. "C'mon, let's find them."

****

Two days of tracking with sign but no sight of their quarry. Two nights with snatches of fitful sleep because he dared not rest when he was in the company of the most lethal killer in the civilized world. At this point, it was all Drake could do to keep from groaning aloud with fatigue. He splashed a bit of cool water onto his face from the brook nearby and sat, back against a tree, to let his horse drink his fill.

While he waited, he made a few important decisions. This would be his last job. Even though chronologically he was only forty, he was getting too bloody old for this and he had enough money to last a lifetime. Disappearing seemed like a very attractive option, one he ought to take advantage of before it was too late. Before he tempted the gods one time too many.

Moderately refreshed and somewhat easier in his mind, it was time to return to Warwick, whom he had left breaking camp. With a sigh, he took up the reins of his horse and led his stallion back toward the path. The loud crack of a twig was the only warning he got before two strangers appeared.

The first lifted a bow and arrow while the other unsheathed a sword. Drake cursed and unsheathed his own blade.

****

The damn man ought to have been back long since. Warwick waited for quite some time, but at last, tired of the delay, he left to go fetch him. Drake would not be happy when he did. Setting off in the direction the other man had gone, he muttered curses and imprecations as he tramped through the forest.

Wary at the sounds of fighting, he approached with caution and chose his spot. He thought it best to hide and assess the situation rather than to flee or interfere. So he observed the proceedings from his position in the brush with great interest.

Two men had Drake well and truly captured. Since he had no desire to meet the men himself and suffer the same fate, Warwick left as quietly as he had come.

****

Drake gave the first man a bad gash in the thigh. The other he ran through. But not before he'd had a knife to his throat. Although air shuddered in and out of his lungs, he could not take a full breath. He had come within inches of having his throat slit. The job was often perilous. No one ever said being an assassin was without risk but never had he come so close to dying. If his reactions had been a trifle slower or if his opponents had been the slightest bit stronger, he could be the one stretched out on the ground lifeless.

More deeply shaken than he had ever been in his life, he wasted no time. Without further delay he mounted and got the hell out. It seemed he wouldn't complete this last job after all.

****

"You really ought to tell him, you know."

Lyssa made the statement in such an offhand manner that Joan did not at first register its full meaning. One week in company together had made the two women more comfortable with each other, but not so comfortable that Joan could expect a comment like that. First surprise, then trepidation filled her.

"Tell him that I have a silly schoolgirl crush on him? One he doesn't return? No thank you."

"Oh, come now, you don't know whether he does or does not return your feelings. He might not be the kind to volunteer that sort of thing. He may be waiting for some sign as to how you feel. He won't know unless you tell him. Or better yet, show him."

The light in Lyssa's eyes made Joan quite nervous. "Whatever you have in mind, the answer is no. Whatever scheme you are hatching in that fertile brain of yours, I want no part of it."

Lyssa pursed her lips in a distinctive pout. "I'm not proposing anything rash. Just a bit of a change that's all. All I'm suggesting is that you clean yourself up and wear your most flattering gown when you sit near him tonight at dinner. There are many ways to let a man know you are interested without having to say the words out loud."

Joan snorted. "I wouldn't know where to begin."

Lyssa beamed. "I can help you there."

Joan sighed. "Lyssa—"

"Oh, please, for me. I only want to see you as happy as I am."

Joan sighed once more then gave up the fight.

****

When she entered the large pavilion designated for taking meals, a few of the men glanced up then did a double take. Instead of her usual homespun kirtle, Joan wore a forest green silk cotehardie gown which brought out the lighter green of her eyes. The cut of the dress flattered her, as did the low neckline. Rather than the uncomplicated, practical, single braid it was her habit to wear, her hair was piled high atop her head in the latest style which Lyssa assured her was very becoming. But Thomas hadn't even glanced her way yet. He was too busy talking to some blonde lady in an elegant but quite revealing rose-colored dress.

When at long last he looked toward the entrance where she purposely dawdled, his gaze lingered for one sizzling instant on her. He looked her over from top to toe, paying particular attention to her cleavage unless she was much mistaken. The look, at least in her assessment, was an appreciative one, but then his companion asked him a question, breaking the spell. With an absentminded gesture, he took up his fork again then turned back to the woman seated beside him.

Fighting off an attack of nerves, she walked to the empty place at the table across from him. As she approached, Thomas stood, came around then held out her chair for her.

"You look positively fetching this evening, Joan.

Quite a breath of fresh air. This is a change from your customary more utilitarian mode of dress, if I may be so bold."

Her cheeks colored. The compliment he first greeted her with ought to have sufficed. Instead, he made her sound like some ragamuffin. He made her look a tomboy, or worse, like some waif with no idea how to dress. How dare he, she fumed. So what if it were to a certain extent true? He ought to be more gallant and she had seen him have far better manners. Thomas's smooth voice interrupted her fierce inner diatribe.

"Lady Joan, may I introduce Miss Katherine Lockwood. Katherine just joined us this afternoon. Her father is a merchant in Camden town and they brought us much-needed supplies. Katherine and I met a few years ago when I purchased some items from her father."

Something about his tone, a certain intimacy perhaps, alerted her to the fact that they'd been lovers. Oh, he was careful to mask it, but she knew him well, far better than anyone else. The look in his eyes when his gaze met Katherine's put the matter beyond doubt. She fixed her own mask into place and steeled herself to behave in her customary polite way in spite of the pain ripping at her heart.

"It is lovely to make your acquaintance, Miss Lockwood."

"Lady Joan." They nodded heads in lieu of curtseys and Joan settled down to her meal.

****

So far what Joan secretly dubbed the flirtation experiment was going nowhere. It was in fact a dismal failure. She could barely get a word in edgewise. Miss Lockwood was quite chatty. Of course, Thomas did nothing to discourage the girl, in Joan's opinion. He just kept asking Miss Lockwood question after question, picking up the conversational ball when it lagged and ignoring his best friend in the world almost entirely.

The longer it continued the more her ire increased and the more mutinous she felt. Yet she would not, absolutely would not, let it show. There was no sense in making more of a fool of herself than she already had. Pretending not to notice while Thomas fawned all over the prim Miss Lockwood was almost more than she could stand, however. Her stomach roiled and churned with self-disgust and jealousy but deep inside there was also a thick icy ball of fear. What if she was deluding herself? He'd never taken any note of her before; why would he now? Had she been foolish to pin all her hopes on him and the memory of one kiss?

Well, no matter what, she wouldn't go down without a fight. Either way, she would make an effort to if not outshine the fabulous Miss Lockwood, at least keep up. She might not be able to compete with the other woman in the area of pure feminine allure, but she could remind Thomas of her particular value.

To that end, when there was a lull in the conversation at last, she made the most of it. "When do you hope to see his majesty return?"

"If the gods are with us, I expect to see him on the morrow. He wanted to scout the perimeter of the capital city. I sent a messenger the night of my impromptu departure detailing the situation as far as I knew it then, but things may have changed by now and he insisted he must see for himself."

"I wonder you did not go with him."

Thomas grunted. "I would have, but his majesty was adamant I remain here. He said he needed me to continue to organize and prepare. I don't much like it, but you know what he's like once he's fixed on a course of action."

Joan sent him an understanding look. "He can be very difficult to dissuade."

"Mmmm-hmmm."

"You mentioned an impromptu departure?" Katherine inquired sweetly, bringing Thomas's full attention back to her.

Before Thomas could respond, however, Joan answered for him. "The usurper, Lord Simon Fairfax, was arresting all of his detractors. Chief among them was Thomas. I warned him then helped him get out."

"I see. How thrilling."

Although she had already consumed several glasses of wine, Joan accepted another, beamed just a little blearily at the footman as he poured, then returned her focus to Katherine. "It was, I assure you. You can't imagine the subterfuge and the risk involved. Well, let's just say every minute of that night I was sure my heart would jump out of my chest, especially when Thomas kissed me. All part of the subterfuge I mentioned, you understand. He is a wonderful kisser," she confided.

Katherine's eyes hardened but otherwise her manner did not change. In spite of the flush painting her cheeks, she said nothing. Instead she toasted Joan as if to say, "Well-played."

While her confessional tone and revelation had little visible effect on Katherine, not so on Thomas. He clenched his jaw so hard Joan could see it from across the table. With deliberate care, he set down his own goblet, pushed back his chair and rose. "Do excuse us for a moment, Miss Lockwood. I'm afraid Joan has had a bit too much to drink. She needs some fresh air."

Before she could utter so much as a squeak of protest, he had her by the arm, up and out of her seat and halfway to the entrance of the tent.

As soon as they were out of sight of any interested onlookers, she jerked her arm from his grip. "What do you think you are doing?"

"Me? I've never seen you behave like this in your life."

"Like what?"

She hoped her low dangerous tone would warn him he was treading on rocky ground but he was too wrapped up in his own temper to pay it any heed. "Like the most determined flirt I've ever seen, and a drunken one at that. What on earth are you thinking?"

"Flirt! Why don't you say what you really mean, Thomas? The word you want to use is whore."

His eyes widened with shock and his mouth gaped. After a heartbeat or two, he managed to sputter, "I would never use that word in reference to you or any other woman, even if she actually was a…courtesan. How could you ever think I would?"

In the back of her mind she registered he was no longer quite so angry, that his tone was now one of shock but her own emotions were too stirred up for her to care. "Oh, well, if not whore, then perhaps the right word is ridiculous. Is it so absurd that I might put myself out to please a man? Set out to gain his attention? Or am I so unattractive, so unfeminine that the very notion is preposterous?"

"No, of course not. I only meant to point out that your behavior tonight has been far from typical and it made me wonder what in the name of all the gods is going on with you. That's all. Yes, you were a dreadful flirt tonight but you were also exquisite and charming and any man would find you desirable."

Tears abruptly threatened. They burned hot in the back of her throat, but she swallowed them. "Except you," she muttered, not loud enough for him to hear.

"As for ridiculous, Joan, I never said that! You are many things, ridiculous is not one of them," he repeated. His voice rose a little and he ran a hand through his gorgeous black hair, leaving it a disordered, albeit attractive, mess. "But I must admit I am getting a little tired of you putting words in my mouth. How can you know how I feel when I haven't the foggiest idea myself?"

"Well, let's stop discussing this then, shall we? I for one have nothing more to add."

"Infernal woman! Have it your own way."

Without another word exchanged, they parted and each went to their own corner to stew and sulk.

Chapter Twelve

The next day was a fine one for hunting. The morning was cool but not uncomfortably so, with the fresh, sweet scent of spring in the air. Thomas appreciated the change in the weather as he and Finn rode out as much as he appreciated the distraction.

As soon as they were well on their way, Finn said, "So, who is she?"

"I beg your pardon, majesty?"

"The woman you've fallen for. Who is she?"

Thomas swore while Finn just smirked. "Did you think I wouldn't notice? It's been written all over your face since I arrived. Come on, you can tell me."

Thomas swore again, more creatively this time then gave up any attempt at subterfuge. "It's Joan."

Finn's eyebrows soared as his mouth plummeted. The king all but goggled then managed, "Joan? You are falling in love with Joan? Little spitfire, good with a bow, known her all our lives? *That* Joan?"

"Yes, that Joan," Thomas admitted in a clipped tone.

"Well, that's…surprising and wonderful. In fact it makes a kind of sense, all in all," Finn concluded. His often too-serious face broke into a broad grin.

"Surprising is right," Thomas muttered. "I'm not so sure about wonderful. She has no idea how I feel yet, as I'm only just beginning to explore the question myself."

"Hmmm."

When his friend said "Hmmm," in just that tone, Thomas knew there was something he wasn't saying. "What?"

"Ahem. What do you mean, what?"

"There's something you aren't telling me. Does she secretly find me unattractive? Think of me as a brother? What?"

Finn narrowed his eyes a moment, considering. "Actually, I think she might fancy you. In fact, I'm almost sure of it. I am a bit astonished you haven't figured this out until now, to tell you the truth."

Stunned, Thomas could think of nothing to say, but in the end it mattered little since Finn continued to elaborate. "She's easier in your company than almost anyone else's. The two of you share many common interests. She admires you in a way she admires no other. Once, when she saw you with another woman, I caught her crying all alone a few minutes later. She wouldn't admit it, at least not to me, but I think it was because seeing you with another woman was hard on her. But even more telling, she's careful not to touch you if she can help it. And it's not because she doesn't want to. Finally, she trusts you more than anyone on this earth. Taking all this information together...face it, my friend, she fancies you."

The events of the previous evening flashed through his mind. "Well, when you put it that way." He shook his head, bemused. "I never realized. But what if you are wrong, what if we're both wrong?"

"We're not, but either way don't you owe it to yourself and her to find out for sure?"

"Maybe, but we aren't exactly speaking at the

moment." Thomas related the events of the previous night then concluded with, "I swear I never thought of her that way until that kiss and I have never seen any indication she thought of me that way. But the other night, she behaved so strangely that even I noticed it. Have I been blind?"

"Very probably. But back up, a kiss? How did that happen?"

In a few sentences, Thomas told his king the story of his escape and the part Joan played in accomplishing it.

After hearing the entire tale, Finn whistled. "A brave woman, but then she was always so. Since it is obvious you've recently developed an interest in her and perhaps she has in you, you have my blessing. See if anything comes of it. You'd be a lucky man if it does."

"So I would," Thomas agreed, easier in his mind now that he had spoken of the matter to a friend. "You, majesty, already are."

"True, and well I know it. As you are my closest friend and Lyssa and I are to be married, I'll tell you plainly there's not much better in this life than having the woman you love by your side each day and in your bed with some regularity."

Thomas grinned. "I'm sure." Upon meeting Lyssa, Thomas had made a detailed assessment of his future queen. What he found was a woman of unrivalled beauty, as distant as she was cold. He wondered how his king would fare with such a woman.

They rode for some minutes with nothing but the sound of the horse's hooves then he asked, "So things between you are going well then?"

Finn nodded. "I feel stronger than ever before, in every way. An arranged, fated, all but forced marriage that was little more than a political alliance could have been a disaster. Instead, I found love. I love her, and miracle of miracles, she loves me. I find myself ready to embrace my fate. I have no desire to fight it anymore. Why would I?"

"Indeed." That was all Thomas could think to say.

They lapsed into silence and let the horses and the hunting carry them where they would.

****

As the note from Joan directed, he met her at the large oak near the river that evening. It was a useful landmark and made an excellent private meeting place. "So," Thomas began, but could not think how to go on. When Joan said nothing, he continued, "It's you who called this meeting. What is it you'd like to say?"

"What? No, it's you who wanted to see me. It's you who has something to say."

Thomas shook his head. "No, your letter indicated an apology might be forthcoming."

"An apology? It's you who ought to be offering an apology." Her tone, which had been carefully neutral, went cold.

"What could I possibly have to apologize for?"

"Your behavior last evening was patronizing, arrogant and downright insulting."

"You were childish, at times unfathomable and more than a little embarrassing," he shot back.

He opened his mouth, to spew more venom no doubt, but before he could speak, a disturbing supposition occurred to her and she held up a hand to forestall him. "Wait. You received a letter? I didn't send you a letter." She sniffed. "You sent me a rather lovely one. Not your usual style at all. I found it strange. It didn't sound like you in the least."

"I didn't send you any letter. Since you claim you never sent me one, I suppose then, that you never intended to apologize? But you assumed I would?"

"Yes, isn't that what I just said?"

"Indeed. You should know, I never intended to apologize, at least not first. I assumed you would."

"I see." Patience at an end, she demanded, "If neither of us intended to apologize and neither of us sent a letter to the other, then who did? How did this happen?"

"Lyssa." They said the name simultaneously. Joan shook her head while Thomas cursed.

"Why on earth would she do this? Why throw us together this way? Why stick her nose in?"

Joan bit her lip, hesitated then spoke. "She's gotten it into her head we're meant for each other. She's to be married and she is happy and so she—"

"She wants everyone else to be the same," Thomas finished on a sigh.

Joan inclined her head then mumbled, "Shows how much she knows. You seemed far more interested in Katherine."

"Who?"

The puzzled look on his face might have made her laugh at any other time. Now it only brought raised eyebrows. "Miss Katherine Lockwood, the woman you ignored me for during the entire night in question." When he still looked nonplussed, she elaborated, "Your former paramour, the one that you threw in my face. Surely you remember her."

He waved the woman away with a hand. "Oh, her. So what if she used to be my lover? She isn't anymore and she shares that honor with more than a few others. Since when is it any business of yours?"

"Since you kissed me the night of your escape." The words burst from her before she could stop them and regret filled her the moment they were out of her mouth, but it was too late and they could not be unsaid.

"The situation called for it. It wasn't planned..." Unable to explain the impulse which had led him to kiss her that night, his voice trailed off. He focused instead on the issue at hand. "It never bothered you before." He seemed intrigued rather than puzzled.

"No, it didn't bother me before. But if you think you can kiss me then move on to another woman and expect me to be happy about it, well, think again."

"I didn't realize one kiss under strained circumstances meant you owned me." His voice held an edge now.

"I never believed one reckless moment meant you were mine, but I did hope it meant something to you."

When he said nothing in response, just stared at her, she mentally threw up her hands and gave it up as a bad job. "But I suppose I've been a fool as well as a wanton," she muttered, whirling away.

She should have known it would not be so simple. Thomas placed himself right in her path. His stubborn expression made it quite clear to her that he was not finished with her yet, not by any means.

"You are neither a wanton nor a fool and if you'd let me explain, maybe even apologize, then perhaps we can come to some sort of an understanding."

She squirmed, wanted to be anywhere else in the

world, but she stayed put.

At length, he spoke again. "I never meant to hurt you. Not then, not last night and not now. The pain I now see I have caused you was not deliberate, I swear it. Since I had to focus on someone other than you last night, I figured it might as well be her."

A trifle bewildered now, Joan demanded, "Why did you have to focus on someone other than me?"

He cleared his throat and wouldn't meet her eyes. "Well, I could hardly let everyone know my changing feelings for you, not when I wasn't entirely sure of them myself."

Changing feelings? Changing how and to what degree, she wondered? Was he starting to notice her at last? Was he beginning to see her as more than friend, sister, or comrade-in-arms? Her heart tripled its beat even as she chided herself. Absurd to let herself hope on so little.

"Do you believe me?"

Joan nodded, and realized it was no more than the truth. She did believe him. Deep down in her soul, she was sure he would never hurt her on purpose, not for the world. Since she did, and as he was only willing to go so far, perhaps it was up to her to take one last risk. If she wanted him, maybe she should do as Lyssa instructed and let him know. "Lyssa advised me to tell you how I feel."

With his hand halfway up to run through his hair, Thomas froze. "Do you plan to take her advice? How do you feel, Joan? Will you tell me?"

"I…" Her throat was so dry she could hardly get the words out, but at last she managed, "Yes, I will." Then on impulse, she rose onto her toes, brought her lips to his.

It was all as she remembered, hot and soft and piercingly sweet. For a moment he was still then his lips stirred beneath hers, just a whisper of motion, making her tremble. Strong arms wrapped around her and for one instant she couldn't breathe.

Finn's voice calling for Thomas sent her back to earth with an unwelcome thud. More than a little shocked by her own forwardness and not a little shaken, she had no desire to meet the king just then. So she slipped out of Thomas's arms and raced away. When she heard him call, "Joan, wait," she paid no heed.

****

Over the years he'd seen her avoid those she did not wish to encounter with inordinate skill. It never occurred to Thomas she would use the skill on him until she did so. With great success he was forced to admit. After three days of such tricks, he had to concede she was good. By that time it was also quite clear to him that he should never have let her go. He let her slip right out of his arms, foolish man that he was. He wouldn't make such a tactical error ever again.

Yet all was far from lost. In fact, he possessed a distinct advantage. He knew her well, better than anyone, and so at last he managed to track her down. Her habit of an evening walk in the woods made it all somewhat easy in the end. As she passed the place where he was concealed, he only had to fall into step with her as he so often did.

"You've been avoiding me," he said by way of greeting. Her startled eyes narrowed then found his and he put his hands up in supplication. "Not that I blame you at all. I apologize for everything that's happened

185

over the past few days. I should never have spoken so harshly when you asked me about Katherine. I was also clumsy and stupid the other evening which only added to it. I was relieved and happy to be back on good terms with you. Happy when I thought you would come to me because I was too proud and foolish to go to you. I won't make the same mistake again now."

Joan sighed. "It's all right. What could I expect when I made such a fool of myself?"

His quizzical look prompted her to explain. "By throwing myself at you the other night then again the next evening and even going so far as to kiss you that time."

"Ah, that."

"Yes, that. Don't worry. It won't happen again now I know for certain you don't think of me that way."

****

For a long time, he said nothing and Joan wished the earth would swallow her up, anything to avoid the rest of this conversation.

"It's true, I never thought of you that way. Not, at least, until the night you rescued me and I kissed you. Then when you kissed me, I confess I was shocked for just a moment. I never truly believed *you* saw *me* that way until that instant. Then we were interrupted."

"Are you saying if we hadn't been, you would've kissed me back?" Her incredulous tone made it clear she did not believe this at all. Still, the heat which flared in his eyes made her quake.

"Given half a moment more? Yes."

Such words coming from him made her bold. "Would you want me to kiss you again?" Everything inside her thrilled, stilled, held its breath.

He shook his head, but rather than be upset, disappointed or disheartened in any way, she remained mesmerized by the look in his eyes. "This time, let me kiss you."

When he studied her face, he must have read her acceptance there because he pressed his lips to hers.

Had she ever been truly kissed before? No, she decided. The amazing things he was doing to her mouth bore little resemblance to any of her awkward previous experiences. Boys had kissed her. Thomas was a man and hers. Everything about the exchange made her believe that. The two kisses they'd shared before had been wonderful, but far too brief, too rushed. This time he captured her mouth like they had all the time in the world.

He traced the seam of her lips with the tip of his tongue, begging admittance and she parted hers before she'd thought. Lord, she could get addicted to this, she realized. Then his mouth sank into hers and she stopped thinking altogether. The only other place he touched her was the nape of her neck, which he'd grasped to tug her to him. Then he changed the gentle hold to a caress, one which sent shivers all through her.

Joan could hardly believe what was happening. Thomas had his hands on her at last and it was as if her most erotic dreams had come to life.

When he released her mouth, she would have protested but then he whispered, "Joan." Her name was like another caress when said in that dark sonorous voice of his. She shifted, blindly searching for more, then met his lips with hers again.

If he was this good at kissing, would he be just as wonderful at the rest of it? His reputation suggested he would be. The idle speculation flitted through her distracted brain and simply wouldn't let go. After several long pleasure-soaked minutes, the temptation to find out was too great.

****

To his surprise, she broke the kiss. Never taking her gaze from his, she captured his hand, which had drifted from her neck up to her cheek. She held hers over his a moment then drew it down, pressed it to her breast. His every muscle locked tight. With a ragged breath, he closed his long fingers gently about one firm mound, which fit his palm perfectly. He'd only intended to kiss her. He hadn't meant to go so far, but in the face of such blatant desire he lost all strength to resist. Not that he'd ever really wanted to. Soon his fingers loosened, tracing paths and finally brushing over her already peaked nipple.

Joan gasped with pleasure. Her eyes widened and locked to his. His caught and held hers. Deliberately, he skimmed a finger over the tip of one breast, then back again.

As he treated her other breast to the same and lingered, he was rewarded with a moan. Thomas's own breathing seemed to back up in his lungs at the evocative sound. Beyond rational thought, he grasped the laces of the leather vest she wore. Pure instinct had him simultaneously backing her against a nearby tree. With one rough tug, he tweaked aside the thin blue cotton she wore beneath the vest. One heated instant later he finally made contact with her bare skin. A triumphant groan escaped him as he caressed her heated flesh.

Joan's sharp intake of air at his touch was

encouraging. Then as he caressed and stroked and claimed, she simply let her head fall back to rest against the tree trunk. When she arched to give him better access, he took full advantage. Her response was ardent and entirely unfeigned and he longed for more. Loosening her vest still farther and sliding it down her arms then off, he was free to touch her without that restriction.

The look on her face as he caressed her was so incendiary that he nearly lost all sense. He threw himself into the moment with wild abandon. The desire to take her where they stood was almost overwhelming, but after one long fraught instant, he got himself back under control.

After that, time stood still for him so he was not sure how long he lost himself in her but when the distant call of a night bird filled his ears, he came back to earth, at least enough to realize he must be the one to bring this engagement to a close and soon. Gently but firmly, he ended the kiss; yet he couldn't quite seem to let her go. His hands continued to knead her exquisite body of their own accord.

"Joan, we have to stop," he forced himself to mutter. A moment later he suited words to action; he wrenched himself away from her.

The loss of her touch was as unpleasant for him as an unwanted dip in frigid water after being in the warm sun. Judging from the abrupt stiffness of her body, she felt much the same.

"Why?" she demanded.

Since she shook with reaction and was almost as badly off as he, he gave them both a moment to settle. When he had her full attention, he continued, "Because this is neither the time nor the place. Again."

When she merely lifted a brow, unconvinced, he admitted, "And because if we don't stop soon, I won't care about any of that."

Perhaps seeing the lust, which surely must be clear on his face, appeased her somewhat. Whatever the reason, it was at least enough for her to step back just a bit from him and murmur, "Later then."

The distinctly imperious tone of her words should have been another cause for caution but he could not bring himself to care in the least. "Later," he agreed, knowing his inner untamed self would not be able to resist. With no more talk, they returned to camp.

****

Her feet never touched the ground. Logically, Joan knew this couldn't be so, but damned if she could feel the earth beneath her. When she caught herself humming an old tune about love triumphant Rowena sang to her when she was a child, she clamped her lips shut. Yet they continued to curve up if she wasn't vigilant.

Reaching her tent to find Lyssa at the entrance sobered her more than a little. She fumbled through yet another curtsey and greeted the other woman.

"Good evening to you. I was just coming round to see if you would care to walk down to the river."

"That sounds lovely. Let me just set down my bow." She disappeared into the tent but was back a moment later, ready to leave.

The two women walked along arm in arm for some time in silence, both taking advantage of the fading warmth and enjoying the peace and the beauty of the day's end.

Taking note of Joan's relaxed state, Lyssa commented, "You seem far more cheerful now than when last we met."

There was no hope of hiding her blush, but for once Joan didn't care. "I am." Not trusting herself to say more, at least not without gushing, she left it at that.

Lyssa was not so easily satisfied, however. "Is there any particular reason?"

Her cheeks were aflame now and she had no idea what to say. "Well…"

"I did see Thomas heading in the same direction as you. Did he find you?"

"Umm, yes he did."

"And?"

A little amused now at her new friend's eager questions, Joan played dumb for just a little longer. "And what?"

"And did the two of you settle things between you?"

Joan grinned at the exasperated tone and relented. "We did. Very satisfactorily, I might add. He does not think of me as a sister anymore; he made that quite plain."

"He kissed you again!" The future queen squealed like a young girl and bounced on the tips of her toes.

"He did and a good bit more besides," Joan acknowledged. "I'm not sure what will come of it, but either way, it was lovely and I don't think it'll be the last time."

"Marvelous." Lyssa sighed happily then linked Joan's arm in hers again and lead her farther along the path. "I did so hope something like this would happen. And so it has, now that the two of you have stopped arguing for five minutes together. You seem so well suited."

"That remains to be seen. I can report, however, that he is an excellent kisser."

The ladies giggled and sat by the river's edge to go over all of the details.

****

Strategy was a bitch. Or so Finn began to think after hours in the pavilion designated as the war room discussing it, arguing over it and poring over every minute detail. With his best and most trusted soldiers and associates gathered around him, a battle plan was being formed with slow painstaking effort, with the emphasis on pain.

"It is vital we force the enemy to fight on two fronts," he maintained. "My castle is all but impenetrable. We will never be able to breach its walls without immense loss of life and with the great number of Simon's soldiers inside, we need the advantage of surprise. I'll be damned if I'll lay siege to my own bloody castle. It would be far too demeaning and more to the point, would take years. We don't have that sort of time. No, I intend to storm it, to take it back from within and without. If I enter with one platoon of my most seasoned troops through the secret passage and take out the sentries stationed at these strategic points then make my way to the main gate, I can let our troops in."

"If we haven't already forced open the gates ourselves from the outside."

Finn acknowledged Thomas's statement with a nod. "No years-long siege, no massacre, just victory."

"Even if we manage to enter by stealth and trickery

as you suggest, we still need a distraction, majesty." Thomas had insisted on this from the beginning and had not budged.

Finn raked a hand through hair already unruly. "I agree but we have yet to come up with a suitable one."

"What about me?" Lyssa's question hung in the air, greeted by stunned silence.

"Not many know of me or my abilities. In fact many, if not most, think abilities like mine are a myth. I could be just the distraction you need. I could use my powers to aid our troops and as an added bonus, stun and astonish the enemy. What better diversion could there be?"

"And bring the attention of the entire army directly to bear on you? No, absolutely not."

"I've been listening to you debate the effectiveness of various distractions for hours. This is our best option. I'm scared to death, but I want to help in any way I can."

"The danger is too great. I won't risk you."

"It is my risk to take," she countered.

"Not if I say otherwise."

The entire room, already silent, went motionless as well while everyone present watched them like spectators at a tennis match.

For five humming seconds, neither said a thing then Lyssa rose. "So this is what it comes down to? You are king and you hold sway over me although I am a queen in my own right? I think not."

Without another word, she departed in a swirl of cool wind and icy skirts. Finn stared after her for a moment, swore then followed.

****

Lyssa's walk was as quick as her temper so Finn did not catch up to her until she was halfway to her tent and that was just fine. She was not at all sure what she might have said or done had she remained or had he caught her any sooner. If he had any sense at all he would let her be. Instead, he was following her, chasing after her, all but guaranteeing an argument. Well, if his skull was too rock-hard to realize this, then she could and would oblige him with not just an argument but a bloody good fight.

She whirled and as he was a mere step behind her, soon they were all but nose to nose. "You have more to say I take it? More orders to give? Well, bollocks to that. I don't take orders from anyone, not even you."

"Lyssa—"

She cut him off with a sharp gesture of her hand. "No, don't say another word. I want you to be quiet and ask yourself one thing. What has this all been about? For weeks, no months now, you have been training me, developing my skills and my confidence. Telling me I was valued." Her voice nearly broke on the words, but she swallowed hard and continued. "You told me to trust myself and the second I do, you say no. You say no like it's your call, as though my opinion means nothing."

"I wasn't trying to—"

But she bowled over him again. "You said you wanted an equal partner. Was that all lies? Or did you just not realize how difficult it would be to love a woman with a mind of her own?"

"Lyssa." His voice held a plea now. His tone also conveyed an equal amount of offense, but she ignored both.

194

"No, don't. Either way, understand this, majesty: I will do this with or without your approval. I'll do it because I know beyond the shadow of a doubt that I can. I know too that I am the only one who can."

"It isn't that I don't trust you." His quiet words cut through her tirade, even if only for an instant.

"Really? Then what is it?"

"It's as I said, I won't risk you."

"No, you don't believe I'm strong enough. You don't believe I can do this."

"It isn't that at all, that's what I'm trying to tell you. I believe you can do anything you set your mind to. You are the strongest woman I know. It's...you have become important to me. Vital. If something happened to you, I'm not sure I could handle it."

Lyssa tilted her head, considered this for a moment. "You said over and over you wanted a true partner and until tonight your actions have always shown that. Don't stop now. Don't be a hypocrite and stop doing what's right because it's hard. Not now. It's more important than ever for you to demonstrate your desire for a proper partner by your actions. You must decide. Do you want a mere companion to share your bed and birth your heirs or do you want a true queen?"

For a long time, he said nothing and Lyssa began to wonder whether she had seriously misjudged him. At last he spoke in a calm, if tentative voice. "I'm not agreeing to anything mind, but if I did, what would you have me do?"

She had her answer ready. "Let me be your distraction. I assure you I can create one hell of a diversion. Trust is a two way street. Trust me to do this while you do what you must. Help me trust myself, just as you always have."

He nodded, coming to a decision. "I agree. With two conditions. One: we plan your moves as precisely as we can manage. I want every step choreographed, practiced, rehearsed and re-rehearsed until you know it backward and forward. Two: we teach you how to improvise."

"That sounds perfect. Let's get started." With a smile which was far too sprightly, she took his arm, and ignoring his pained look, led him back to the others.

Chapter Thirteen

The spring night was warm, almost sultry, and it did little to help Thomas's frame of mind. Joan could see that much in the way he kept casting his stone-cold gaze in her direction. The stiff way he held his body was also a clear signal of his agitation, at least to her. She knew from experience that it was best to ignore him when he was in such a mood. Eventually he would calm down enough to tell her what was wrong; until then giving him a wide berth was best for all concerned. So she put him out of her mind and did her best to enjoy her evening.

She sensed more than saw him approach so she wasn't surprised to hear his smooth rich voice.

"If you'll excuse us, gentlemen? Someone has to patrol." Without so much as a by-your-leave from any of their companions, much less her, he took her arm and steered her out of the tent.

"Thomas, what on earth? That was very rude."

Despite her desire to be in his company, especially in his company alone, she could not keep a certain amount of testiness from her voice. She had been in the middle of a very enjoyable, most engrossing conversation with a man called Fletcher involving new techniques in swordplay and she really was a bit put out at being dragged away so summarily. Just as if she were his to do with as he pleased. Well, they'd see about that, now wouldn't they?

"And what was all that about patrol? You know very well Marcus and Jack drew the short straw in our division tonight."

"We did say later, did we not?"

Later? For a heartbeat she wondered what he could possibly mean then she remembered. Those moments beneath the trees played back through her brain at top speed. She stole a quick glance at his face and what she saw there made every inch of her skin heat. But surely he couldn't mean now, not after the two of them left together so publicly? She risked another peek at him and found his gaze fixed upon her. She was captivated by the look in his eyes, which she could only describe as hot, hard, and possessive. Yet it was mixed with something else she couldn't quite put a name to. Since whatever it was made her very soul shimmer, she simply nodded in acquiescence.

He marched quickly, purposefully, toward a thick copse of trees and she could only just keep up with his longer stride. He didn't call a halt until they were well and truly alone, quite away from any who might happen by. Before she could draw breath to speak or indeed react or comment in any way at all, he captured her.

Soft lips claimed hers. Hard hands roamed her body and everywhere they did, she burned. And she wanted more.

He seemed to realize, as he wasted no time. He spread his cloak on the ground beneath an oak then lay back. Taking her hand, he drew her with him. It ended with him half atop her. Then in short order he loosened the bodice of her simple gown and his hand found her breast. His other drew up her skirts and ran a hand down the length of her thigh. When he placed some slight pressure on her knees, she hesitated but then she trembled and opened for him. She was in no mood to refuse him or deny him, much less herself.

"You don't belong to Fletcher. You are mine."

Desire for him coursed down every vein as he found her center then stroked. Her shock was exceeded only by her pleasure.

His tone was low and so gravely as to barely be discernable, but she heard. She heard and could not allow such an arrogant statement to go unchallenged. "I am. Just remember, it works both ways. *You* are *mine*."

"I am. May the gods protect me."

Her breathy laugh ended on a moan as two long smooth fingers entered her. As his palm skated over an exquisitely sensitive spot then away, she shivered. When at last his hand found the spot again and pressed, she arched into the touch then let out a satisfied sigh when he stroked firmly. For long minutes he teased her, repeatedly bringing her right to the brink but never over, until she thought she would surely go mad or be reduced to begging. Begging for what she sensed could be between them, demanding what he held right out of reach.

Ten fraught minutes later, begging was looking less and less like a bad idea. If only she could manage the words. At last she did. "Please," she gasped.

With a glance, he took in her thoroughly aroused state then made careful note of his own. Perhaps realizing neither of them could bear any restraint much longer, he acceded to her request. Holding her eyes with his, he rubbed her core with just the right amount of pressure and sent her flying.

She wanted him with her desperately, but she could no more stop her climax than she could the tide. So she rode it out and it was amazing. Hot shivery sensation rippled from the crown of her head to the tips of her toes. She soared and thought she would never come down, but eventually the glorious contractions faded and she was aware of the world around her again.

As soon as she could think, she was possessed of a desire to bring him the same pleasure she had just experienced. In no frame of mind to put herself in check, she pushed him gently but firmly from her then with no further warning, she reversed their positions so that he was on his back beneath her. "Turn-about is fair play."

Longing to have her hands on him once more, she dispensed with his shirt. Then she fell on the tie of his breeches. With those loosened, she plunged her hand in and found him. Hard steel encased in the velvet softness of his skin met her palm. When she slid her slim fingers up his length then down, he groaned. Startled, she shifted her eyes to his face, saw passion there. She repeated the motion and his head fell back onto the soft fabric beneath them. He let her have free rein for a few superb minutes then placed his hand over hers, teaching her his preferences.

Just the right touch, the most flawless position, and the perfect pressure were soon seared in her memory. Time passed; it may have been minutes or hours, she had no way of knowing which. His hand fell away and he left her to continue on her own. Not long after, his breath started to come in soft pants and when she increased the pace, she was rewarded with a throaty moan. Instinct had her tightening her grip slightly and hot and hard, he exploded.

As his respiration slowed, her own breathing wasn't exactly steady as a sense of triumph filled her. She could give as good as she got. Minute by minute her feeling of triumph faded, however, as he said nothing but instead leaned back, eyes closed.

Finally, jittery with nerves, she could not stand the silence any longer. "Thomas?"

He opened his beautiful eyes, turned them toward her. When his hand rose languidly to touch her cheek, she let out a sigh of relief.

"Are you all right? I hadn't intended…"

The dreamy smile on her face was one she was incapable of concealing. "Oh, I am fine. What just happened was lovely. But how about you?"

He shook his head a little as if to clear it. "I haven't felt this incredible in a long time. But Joan, we really shouldn't have—"

Tossing her head defiantly, impatiently, she retorted, "But we did. It was what we both wanted so why regret it now?"

His eyes studied hers for a long moment then he laid a gentle kiss on her lips. "Indeed. There's little time for regret especially now."

For the first time, the deepening dark registered and he sighed. "We should be getting back." He offered her his hand and led the way back to camp.

More than satisfied with the night's events, she followed.

****

Exhaustion dogged Finn yet sleep continued to elude him. For an hour, he'd stayed abed, staring at the canvas above him unable to surrender to unconsciousness. So much was rolling around in his head that his mind flatly refused to quiet. Restless, he turned over to find a more comfortable position and it was this impatient movement which saved him.

The glint of the knife caught the corner of his eye and as it came down in a graceful arc, he rolled right out of bed and onto the floor. With the weapon stuck into the mattress instead of him, it took some force and precious seconds for his assailant to pull it out. By the time the man retrieved it, Finn was up and on his feet on the other side of the bed.

They took each other's measure for a few humming moments then Finn made the first move. With an almighty yell designed to wake everyone within earshot, he tilted the bed over onto its side then upended it into the other man.

The assassin grunted as his breath whooshed out from the impact. Quick reflexes allowed him to sidestep the worst of it, however, and get out from under the mess quickly. Far too soon the stranger focused on his prey once more. The action, Finn realized, had bought him time and certainly kept him alive but he wasn't out of danger yet, not by any means.

As the intruder swiped at him with a wicked-looking dagger, Finn realized the man was more than capable of wielding a blade. This was no random act of violence. It dawned on him that this was an assassination attempt. Someone was trying to take him away from his kingdom, his family, his friends, and worst of all, his betrothed. That, he decided, would not happen.

In one lightning quick motion, he grabbed for his sword. Tossed across the tent in the struggle, it was now feet from him where he couldn't quite reach it. The knife grazed his forearm and blood spurted and spread. Furious now, he knocked the knife from the man's hand and sent it flying. It hit the canvas across the room with a dull thump, bounced then hit the ground.

On equal footing now, Finn proceeded to beat the man to a bloody pulp. The intruder, no stranger to hand-to-hand combat, landed several punches. Blood poured from his wounds and into his eyes until he could barely see. Reduced to grappling blindly on the floor, Finn was temporarily trapped beneath the other man when suddenly the weight was removed. Sounds of a struggle reached him through the ringing in his ears, next came the satisfying crunch of a nose breaking, a dull thud then silence.

Then Thomas said in a calm voice, "Well, what is this then?"

"Thomas, restrain him," Finn managed to gasp.

"With pleasure." Thomas tied the man's hands and feet with sturdy tent cord, which he produced from the gods alone knew where. When the man grunted in pain and struggled against the snug ropes, Thomas wrenched them even tighter. Finn wiped his bleeding mouth with the back of his hand then tried to catch his breath.

Still a bit winded, he nevertheless struggled to his feet and took in the situation. Not only Thomas, but several more had come running. Joan was among them, looking first annoyed at being awakened and then utterly furious that anyone would have the temerity to attack her king. She was more than ready to take out her frustration on the unwelcome visitor. Lyssa was also there; she was pale as death.

"He's secure," Thomas announced.

"Good." Finn turned to address his attacker. "Who sent you?"

The man said nothing, just stared unblinkingly at him.

Finn grabbed the man's throat and squeezed. "This was an assassination attempt. I want to know who ordered it and why. If you don't answer all of my questions, I can make things very unpleasant for you. Believe me, it would be in your best interest to do exactly as I say." He released the man, but the prisoner still said nothing. This time, Finn took up then unsheathed his knife and placed the tip beneath the prisoner's chin. "I won't ask again."

A small bead of sweat trickled down the man's face and he swallowed audibly, but when he spoke, his tone was as calm as if he were discussing the weather. "All right, I'll tell you what you want to know, just put the knife away."

"Good. But know this, speak one untrue word and I'll cut out your lying tongue."

"Have no fear on that score. I'll tell you the truth. My name is Charles Warwick. You are right. I was paid to assassinate you. But what good is money if you aren't alive to spend it?"

"Quite," Finn replied, the irony of that not lost on him. He sheathed his blade then pulled up a chair. "Who paid you, Warwick?"

"Queen Adriane."

Though the other spectators gasped, Finn only lifted his eyebrows then he gestured for the prisoner to proceed. "Why would she do that? What does she have to gain?"

He snorted. "Everything." He leaned forward. "I

am a mercenary. The queen pays me a retainer to keep myself available. I traveled with her to Ravenstone. From the moment we arrived it was clear she and Lord Fairfax had been planning this for some time and that they wanted certain obstacles such as yourself out of the way. When I received this commission, Lord Fairfax was there."

"Are you saying he gave the order?"

Warwick shook his head. "He said nothing, did nothing, but he was there. The queen gave me my orders. Track down King Finn Hale and do away with him as discreetly and efficiently as possible. She didn't care to have it known the queen of Minden sent her own people to assassinate rival royalty. I mean, if that got out, who's to say she wouldn't be next?"

Considering this very astute observation made a cold chill run up his spine in spite of the warmth of the tent, but all he said was, "I see. What is the present situation there?"

"Fairfax imprisons anyone who opposes him although there are few bold enough to gainsay him now. My queen's troops mingle with those he handpicked from his own personal guard. The palace guard as you knew it is no more. The same could be said of the council. Only staunch supporters of Fairfax remain. When I left, the coup was all but over."

"Then why send assassins? If it's all but over, why bother?"

"He knew he would never be safe, not with you running around alive and well. The same goes for the snow queen and Lord Thomas. It was only with the three of you gone that the fate of the kingdom would be assured."

Fear, like the coldest sharpest knife, cut through him. "He sent more than one."

"One for each of you," Warwick confirmed.

Only the fact that Thomas and Lyssa were right beside him, hale and whole and entirely unharmed kept Finn from killing the assassin right then and there. That and the need for further information. He took up his knife again. In one smooth fluid motion, he stepped behind Warwick and yanked the man's head back by the hair. Thomas half-rose, Joan exclaimed in shock and Lyssa said his name. He ignored them all.

"Who were the others?"

"I don't know."

Finn pressed the knife just one satisfying millimeter in, enough to draw blood but not enough to seriously wound.

Warwick didn't even flinch.

"Don't lie to me. I told you I'd cut out your deceitful tongue. Maybe I'll just slit your dishonest throat right now instead."

"Let's try it this way. How do you know there were others meant to go after me and the snow queen?" Thomas asked.

When Warwick said nothing, Finn scraped the knife along the sensitive skin of his throat.

He winced, swallowed hard and answered, "Along the way I met a colleague of mine. We both ended up at the snow queen's palace at about the same time, but got there by different routes. I realized he must be tracking her and that he must have been the one contracted to kill her. But he was captured, so I thought why not get the both of you?"

Hot fury rushed into Finn, but all he said was,

"Indeed. Why not? Who was the third man?"

Warwick stood his ground. He didn't beg, plead or even tremble. "Kill me if you like. I can't tell you what I don't know. I don't know the other man's name. My queen is no fool, nor is the new king. I never saw the third. He never saw me. I only know there were three of us because I later overheard the queen speaking of it to him."

Disgusted, Finn lowered the knife then released Warwick none too gently.

"The second assassin was sent north to find the snow queen. I was sent east to find you then tracked you to her. As for the third, he was sent south to track down Thomas."

"And none of us were found until now, obviously."

Warwick inclined his head in acknowledgement.

"If you failed, what were you to do?" asked Thomas.

"I never fail. Neither do the others, I suspect."

"But if you did?" Thomas persisted.

"I don't know about the others, but speaking for myself, if a job goes bad, I disappear. I keep the means to do so on my person and hidden in certain towns located at strategic points with certain contacts, in case of need. I presume the others would have similar arrangements in place if they are smart."

"And what of my mother?"

"She keeps to her chambers. Even now the king doesn't dare touch her. It is said she plots against him from her sickbed, however. It's rumored she secretly smuggles out those who wish to leave court. Since the rumors are only that and can't be proven, he has not bothered with her just yet. If she doesn't die first, he will handle her eventually, never fear, but for now…" Warwick shrugged.

Relief nearly brought Finn to his knees. His mother lived and was safe, or at least she had been a fortnight ago.

"Anything else useful you can tell us, Warwick?"

"Yes, you're supposed to be dead."

Finn was silent for a moment then replied, "I know that already. We've heard the rumors. Rumors you tried to make a reality. You'll be executed once this is all over and done. In the meantime, sleep well." On that ironic note, Finn turned on his heel and headed out. Not willing to leave his king alone just yet, Thomas followed.

When they stepped into the evening air, Finn breathed deeply then turned to his friend. "Thomas, keep him chained and under constant guard. Let our guest stew for the rest of the night, but come the morning, question him more closely. I want to know everything he knows, about Simon, about Adriane, their plans, the other assassins and any other new developments."

Thomas bowed immediate acquiescence to his king's request. "I will see it done, sire."

"Good. Now let's see if we can find me a bed for the night. Until my tent can be set to rights and relocated, I'll not sleep alone."

"That is wise. Come with me."

Chapter Fourteen

Joan believed in being prepared. Given her last encounter with Thomas, she wanted to be ready for any situation, particularly the inevitable end to what they had started under the stars a few nights ago. While she would not yet presume that they would become lovers, she could not deny that they were getting closer, physically as well as emotionally. The possibility was there and she would meet, even embrace it.

Many shield maidens took lovers and it was not a foregone conclusion that they would then marry. As one of them, she had the knowledge to mix a dram of herbs that would prevent pregnancy until she so desired. With war looming and things between she and Thomas so new, the time was not right for a baby. Even though she longed to have his child so much that her heart ached, she would take advantage of this opportunity to minimize the risk. Once that was done, let fate and Thomas take her where they would.

Decided, she headed to the forest to find all she needed.

****

This was right. Joan had to believe it. She had loved him all of her life, as child, girl and woman. Ever since the night she'd helped him escape she had wanted him, not as a girl wishes for her fantasy but as a woman craves her lover, with an almost overwhelming intensity. Besides, she was a shield maiden, not some sweet elegant miss. Such women took what they wanted, did they not? Well so would she and what she wanted right now, more than anything, was Thomas.

Added to that, the waiting was maddening. The assassination attempt on the king two nights before made it quite clear that anything could happen, at any time. She would not risk delaying any longer. Decision made, she ambled in the direction of Thomas's tent. With any luck, she would wind up in his bed.

The moon lit the path well enough and she arrived without incident. Taking a deep breath and her courage in both hands, she scratched on the rough cloth. When she got no response, she whispered, "Thomas. Thomas, it's Joan."

There was a muffled exclamation, a soft thud then he appeared at the entrance. He was clad only in a loose linen sleep shirt and drawers which left little to the imagination. One small inch of his skin showed in the v of the shirt and his golden hair was tousled from sleep or restlessness, she wasn't sure which. Either way, he looked entirely delectable.

"Joan, what's wrong? Are you all right?"

"I'm fine. It's…" She moistened lips suddenly dry. His eyes followed the movement. Encouraged, she drifted closer and placed a hand over his heart. "I don't want to be alone tonight."

At her words his heart beat faster under her hand. "Joan, you don't know what you're asking." His tone was full of warning, but of longing too.

It was this longing which gave her the nerve to stand her ground. "I do know. Do you know I have waited years for you? Waited years for what happened in the woods a few days ago to happen? I've dreamed of no one but you since I was fifteen. Believe me, I know what I'm asking. I know what I want: you."

He took hold of her hand, whether to keep it where it was or to fling it away she wasn't sure. Nor was he, from what she could tell, judging from the almost imperceptible tremor in his voice and the muscles locked tight.

Yet his words were harsh. "Stop this. It is one thing to have a bit of fun, but what you are talking about now is deadly serious. I won't take your maidenhead."

Her mouth gaped open. "A bit of fun," she muttered. Taking a deep breath, she put that issue aside, focused instead on the more important one.

"In days, weeks at the outside, we will be off to war. I don't want to die never knowing what it's like to be in your arms. Will you really deny me and yourself?"

"I won't leave you to mourn me." He stepped back from her, leaving her cold, but she wouldn't let him go without a fight.

"Haven't you been listening? Did you ever consider that you might be the one mourning me?" Without conscious thought, she entered the tent and forced him farther inside until his legs hit the makeshift bed.

"I'm a warrior born and bred, just as much as you, as equal and opposite as any fire lord with his snow queen. I could die as easily as you. So I repeat, will you deny me and yourself?"

He said nothing for a long time, so long that she began to wonder if she had made a horrendous blunder, which would cost her everything. Then his strong hands reached for her through the dark and an instant later she heard his voice, low and fierce.

"Not anymore by all the gods," he murmured. Then he kissed her and she forgot everything else.

****

"You need to be absolutely certain about this, Joan." He was determined to give her one last chance to back away; his sense of chivalry demanded it. Demanded it even as he divested her of her cloak and untied the pretty ribbon of her chemise. Demanded it even as he prayed she would not heed him. "If you want me to stop tell me now," he murmured.

"Not a chance."

The breath he held whooshed out in what at any other time would have been a chuckle. "Thank the gods. Because I've just realized something, I've waited years for you too. I just didn't know it."

Without his being cognizant of the action, he drew her toward the one well-lit corner of the tent, the better to see her. The moonlight was bright that night even through the gauzy filter of the canvas and he silently blessed the gods for it. It was only then that he took his first proper look at her. Her skin was pearlescent in the starlight and her long honey-colored hair was still in its practical braid. Since the night he'd first kissed her, he'd fantasized about her hair, imagined unbraiding it slowly and running his fingers through the silken mass of it. Well, why not live that dream?

Task completed, he placed hot opened-mouthed kisses down her neck then across her shoulder, until he came to the straps of her chemise. He lowered first one then the other to expose another few inches of soft flesh. Fingers splayed, he caught each thin strip of lace and cotton with his thumbs and skimmed his palms down her arms, taking the diaphanous garment with them so it fell to her waist. For the first time, he feasted his eyes on what he'd already had his hands on. His gaze landed first on her flat stomach, then the curve of her hips, finally travelled up to take in the abundance of her cleavage. Her face, and he could now personally attest, her form were both exquisite. Lush and firm, her breasts fit his palms as if they were made for him. "You are so beautiful. Belong to me now."

As he ran his palms over every inch of her, he could only hope she would be his in every sense, for he knew to the very depth of his soul he was hers. A fierce desire, as unexpected as it was unprecedented, to leave his mark on her spirit as well as her body swept through him. Every time she looked at his hands, he wanted her to remember them on her, caressing her, giving her pleasure. In fact, he wanted her to know him and only him in this grand sensual landscape.

"Look at me. I want to see your eyes when I touch you." When she raised her gaze obediently to his, he added, "When I finally take you, I want us both to be able to recall the moment in precise detail."

Gaze locked to hers, he let his hands roam and let instinct and the myriad expressions on her gorgeous face guide him. How strange and lovely it was to know her in this whole new way. How right it seemed and how exciting. Growing up together meant he knew everything about her, every nuance of mood, and every alteration of attitude. Each one but this. And oh, how he yearned to know her in this way as well. In the brief time they'd already had together, he'd learned to crave that, to crave her.

So his eager mind cataloged all of her responses. For a start, where she liked best to be kissed. What caress she most favored was also high on the list of things he wanted to—no, would—learn. That she was as eager to embrace this experience as she had all others offered by life did not surprise him. That she would take the lead occasionally, for example, astonished him not a jot. Yet it was a revelation to watch her discover her own sensual nature. Although it was increasingly difficult to think with her so beautiful and willing beside him, he tried to use all he knew of her to give her all she might wish for in this sphere.

****

When he kissed her ravenously and started to guide her toward the darkness of the bed, she tore her lips from his. "Wait."

"Joan…"

His voice was one part plea, one part sensual command; she hoped to answer both, but first… "I want to see you too, Thomas."

His jaw tightened so much she worried it might shatter, but he nodded. Without further comment, he crossed his arms, drew his shirt up and over his head. Where it landed she neither knew nor cared. She was far too engrossed in the glorious expanse of chest revealed. Smooth skin over sculpted muscle and hard bone. She put out a hand to touch, just as she had upon her arrival, only now there was no cloth between them. With the tips of her fingers just barely brushing his skin, she explored his well-defined pectorals then traced down to his abdomen. Taunt muscles quivered and he sucked in air.

Never taking his gaze from hers, he started on the

drawstring of his drawers. With the tie undone, he slid them down his hips, let them fall. He was exquisite, like some pagan god or fallen angel bathed in an ethereal glow. Indulging herself, she let her gaze travel over every inch of him. Sleek skin, firm muscle, a gorgeous face and blatant arousal was what she found. Her stomach jittered slightly at the sight, but she didn't look away. "I take it you know what you're doing?"

His grin was swift and intense. "I've never had any complaints." He sobered quickly enough, however, and framed her face with his hands. "You trust me with your life every day, just as I trust you with mine. I swear you can trust me with your body as well."

And what about my heart, she thought but didn't say, since hers was already well lost to him.

Time spun out and lengthened while he touched her everywhere in impossibly erotic ways. Until at last, she found herself lying beneath him, with him poised at her entrance. He took her hand in his and eased in that first fraction of an inch. Her mind was suddenly clear and feeling a wild recklessness unlike anything she'd ever experienced overtake her, she arched up in one swift rough motion, clasping him to her at the same time. The combination was enough to rupture her maidenhead, leave him buried to the hilt within her. The small involuntary cry of pain she couldn't suppress was a small price to pay.

Thomas's reaction was far less subtle. His curse was brief, to the point and fervent. For a moment, they both simply lay there, panting slightly.

"You might've warned me you were going to do that," he muttered, once he got his breath back.

Joan was quite certain that had she been able to see

his face, he would be glaring at her. Eventually, she ventured, "I'm sorry. I just wanted the worst of it over."

Thomas cleared his throat over what sounded suspiciously like an unwilling chuckle then sighed. "You took control of your own fate, the way I've often seen you do. This is not something you ever need to apologize for. Gods, you feel incredible. Are you in any pain now?"

Joan did a quick inventory. "No, I barely felt a twinge."

"Good. This shouldn't hurt at all then." With no further warning, he rocked against her, caressing an exquisitely sensitive spot between her legs. This time her gasp was of an entirely different variety and her heart thudded until it was fit to burst. Biting her lip in concentration, she did her best to meet and match him.

****

Thomas's head spun. All he could see or feel or know was her and when she had taken him fully inside of her with that quick, almost brutal burst of pleasure, he'd almost come right then and there. With his control hanging by one flimsy thread, he did his best to assure himself she was all right. Once certain he hadn't hurt her, he let that delicate thread snap.

When he started to withdraw, she clung to him, protesting. He shook his head and smiled just a little, though the expression was a bit strained. "Don't worry. I'm not going anywhere except right here."

He suited words to action and glided deeply back inside of her, back home. The delicious friction left them both breathless and he stopped thinking at all.

She was inexperienced, but any vague concern he might have had over how she would take to the activity dissipated quickly. Her active lifestyle, full of so many physical pursuits, had subtly prepared her for this one. She soon picked up his rhythm and they moved as one, all heat and friction and endless pleasurable sensation. Yet it built and Thomas knew they would soon reach flashpoint. He could feel her tightening around him and any second her release would come.

"Joan, look at me." Her eyes, closed in appreciation, opened wide and flashed to his. "I told you I wanted to see you. Let me see you."

She gave him his wish. Her breath caught then he watched her go over, watched her give herself up to a storm of glorious sensation. The pulsing contractions around him triggered his own release and an instant later he followed. As he joined her in the whirlwind, he held onto to her and let her see. He let her see every part of him and gave up the very last of his heart to this beautiful woman he'd known forever.

Spent and stunned, he simply lay there on top of her trying to find the strength to move. Eventually he disengaged and rolled to his back, taking her with him and tucking her into his side.

After some little time, she murmured, "Thomas, I know this isn't how you expected to spend your evening."

"It wasn't expected," he conceded, "but it was wonderful and I am not complaining. Believe me."

"I'm glad and I hope you can take another shock."

He grinned and kissed the top of her head. "If it's a shock anything like the one I just experienced, then please lead on." He expected she might smile or even laugh at that, but she did not and a small frisson of worry pulsed through him.

"I love you. I have for years and clearly not as a sister loves her brother."

When he didn't speak, couldn't find the words, she rushed on. "I know you may not necessarily feel the same way and please don't feel obligated to do or say anything. I only wanted you to know how I feel, especially after tonight. I want you to know I don't throw these words around willy-nilly—"

"Any more than you give your body to just anyone," he finished for her in soft voice.

"Right. I—please believe, when I say I love you I mean it. No matter what happens, even if you don't ever touch me again or want to see my face again after tonight, that will never change. Promise me that even if this aspect of things"—she gestured vaguely to encompass themselves and the tangled bed sheets— "ends tomorrow, we can still be…at least somewhat as we were before."

"You mean friends?" When she nodded, he considered for a moment then tilted up her chin to study her face. "Is that all you want from me? Friendship?"

She hesitated and bit her bottom lip. Covering herself, she sat up and picked at the coverlet before answering.

"Of course not. I want more. But I want your word that our friendship will remain intact."

He also sat up then took her hand in his. "I can't promise that."

"What?"

Shock was clear in her tone and he wanted to sooth it away but he took a moment to gather his thoughts. Now it was his turn to hesitate. When he finally spoke it was with great care. "It's a very complicated question.

Things aren't the same for me, you see. For a long time, I only loved you as a sister. Then you rescued me and everything changed. I finally admitted, at least to myself, what a beautiful attractive woman you are and that I wanted you. Not only that, I saw a woman willing to risk her life not just for her country, but for me. That is when I fell in love with you."

Even though her mouth gaped, she still looked exotically beautiful. He registered her bemused expression, then refocusing, hastened to explain himself further. "So you see, if friendship is all you can offer, I cannot promise to be satisfied with that. Not any longer. Joan—" Abruptly he found his mouth stopped in the most pleasant way imaginable: with hers.

Joan lunged for him, fit her lips to his and bore him back into the pillows.

"You love me!" She cried out the words in between reigning joyful exuberant kisses over his face.

"I do. I do," he managed. He couldn't help laughing as her kisses became even more enthusiastic. In defense, he reversed their positions and had her on her back. It was only then that he became aware of the tears shimmering in her lovely green eyes along with the laughter.

"You love me." The words were soft and her eyes glowed with wonder as well as tears.

"Yes, always."

****

When he woke, she was gone and for a moment he wondered if he'd dreamed the entire interlude. Then he breathed in the scent of her that still surrounded him and caught sight of the note on the bedside table informing him that she left early in order to prepare for the day. Contenting himself with that since he had little choice, he rose and made himself ready for his own day which was sure to be full of far less pleasant things.

The current precarious state of affairs necessitated that he give the entirety of his attention to the coming battle and its plans. Yet sitting in the pavilion dubbed the war room, he still found his mind wandering at odd times to Joan and their night together. All day, one part of his brain worked to find an opportunity to get her alone again while the rest concentrated on the coming war. Knowing she would welcome him made it all the more difficult to maintain his control. One word from him and she would be in his arms. This certainty fractured his normally unwavering focus.

Not for the first time, he wondered at the caprice of fate. She was a blessing he'd never had the wit to look for, but she was now as essential to him as the very air that he breathed. Nevertheless, as she had said, they were both going into danger and anything could happen. It could all end tomorrow with her death or his; he had no illusions about that. It surprised him that he felt far less prepared to die than ever before, perhaps because before, he'd had less to lose. But now a beautiful woman, one he loved, respected and admired, loved him. He had the beginnings of a life and the last thing he wanted was to lose it.

As for her death, he scarcely had the strength to contemplate it. If he lost her…it did not bear thinking about. Only thoughts of seizing the moment could keep such dark imaginings at bay. As she explained some complicated tactical maneuver and he didn't hear a word of it, Thomas made a decision. He would make the most of their time together, in every respect. The first step toward that end would be to arrange another private meeting with her as soon as possible.

When the king suggested they take a short break and adjourn for a meal, he grew hopeful. He waited while everyone else headed to the dining tent, hoping she would linger. She did. This was a very good sign to his way of thinking. The moment they were alone, he began the speech he'd carefully prepared in his mind, the speech which would convince her to join him in his tent and possibly his bed that evening.

"Joan, would you like to—?" He got no further as Finn chose that precise moment to return.

Finn fell back a step when he realized his two friends were in the midst of a private discussion. He gave them a moment then stated, "I'm sorry for the interruption, but I need your expertise, Thomas, on a matter of strategy. It won't wait. Forgive me."

Thomas sighed and cursed inventively but silently. "Very well." To Joan he said, "We'll talk later, yes?"

"Yes," she agreed. The tentative smile she sent him was almost worth the temporary delay.

The remainder of the afternoon was busy, with precious little time to talk or even think of anything apart from war. He didn't anticipate she would come to him that evening. He could hardly expect her to be so bold a second time, could he? No, he couldn't, particularly when he'd not seen her the rest of the day and they'd had no chance to have the promised conversation. He resigned himself to a sleepless night alone.

The day was long and the night would be even longer, so finding her waiting for him in his tent once more was a godsend. This was another boon he hadn't foreseen but wouldn't question. Instead, he simply took her into his arms then to his bed.

****

"Marry me, Joan."

It took a moment for his words to register in her desire-clouded mind and once they did, she did her best to make her disbelief plain. "What?"

"Marry me," he repeated. Gaze locked with hers, he rocked deeply into her until she shuddered.

She clung and for once fought against the overwhelming pleasure. She didn't dare speak. She knew no words would come, only incoherent sounds of longing. Instead, she shook her head.

"Stubborn woman." Voice, countenance, his entire body, everything about him turned to steel under his indomitable will. "Marry me."

He withdrew almost completely then rocked into her again, this time caressing her inside and out. They both moaned; the pleasure was so intense. Yet… "No."

He opened his mouth, probably to curse, but she didn't let him say any more. Instead, she set about directing his full attention to the here and now, the moment and her.

****

Later, spent and sated, he slouched half atop her and ran his hands through her hair. "I meant what I said before. I want you to marry me. I have never been more serious about anything in my life."

"I'm aware," she replied acerbically after a long moment. "Oh, Thomas, don't spoil things with such ridiculous fancies."

He stiffened then eased back to study her face. "Ridiculous fancies? Why ridiculous?"

"A marriage between us can't, shouldn't be, for many reasons. You know that."

"No, I don't know that. Explain."

"First and foremost, we are both so devoted to this country. How can we give proper attention to a marriage, or if the gods will it, children? I wouldn't begin to know how to find my balance. How can we focus on any children we might have, especially since we're both about to be right in the middle of a bloody war we might or might not win? Furthermore, whether we win or lose, we will also have to pick up the pieces afterward. I won't bring a child into that."

"It's a little bit late to decide that isn't it, Joan? You might already be pregnant." He was a little surprised to find himself not exactly displeased with the notion. A momentary vision of her grown huge with his child held him riveted. The image shattered and his belly clenched when she shook her head.

"I've taken steps to prevent pregnancy. I would never have come to you otherwise."

He stilled and for a long time he said nothing. Then he murmured, "I see. So if we were to wed, you wouldn't ever want to bear my child?"

She made an impatient sound. "Don't be daft. I love you and I've longed to give you a son or daughter since the day I watched you playing with your young cousins on the Strand. Of course I want to have your child, just not now, with things between us so new and war staring us in the face."

His breath when he let it out quivered all but imperceptibly with relief and he could only pray she wouldn't see it. "Well then, let's get married."

"Thomas, it's only been days since we spoke of

love. Don't you think it's too soon to talk of such matters?"

"Not at all. I've known you all of my life. Now I've fallen in love with you and I want to marry you. We don't have to marry right away, but I know I want a life with you once we are both ready."

"You are forgetting something else." He gestured for her to go on so she elaborated. "I am no fire lady. I haven't the power to pass on. Even if I wanted to be your wife, you as cousin, advisor and friend of the king, must make a far more auspicious match."

"Bollocks to that." With no thought whatsoever, he found himself on top of her again, poised at her entrance. "Being with you is the best thing that has ever happened to me. I've enough power to pass on for us both. As for your blood, you are hardly a peasant. Aside from all of that, we're stronger together. I'll say no more about it now, but this discussion is far from over." He slid inside her again. "I won't force you. I'd never even try. But make a concerted effort to bring you around to my way of thinking? Well, that's another matter. I can be very persuasive."

****

Joan didn't try to fight him; she simply let him have his way and allowed him to do as he wished, as he would. Why wouldn't she when what he wished was to steep her in sensual delight?

Still, as she lay awake beside him sometime later, she couldn't help but worry. When Joan reflected on his words as well as his actions this evening, she could not deny that she was tempted to say yes. A life with him was all she had ever wanted, but there were more things to consider.

That he was a man of conviction was undeniable. If he said it, he meant it. If he meant it, he would certainly do it. What was more, he was a man far too accustomed to getting whatever he wanted.

This meant she would have to make a decision and soon about what *she* wanted. Did she want to spend the rest of her life with him? Did she trust him enough to bind her life permanently to his? Did she love him? The simple fact of the matter was she already knew the answer to all of those questions was yes. She had been bold enough to get him into her bed and brave enough to tell him she was in love with him. So why was she balking at making it official?

Unable to refute any of these disturbing observations, powerless to come to any firm conclusions and with her exhausted mind still full of that last unanswered question, she followed his murmured directive and slept.

****

He ought to take his own advice and sleep, but Thomas found it impossible. He was restless, edgy and absolutely unable to settle. Every possible disastrous scenario played over and over in his head then the impossible ones began. Enough repose was essential right now, but he was afraid to sleep, certain nightmares would plague him. Eventually, however, he clung to Joan and drifted off. Though he woke alone again, he woke more refreshed than he had hoped to be and found he'd dreamed only of her.

Chapter Fifteen

The days rolled ever onward, bringing them closer to the brink of war, yet it was the nights Joan found the most difficult to cope with. Routinely, she would walk the camp's perimeter in the late evening before retiring for the night and while these days she often joined Thomas afterward, her nightly ritual was one she was loathe to give up. More and more now, she encountered others who walked the grounds as she did. On this moonlit night, however, she was startled to glimpse Lyssa's slim form on the river bank.

"Can't you sleep?" Joan asked in a soft voice as she approached, having no wish to startle the king's betrothed.

Lyssa jerked at the sound even in spite of this precaution and turned her head toward it. Seeing it was Joan, she sighed with quiet relief. "No, I'm too nervous. I've never been in a battle before. I've never had to fight, not really. People were just frightened of me. Now it's me who's scared to death. That's not my only problem. I've also never had people counting on me to do my part. What if I can't? What if I mess up? I could freeze, literally or figuratively."

Joan could not quite stifle a snort. She sat and gestured for Lyssa to do the same. Once the other woman joined her, she made an apology, of a sort. "I suppose I shouldn't find that funny, but it is a little."

"Maybe right now," Lyssa conceded, "but what happens if I can't do what needs to be done or I make a mistake and I hurt our own people? I would never forgive myself."

"You might. I won't lie to you or sugarcoat things for you. No one knows how they will react in a battle until they are in it."

Lyssa let out a little huff of breath. "Well, that makes me feel better, thanks."

Chuckling a bit, Joan shifted to a more comfortable position on the hard dry ground. "I'm not saying you will mess up. I'm just saying it's a possibility, like it is for everyone every time they go into combat. Personally, I think you'll hold up just fine."

"Really? Why? What makes you think so?"

"You have courage. You aren't afraid to say what you think and go after what you want. You've found a way to manage His Majesty Finn Hale, the most powerful man in the kingdom, possibly the world. You are no lightweight. You'll do your best no matter what happens. That's all anyone can ask of you."

Lyssa digested this a moment. "Thank you. Your confidence in me means a lot."

"I'm glad, but it's better for you to have confidence in yourself."

"I'll try, but the fact remains, I've been trained but I've never been tested. I am out here at this time of night because I'm on edge. I am about ready to jump out of my skin, actually."

"Hmm." Joan considered a moment then continued, "There is one thing I could recommend which might help settle your nerves."

"Oh? I'm all ears."

"Bed your betrothed."

On a half-laugh, Lyssa burst out, "What?"

"Bed Finn if you haven't already. I've been in a lot of battles and been close to death more than once and I can say from personal experience, taking a lover is a wonderful way to feel alive. I never had the option before, but let's just say I'm glad I have it now."

Lyssa sat up straighter and took a good look at her friend. "You and Thomas spent the night together? When was this?"

"We spent most of the night together," Joan corrected. "A few nights ago. The truth of the matter is I didn't want to die never knowing what it was like with him. Now I know."

"And?"

"And it was wonderful. Everything I dreamed of and more." Joan knew her tone was self-satisfied, not to say smug, but she couldn't help it.

"Since you were willing to share something so personal with me, I will do the same." She cleared her throat, then blurted out, "Finn and I, we've already shared a bed."

Joan's eyebrows shot up and her eyes widened. "Have you? You kept that quiet."

"To speak nonchalantly of such things is unseemly, especially in a queen." This time Joan heard the prim disapproval in Lyssa's voice, but then she cleared her throat and returned to the topic at hand. "Be that as it may, I feel confident you won't spread idle gossip, so I believe I can tell you a bit about how it was for me as well."

"I never gossip," Joan stated in a solemn tone, though she was glad the night was dark so Lyssa would not see her lips twitch.

"When he found me, it started out as an experiment. Could we touch each other and live? Since that wasn't the case for either of us with any other, we hoped the experiment would work."

"And it did."

"It did. We touched, casually at first, then more intimately. Then we couldn't stop; we found we didn't want to."

Slowly, sometimes haltingly, Lyssa told her the rest or at least, Joan suspected, most of it. Some moments, Joan believed, were for Lyssa and Finn alone, but those that weren't, Lyssa shared freely. Joan found it lovely to share her own joy with another. To their mutual surprise, they also discovered that they were in much the same situation, in love for the first and the last time in their lives and unready for war.

Soon Joan found herself confiding fears of her own. How Thomas had asked her to marry him and she had refused. How now she was worried she would lose him entirely. Unburdening herself to another living soul made Joan feel as though a heavy weight had been lifted. When she asked Lyssa for advice, however, the answer she got surprised her.

"I am hardly an expert on matters of the heart, having only just discovered I had one myself."

"You and the king seem so happy together. I hoped you might be able to offer me some guidance." She tried not to sound too disappointed, but she wasn't sure how well she managed it.

"I find that even when people ask for advice, they don't often take it."

"Oh, come now. I promise I'll at least consider any

wisdom you might have to offer. Please, I want someone else's opinion on this. No, that's not accurate. I want your opinion. In these last weeks, I've come to value and respect you. I truly want to know what you think."

"I think you must let your own heart decide. You've done well thus far in that regard. You've followed your heart and where has it lead? To happiness for you both from what you tell me. I know you are worried. Some of these worries are valid and some are not, but in the end, you must choose. Are you willing to take the risk? Are you ready to settle on one path and let all the others go? No path in this world is perfect. There is only the choice." She paused a moment, shrugged. "This is what I've learned anyway."

They continued talking of the matter for a while, but soon they began to tire and admitted it was time to at least attempt to sleep.

"It sounds to me as though you've learned quite a lot in a short while. Thank you for sharing all you've discovered with me." Joan rose. "You've given me a lot to think about. Come, it's late and we should both get what rest we can."

****

The next morning, Joan looked for Thomas. She found him about to go on patrol and asked if she might join him. Although he looked as if he would have liked very much to refuse her, he gave his grudging consent.

"You said you want to marry me. Do you still?" she began without preamble once they were alone.

"Yes." Thomas's answer was far more curt than it normally would have been and it dawned on her afresh how much she must have hurt him with her rejection.

"Then I would like to know what you would expect. Of me," she clarified when he looked blank. He said nothing so she elaborated. "Would you expect me to give up my sword, for example? Like you, I am a warrior. I am a shield maiden; that is who I am. I tell you plainly I cannot deny that part of myself."

At last he found his voice. "I would only ask you to lay down your sword temporarily, whenever you are with child."

"Considering how much we…" Joan was horrified to realize she was blushing and she could not complete the statement.

"Indulge ourselves?" Thomas helpfully supplied. The look he sent her way was a very attractive combination of amused and heated.

The sound of his voice rolled over her like a hot caress. Joan shivered once then gave him a quelling look. "Yes considering that, well, I could be with child quite a lot. What happens when I don't want any more children?"

Instead of answering the question directly, he asked, "How many children would you like?"

She gave an impatient shrug. "I don't know, three or four perhaps."

"That sounds about the right number to me. You said you know how to prevent conception, yes?" When she nodded, he continued, "Then I don't see a problem so long as we make any decisions regarding children together. I would want us to discuss matters before taking action either way. Oh, and as long as I can still share your bed."

She blinked, surprised at how easy the conversation had been, then blushed anew when the last of what he said registered. After a moment, she inclined her head.

"Good. What else is troubling you? What else is holding you back? You mentioned your lack of magic. I don't see that as a problem, as you have many other laudable attributes."

"Thank you," she replied drily.

"So what else? I swear I will do all I can to reassure you and get rid of any obstacles to a union between us."

It was difficult, more difficult than she ever imagined it would be, to say what was in her heart, but she understood all too well that if they were ever to develop a true partnership, a true marriage, she must. "Since you asked me to be your wife, I've thought of little else. What it comes down to is this: I've been my own mistress for a very long time. I've also been alone for a very long time, for almost as long as I've loved you. I am my own person and it would be unfair to let you go into this thinking I can or will change. As much as I love you, long to keep you and be with you always, I fear I would not make a very good wife. You should know that."

"You think telling me all this will put me off?"

"I was afraid it might. I think perhaps it should," she admitted with some reluctance.

"It doesn't. I like who you are and I do not want to change you."

"You say that now but—"

"Joan, we have known each other since we were children. When have you ever known me to say things I don't mean? Or change my mind on a whim?" He didn't sound angry, but he did sound a trifle stern.

"Never," she murmured and her voice was small even to her own ears. "I'm scared that is all."

"Why?"

"Because I want this, I want you so badly. I want you so much I can hardly see straight. I don't want to make a mistake and lose you."

"Then don't. Marry me."

Joan searched his eyes for a long moment. Then she examined her own heart and gave him the one answer she could, the answer she wanted to give him from the very start. "Yes."

"Yes?"

He looked to Joan as though he could hardly believe her or his good fortune, so she reassured him. "Yes."

Thomas threw his arms around her and kissed her for all he was worth. He also spun her around until it was impossible for Joan to tell whether she was dizzy from that or with love for him.

When he returned her to earth, she demanded, "Where's my ring? We can't get married without a ring."

He took out a small velvet drawstring bag from a pocket in his tunic and then produced the most beautiful diamond ring she had ever seen. If that weren't enough, he knelt before her, took her hand and slipped the jewel onto her finger.

Though happy tears clouded her eyes and a sob wanted to issue from her clogged throat, she managed, "It's beautiful, Thomas."

"You like it? I've had it for ages, and I always pack it amongst my things so it's with me wherever I go. I have always wondered if I'd ever meet the right woman. Now I have. It's been in my pocket since the other night when I first asked you to marry me."

"I love it," she assured him. "I-I love you. I always have. I always will."

"And I love you, always and forever."

They sealed the vow with a kiss, both passionate and pure, knowing the bond they forged in that moment would never break.

****

Thank the gods he'd been taught strategy from the time he could walk, was all Finn could think as he studied the battle plans for the hundredth or possibly the thousandth time. Much of his evening had been spent improving, refining, and finalizing all he meant to do until he was dead certain his head was going to explode. Trying to account for the unexpected was giving him an awful headache. So the sound of Lyssa's light feminine voice requesting entry was a welcome interruption. "Let her pass," he called out.

The lantern cast a soft glow about his tent and he could see her well enough. Holding out his hands, he stepped to her. As she entered the tent, she reached for him, tangled her fingers with his then gripped. It was then that he got his first close look at her face. She was far too pale and her pretty eyes danced about, her gaze never landing on anything. Her hand trembled in his. Never had he seen her so jittery. Although sure she would hate the word, especially when used in reference to her, and he wasn't overly fond of the term himself, it was the only one which accurately described her present mood. "Good evening, my dear. I assumed you would be sleeping at this hour. Are you all right?"

Lyssa denied this with a simple shake of the head.

"I'm feeling a bit punchy. Tomorrow I take part in my first battle. What if I don't measure up?"

"I have every confidence you will. I trained you, remember?" He released her hands and they both sat. Or he sat while she remained in her chair a mere moment before she popped up again. As if the seat was covered with hot coals, he observed, a little amused.

She started to pace. "You are the second person who has told me that recently. I'm trying to develop a little of that same confidence inside myself, but I'm finding it hard to do. I can't get past the nerves."

It was her tone which first alerted him. There was something mysterious, something unusual in it he couldn't quite pin down, but which left him intrigued. His fascination increased exponentially when she stilled then fixed him with her gaze.

"I need something to take the edge off."

His breath stuttered in his lungs and his throat tightened, yet he still forced himself to ask. "A walk in the moonlight? It's a fine evening for it."

On a short laugh, she shook her head. "No. I tried that last night. It didn't help."

Every single muscle he possessed locked tight. He rose and with deliberate unhurried movements, poured her a glass of wine. "Perhaps this?"

She took the goblet he offered and sipped. Then she shook her head again.

More than willing to abandon himself to fate, he took the near-full cup from her and set it aside. "Well then, this will have to suffice." Turning back to face her, he gathered her into his arms, pulled her close and took her mouth. It might be more accurate to say that he ravaged her mouth. It was warm and sweet and glorious. So was she and as a consequence he plundered. She had offered after all. She had all but begged him to take her into sensual oblivion and he had an edge of his own.

How long had it been since he had his hands on her? Since she had hers on him? Days, what with one thing and another, he realized. An eternity, by his estimation.

That being the case, he wasted no time. Her clothes went flying then his own followed until they were both naked. For one heated instant, he held her close, bare skin to bare skin. With a light shove to her shoulder, he tumbled her onto his bed. A heartbeat later he stretched out atop her, between her spread thighs. "This," he breathed the word as he slid into her for emphasis. "Will definitely…" Stroking every inch of her he could, he pleasured himself as well as her. As he withdrew, he gripped her hand to anchor himself, then shuddered as he glided back home. "Take the edge off." As he stroked again they both moaned.

After that, it didn't take long. It was fast but very fulfilling. Sooner than he would have believed possible, they were racing headlong toward the peak of sensation with little of the prolonged tenderness which most often characterized their encounters. The difference was exciting, potent even. Yet so much remained the same. They were just as in sync as they always were in this sphere. Since that was so, they tumbled over into climax together, heedless of anything else in the whole wide world.

He lay back and just breathed. Busy as he was savoring the aftermath and the pleasure still coursing through his veins, it took him a few moments to become aware of the wetness just above his heart. Alarmed, he sat up in one abrupt motion, taking her with him. Then he tilted her chin up so he could see her face. "Darling, what's wrong? Was I too rough with you? Oh gods, I'm sorry."

She wiped at her tears and smiled through them though they continued to fall. "No, you were wonderful, perfect in fact. That's the problem."

The best he could come up with in response was, "Huh?"

Laughing just a little, she tried to explain. "I'm just afraid. I'm so afraid of what may happen tomorrow. I have all these terrible questions spinning round and round in my head. Will I hold up in battle or will I falter? Will we be victorious? What will happen if Simon escapes us even if we do win? But the worst one is, what if I lose you?"

"You won't lose me."

"You can't promise me that, any more than I can promise you the same." Her pretty eyes, so often dreamy and so recently full of tears, were dry now and fierce.

"I suppose you are right but it's not something I want to focus on. We should keep our attention on the positive. Focus on the outcome we are determined to achieve."

"Go forward with optimism?" She smiled a little. "Yes, so we should. For a little while I was able to do that, or at least I was able to put aside my fears. I can't think of anything else but you when I am in your arms. I never have been able to. I suppose I also needed the release of tears after all."

Her bittersweet smile nearly broke his heart.

Then she shrugged. "Lying here in the quiet, listening to the beat of your heart, it all rushed back. I'm sorry."

"Sorry? For what? Being human?"

She chuckled a little at his observation then shook her head. "No, I am sorry for not being made of tougher stuff. My one excuse is that I have so much more to lose now."

"As do I." He placed a gentle kiss on the top of her head. "You don't have to be strong all the time. You don't have to hide your fears. Share them with me and I'll share mine with you. That is sort of the point, isn't it? To give each other comfort?"

She took a deep breath, nodded.

"Well, let's try to keep the dark at bay for just a bit longer then." It was the only thing that mattered, at least for now, and he kissed her.

"Even if it's the last time?" She whispered the words as his mouth traveled down the long delicate line of her neck.

"Especially if it's the last time," he corrected.

He drew her to him, over him, into him and the encounter held all the tenderness the previous one had blurred.

Chapter Sixteen

"I'm sorry. I must not have heard you correctly. Did you just say you abandoned your mission, Gregson?"

The third assassin cringed just a bit at Simon's tone then locked his trembling knees together. He looked his master square in the eye, a last show of defiance. "Above all you said to be discreet. Well, arranging something in the middle of a war camp was the definition of conspicuous, not to say dangerous. So, yes, I abandoned my mission."

Simon slowly nodded. "His death would have been discovered and remarked on."

"Yes," he conceded with an eager nod. "I tracked Lord Thomas to Brighton Forest easily enough, but he was not alone when I found him. Had I tried anything, I would have had to deal with at least two others. He was never on his own; there was always some companion or other with him. While I could have done so, I figured killing those companions would alert someone. So I opted to return here and report."

"I see. You were supposed to be the best. Yet one man eludes you. Then when you find him, rather than doing your job, you walk away. Not acceptable. Is it, Adriane?"

"Not at all. Most disappointing."

The cold sweat which beaded the man's forehead

was a balm to Simon's soul. Slowly, Simon circled around Gregson and stopped behind him. "It's good you returned. It saves me the trouble of tracking you down." In one swift maneuver, Simon knifed the man in the back. One rapid jab to the kidneys incapacitated the man. One more blow and it was done. "I punish failure. Remember that while you're dying."

Simon heaved Gregson away. The man stumbled forward a step then gasped as he dropped to his knees. Guttural choking sounds came from deep in his throat then he subsided. The ill-fated assassin drew in one last raspy breath then collapsed in a dead heap at Simon's feet.

His handkerchief served to clean the blood from his weapon and one gesture had guards stepping forward to remove the body. In the space of a few minutes, it was as if the incident had never happened. So his hands were steady as he lowered himself into a nearby chair, took a deep breath. It had been some time since he'd taken a life. He'd forgotten the illicit thrill of it. That moment of release which rushed over him before the twinge of conscience kicked in was something he savored.

After a time, he sensed Adriane's gaze on him and he turned to her. "Forgive me, my dear, for taking the liberty. You ought to have been the one to dispatch him, but I wanted to do it myself."

She walked to the sideboard, poured herself a glass of wine and shrugged. "No apology necessary. I understand, darling. He failed both of us after all. You had as much right to deal with him as I."

When she sat beside him, he plucked the glass from her hand, drank deeply. "Have you heard anything more of the others we sent?"

Adriane shook her head. "Nothing. We should have had some news by now. It may be that they too have failed."

"Captured or killed is a definite possibility."

"Should I try to call them back?"

"No, leave them be. Let us hope they will be more successful."

"To success." Adriane took back the wine, drank then set it aside. For a time she studied him.

As he bore her scrutiny, the high flush on his cheeks deepened. What must she think of him now? He would not like to hazard a guess.

"Are you all right?" she asked at length.

"Of course I'm all right. It's been a while, that's all, since I've—"

"Since you've gotten your hands bloody?"

He nodded.

"How did it feel?"

A little taken aback by the question, even in spite of all he knew of her, he took a moment before answering. It dawned on him he was as shocked by his own inner response to her query as he was by the inquiry itself. He wondered what it might be best to say and at last settled on the unvarnished truth. "It felt...intensely satisfying." The admission felt almost as good as the act itself. When no recriminations came from her, he felt even better. For the first time, he felt free to be himself with no restrictions.

"I should think so," she agreed. She turned her hungry gaze to him.

He met and matched it. "Killing is the ultimate act of power and it's the power I crave most, you know.

However I can get it," he admitted, his tone blunt.

"That is a craving I share. Perhaps that is why we gravitated to each other. It's certainly why we work so well together now."

"True," He sat forward. "Since we do work so well together, I've something in mind for our next step."

"Do you now? And what might that be?"

"It's time to start planning my coronation. The sooner I solidify my power the better."

She narrowed her eyes as she considered. "It's a risk. Are you certain it's one you should take now? For all we know, Finn is still out there, alive and well, ready and willing to challenge any and all comers including you."

"All the more reason. I must make my claim now. I must be ready for him."

"Very well then. What did you have in mind?"

He grinned and told her.

****

The pounding at her door and the call of, "Open in the name of the king," shot Rowena out of a deep restorative sleep. This distressing noise interrupted the most healing slumber she'd experienced in months and she was not at all happy.

She became even less pleased when the brutes outside broke down her door and entered. The group included several of Simon's guards, whom she privately dubbed minions, Simon himself and a pretty young maid flanked by two of the men.

Sal froze, kindling dangling in her limp hand. "What is the meaning of this?" Rowena croaked, her voice still weak from illness and disuse. "Are you all right, Edith?"

The girl wiped a tear-stained face and a bloody nose on her sleeve then said in a small voice, "Yes, your grace." Yet the desperate look in Edith's eyes was clear to Rowena.

"The damage to the girl isn't permanent," Simon put in. He sounded bored as he studied Rowena and her surroundings with little interest.

"How dare you do violence to this lass, permanent or otherwise. I won't stand for it—" A fit of uncontrollable coughing made it impossible for her to speak for some minutes, yet despite its intensity, it did give her some much-needed time to think.

"You won't stand for it? I rule here now. Did you think I wouldn't find out? You've been aiding and abetting traitors. You have been liberating those who wish to shirk their duty." His voice was not loud, but it was unyielding and filled with an astounding amount of menace.

Rowena forced herself not to shudder. It was vital she keep her wits about her and remember how to play the game. Her life, the lives of poor Edith and Sal and countless others depended on it.

Once her coughing jag wheezed to conclusion, she sipped a bit of water then addressed Simon. "You think so? How precisely did I accomplish that when I am practically on my deathbed and you have this castle locked down tighter than any prison? No one goes in or out." She let just the right amount of haughty contempt into her voice and was gratified when he flinched.

"And yet, you have done these things. I clearly underestimated you; rest assured I won't make that mistake again. I don't know how you managed it, but it stops now." In one fluid motion, he wrapped an arm around Edith's waist, pulled her back against him, drew his knife and stabbed her in the gut several times in rapid succession.

Rowena cried out in shock and horror. Sal flung herself at Simon, her hands raised and curled into claws. One of Simon's minions hauled her away though she fought like a wild cat. Ignoring Sal, Simon stabbed the dying Edith twice more then let her go, allowing her limp and now lifeless body to fall to the ground.

After cleaning his blade, he stepped to the bed to address Rowena. His gaze was direct and as cold as a winter wind. "If one more person, just one, manages to disappear, there will be consequences. If even one escapes, I'll kill ten more who were intending to go. I already know who they are." He grabbed hold of her chin, jerked it up. "Do we understand each other?"

Rowena looked him straight in the eye and she did not break. "We do."

"Good." He released her and turned to go but then swiveled back to face her. "One other thing, from now on you are officially confined to your quarters. I realize, being bedridden, you cannot go anywhere at present. However, even should you recover, you will remain here. In addition, no one else will come or go from these chambers without my express permission. My guards will be here to insure this. Try me any further and I will throw you into the vilest cell I can find and leave you there to rot, which in your present condition, shouldn't take long. Is that clear?"

"As crystal," she replied.

Seeing Simon was preparing to leave, the guards released Sal, who dropped to her knees beside her friend right away, sobbing, hysterical and heartbroken.

"Very well." He gave Sal a disgusted glance. "Stop sniveling, girl, and clean that up."

Rowena saw Sal's profile out of the corner of her eye as the girl lifted her tear-streaked face. Such hate filled the young woman's expression that Rowena gasped. Recovering her own self-possession as quickly as possible, she caught Sal's eye, gave an almost imperceptible shake of her head and prayed the girl would heed her.

Sal's jaw hardened and her hands clenched, but she said nothing as Simon and company took their leave. It was only once they left that Sal spoke. Now her eyes were dry and her face was fierce and set. "She was getting out but that bastard killed her. He won't get away with this. I won't let him," she vowed.

****

The sounds of an inordinately loud disturbance attracted Thomas's attention. He rose and went to the entrance of the command pavilion where he and the king spent most of their days to find out the cause.

A young page boy tore into the camp at a run with no regard for anyone in his path. He knocked aside a soldier then jostled a pretty girl carrying water. Ignoring her shouted, "Oy!" he rushed on at top speed.

At last the boy reached the command pavilion. The soldiers standing guard viewed him with far less interest than Thomas as he panted, barely able to speak. "I must...see the...king. I have news...for him. Very...important."

"The king can't be disturbed right now, Kent. Tell us and we'll pass it along," one said.

Kent shook his head. "No, I'm telling you the king needs to hear this from me now." Scrawny, but with a wiry strength for all that, he attempted to push his way past the guards.

Thomas stepped forward. "Gentlemen, is there a problem?"

"This boy is trying to see the king. We've done our best to stop him and keep him quiet," a guard replied.

"Release him. He's not going anywhere." He addressed the child, who he put at no more than twelve years old. "What is it you need, boy? I am Lord Thomas Marbury and I have the king's ear."

With some dignity Kent righted his clothes and straightened his spine. "I thank you, sir, but my news is for the king alone. I beg you, allow me to speak with him."

Thomas assessed the boy's determined face for a moment then nodded. "This had better be good. Very well, you have five minutes. Come with me."

Thomas gestured for Kent to follow him into the tent. He noticed the boy's awed expression and advised, "Try not to gawk."

"Yes, my lord, It's just I ain't never seen such richness. I bet the palace is a thousand times finer if just an army tent is as grand as this."

Then they were in the presence of the king and the boy bowed as he'd been taught and waited.

Standing behind a rough table with a map spread out on it, Finn looked up at their approach. "What's this, Thomas?"

"The boy says he has news. He will speak to no one but you."

Finn raised his eyebrows but said only, "Speak then, boy."

A pale Kent took a deep breath then blurted,

"Forgive me, your majesty, I know messengers of bad tidings have been killed for less. The new so-called king, Simon, has set his coronation for a fortnight from today."

"That will not happen." Finn spoke as if to himself and his tone was flat and fearsome. Then he seemed to remember Kent was there and addressed him. "You, young sir, are to be commended for bringing this news to us at great personal risk. Thomas, see that he is fed and given twenty gold pieces. Your name?" he asked.

"My name is Bartholomew Kent, your grace."

"We are in your debt, Kent. If I can be of any further service, you have but to ask."

"There's only one thing you can do for me, your majesty."

"What's that?"

"Get that mad bastard off of your throne, my liege. He killed my family, you see."

Finn's face set like stone. "I intend to," he promised. "I am sorry to hear about your family," he added.

"I thank you kindly, your grace." Kent bowed low once more before the guards showed him out.

****

"Can it really be true?" Lyssa asked when she heard of the coronation later that day.

"Oh yes," Thomas answered. "Others have confirmed it. Simon plans to hold the ceremony in two weeks."

Finn said nothing. Instead he let the ire of his people spin itself out. Joan, Thomas and most especially Lyssa, expressed shock and awe then a veritable frenzy of indignation.

After some very creative cursing, Joan's first coherent statement was, "Well, we cannot let this stand. It's time to act."

Thomas nodded. "I agree. We've prepared for this and it's time."

Finn weighed the matter carefully, or he tried to. He was afire to end Simon's charade, but he had to be objective. He had to do what was in the best interest of the kingdom. His personal desire to pummel Simon until he was a bloody mess could not enter into it.

Objectivity be damned, he determined. Emotion aside, no good would come of Simon on his throne. This he was entirely sure of. "It is time," he concurred, "so let's begin."

****

The pounding on his door woke Simon. Still groggy after a night of sport with Adriane, he shrugged on a dressing gown and went to see who had the gall to disturb him in his private chambers at such an ungodly hour.

It was Payne, looking a combination of furious and terrified. Before Simon could even speak, Payne burst out, "He isn't dead."

The shock which ran through Simon's system at the words blew away the last of his fatigue. He discerned right away who Payne meant of course, but he asked the expected question anyway. "Who isn't dead, Payne? Whoever it is had better be very important."

"His maje—" At Simon's thunderous expression, he backtracked. "The former king, Finn Hale, is alive and has shown himself just outside the city."

"What do you mean he's shown himself outside the

city?" Simon demanded.

"I mean the rumors that he is alive aren't only rumors anymore. He has made his way through Brighton Forest down the Great Eastern Road and toward the city. He has thousands of troops behind him and he's picked up every chivalrous knight and bored farm boy ready for adventure along the way. It's turned into a damned royal progress or worse, an invading army. The people aren't just delighted he's returned from the dead, Simon, they are treating it like a miracle."

"A miracle, is that so?" Simon asked drily.

Payne nodded vigorously. "A miracle, yes. And once the people grow tired of that oddity, they will come looking for you and anyone who supported you. They will ask how this mistake happened. They will demand to know how and why this vicious rumor became known as fact when it's nothing more than fiction. That's if the king doesn't come for you himself and kill you outright."

The man was babbling now and it got on Simon's already frayed nerves. "Payne, don't panic."

"Don't panic! Either way, I'm in serious trouble. Whoever comes looking for you will come looking for me. Once they have finished with you, they'll come for all of us. We have to—"

"Stop!" The authority in Simon's tone had the desired effect. Payne's voice cut off in midsentence. When he was certain he had the councilman's complete attention, Simon continued, "You will head out to meet him."

"Me!"

The look of utter alarm on his face was quite

comical and would have made Simon laugh out loud at any other time. He barked, "Yes, you. Find out whether it's really him. If it is, try to get close enough to determine his plans. Also, you will give him a message from me."

"Which is?" Payne squeaked.

"He should have stayed dead."

Payne's complexion turned an unhealthy pasty white and he swayed where he stood. "But I can't do that," he gasped out at last and sat down in a nearby wing-backed chair.

Simon's tone hardened. "You can and you will. Now."

With little choice in the matter, Payne rose on shaky knees and did as his king commanded.

****

They topped the rise of the hill just as the sun rose and Lyssa got her first glimpse of Finn's home. It shone as brightly as a multi-colored jewel in the distance. The spires and domes were capped with colored glass of bright blue, red and green. The entire structure dominated the landscape. It was so beautiful she might have taken it for a mirage had she not known better. Her breath caught in her chest at the gorgeous wonder of the palace. It was like none she'd ever seen.

As she took in every detail she could, Finn told her that inside, the place was light and airy, in spite of being built of solid stone. According to him, the warm sun and the breeze off the southern coast made it not only a stronghold but a lovely place to live. The castle stayed cool in the summer and warm in the relatively mild winter due to clever ventilation, Finn explained.

To the east a half league away from the castle was

Brighton Forest. To the south were the sea and the river, which snaked along to join with it, a silver ribbon in the misty light. It was, in her opinion, a most magnificent oasis situated between an immense desert to the west perhaps five leagues distant and the vast ocean. "It's magnificent," she managed at last.

"Yes, so it is. Come."

Following his lead, she reined her horse to the left and followed the path he had chosen for them.

As planned, Finn and all of his people arrived outside the city just after dawn and began announcing his return and his triumph over his supposed death. By noon, half the city knew of his presence and of the troops with him.

****

The well-equipped carriage halted at the edge of the forest a mile due east of the city where Finn had chosen to end his procession and set up camp. A man stepped down and Finn recognized Payne. In general, Councilman Payne did not perform the duties of a lackey, yet here he was.

The councilman made a beeline in Finn's direction. Neither man spoke and Finn welcomed the opportunity to study the older council member. Sweat beaded on Payne's forehead in spite of the fresh cool spring day. Idly, Finn wondered why but did not deign to ask. What did the man's nerves matter to him after all?

Payne looked as though he was forced to swallow some very distasteful poison, but he bowed to Finn and began. "The new king wishes to send a message to you."

"Oh, he does, does he? Speak."

Payne cleared his throat, went beet-red, cleared his

throat again then at last said, "You should have stayed dead." He took a deep breath then clarified. "That is the message, word for word. Only this and nothing more."

Finn stilled. Rage, black and strong and lately all too familiar, churned through him. It was a long moment before he trusted himself to speak. Even once he did, what he said was not exactly wise. "In a very short time people will know what a liar and thief your master is. Payne, tell Simon I will soon take back what is mine. Let him know that I am very much alive and intend to stay that way."

Payne paled and for a moment Finn wondered whether the older man would pass out.

With a visible effort he pulled himself together. "Are you certain there is nothing more you wish to say?"

Finn took a deep breath and tamped down his fury as much as possible so he could say what he had to. "In order to avoid bloodshed, I will agree to meet to negotiate the terms of his full and free surrender. He has forty-eight hours to decide whether he wishes to meet me or if he prefers bloodshed."

Payne paled even more. "But you know he'll never agree. Please, I beg you to reconsider."

"Forty-eight hours," Finn repeated. Then without another word, he left Payne standing in front of the carriage, gaping.

****

Simon beckoned Payne closer. The council member walked down the long room past its floor to ceiling windows, boot heels clicking on the flagstone floor. At the far end of the audience chamber sat the throne, currently occupied by Simon. The oak chair was painted black with a raven carved into it. The wings and head formed the top edge of the back and a blood red velvet cushion padded the seat.

Wiping the sweat from his brow onto his sleeve then clenching both hands at his sides, the councilman made his way forward.

"You have a message from Finn, I'm told."

Simon waited and the silence grew until at last, Payne broke it. "Indeed I do. In order to avoid bloodshed, Finn Hale agrees to meet to negotiate the terms of..." Payne cleared his throat, attempted to speak but managed nothing more than a strangled sound and cleared it again. "To negotiate the terms of your full and free surrender. He says you have forty-eight hours to decide if you wish to meet or if you prefer bloodshed. These are his precise words, not mine."

"He demands my full and free surrender, does he? I think not." Rage flared up inside of him like a flame, but he tamped it down and tried to think rationally. "Still, in spite of his insults, I will agree to meet with him. It's high time we met face to face again, don't you agree?"

"But you don't intend to surrender to him?"

Simon laughed. "Hardly. But I want him here. I have things to say to him and I want to see his face when I do. Make the arrangements."

Payne bowed in acquiescence and escaped.

****

"Who goes there?" demanded a young soldier stationed on the wall above and to the right of the drawbridge.

"Your king has returned under a flag of truce to negotiate with the pretender Simon. Open the gate,"

Finn shouted back.

With only a small delay, they did so. Finn crossed the bridge and was home. Little had changed during his absence, he noted as he continued into the forecourt. As he proceeded to the mounting block, an officer approached then blocked his path.

The young soldier bowed. "Your—My lord," the man hastily corrected himself. "You are to attend his majesty in the audience chamber. You will dismount and come with me."

Keeping his hands well away from his weapons, Finn slowly descended from his horse. "Very well. That is what I've come for after all."

He indulged the guard, allowing the man to lead him down a path he would have known blindfolded. Upon entering, he could admit that here at least, the changes were more apparent. The Hale coat of arms had been replaced as had the wall hangings. A new banner with a design incorporating both the Fairfax crest and Wentworth coat of arms had been created in a rather distasteful purple. He took his time, studied every detail of the room, then and only then did he address Simon, the man currently sitting on *his* bloody throne. "Well, I'm here and I'm willing to negotiate. I want to avoid any further bloodshed. You must desire the same since you agreed to meet me."

"I'm not and I don't," Simon stated, tone flat. When Finn's expression grew stony, Simon smiled, all teeth. "Surely you did not think I would ever seriously entertain the idea of surrender?"

"Then what do you want?" Finn demanded. Fighting disappointment and feeling more defeated than he liked to admit, he waited for an answer. Much as he tried to stamp it out, when Simon had consented to a meeting between them, a tiny gleam of hope had taken hold of him. Perhaps this fraught situation might end without war after all. Hearing Simon's words now, Finn cursed himself for a fool.

"I long for order, the order which kept this country safe during my youth. While you do everything you can to destroy it."

Finn shook his head, a weary sorrow suffusing his expression. "There isn't any going back. There is only forward."

Simon took a sip of the wine he held and had not offered to Finn. "You are quite right, I admit. The world of my childhood is gone. It's taken me a very long time to understand nothing can bring it back." He leaned forward. "But I tell you this, that being the case, better to let the whole world burn and rebuild on the ashes."

Finn studied the older man's face in the flickering candlelight for a long moment. "You're serious."

"I was never more so. If the world I loved as a boy is gone then I will shape a new one."

"In your own image, I take it?" When Simon nodded, Finn took another careful look about the room to give himself time to regain his composure. "Conflict is destructive so you will end it by using force."

"Yes."

"Such senseless tactics are rarely successful. But you will attempt this with no thought to what the people want and no regard for their lives or their fate?"

"None."

"And what of the free will the gods bless every person with? The free will it is a king's duty to protect?"

"I do not pretend to know the minds of the gods. Their reasons for doing what they do escape me and I have long since stopped trying to understand them. What I do know is men and women and this world we live in. Freedom is an invitation to chaos. Thus it is a privileged few alone who should be granted liberty of any kind. Examine history over the last half-century and tell me I'm wrong."

Finn could not, would not speak to it. Instead he brought up another more salient point. "So no one holds sway over you, not your king, not the gods. No one and nothing."

"That's right, no one and nothing. Not anymore. Not even you, my liege." He bowed his head and the gesture was full of mockery.

Finn's demeanor had been calm but now a fierce light kindled in his soul. "You are not a god. Like anyone else your freedom only extends so far as it does not infringe upon that of others. This is how we hold back the chaos. This world is not yours to mold as you see fit. Not at the expense of everyone else in it." His tone was low and authoritative.

"Not yet, but it will be. Either way, I intend to make quite certain it will never again be yours. Surrender now and we can avoid so much senseless killing and destruction."

"Hear this now; I will not surrender. I will fight to protect the freedom of my subjects if I must. I will defend them to the last drop of my blood."

"And what about their blood? What about their lives? What are they worth to you? Will you defend them to the very last drop of their blood?"

Finn closed his eyes. In his mind's eye he envisioned the destruction Simon threatened and he longed to prevent it. Yet he was sure even if he himself capitulated, his people would not. They would fight and he would be unable, perhaps even unwilling, to stop them. So this being the case, their best chance was to have his full support. Even with all that meant. "Yes. May the gods forgive me."

"Well then, how are you any different from me?"

The soft words pierced Finn's heart as surely as any blade. In that moment, he swore no matter what, he would be different. He would liberate and release them, not conquer or master them. He also vowed that not one drop of needless blood would be spilled. It was these two oaths, the keeping of them, that would make all the difference for his country and himself.

To give himself time to regain his composure, he took a deep breath then fixed his gaze on Simon. He watched as the usurper rose, stepped down from the dais and stopped mere feet from him. Knowing there was nothing he could do to change Simon's mind and knowing his own was just as firmly fixed, he gave up the attempt.

"I see no point in further discussion. Since neither of us will be swayed, to bandy more words about wastes precious time. I will take back what is mine. Surrender to me and vacate the castle by dawn three days from now and I will show mercy. If not, there will be blood. Goodbye, Simon."

"Oh no, Finn, you aren't going anywhere." Simon grabbed Finn's arm and with a jerk, put his knife to Finn's throat. "Guards!"

Finn pulled himself free, but in the few seconds

that took, ten of Simon's men entered at a brisk march and surrounded him in a rough circle.

"You think you can hold me? With just these few?" Barely able to suppress a laugh, he lifted his hand, ready to use his power.

"You might want to reconsider that."

Now Finn did laugh. "Really? Why?"

"Because I have the advantage. Your people are now under my rule. Their lives are mine to do with as I will. As is your mother's. Do you really want to test me?"

Rage filled him. "Do you really want to test me? You dare to threaten my mother and you think that will make me bow down and do your bidding? Think again. She would rather die than bow to you and so would I."

Not at all interested in anymore talk, Finn raised both his hands, spread them in opposite directions and shot fire at them all, including Simon, as he turned in a circle. The two men nearest cried out in pain and staggered back while the others avoided the flames. They shot forward in an attempt to incapacitate then capture him. They failed.

When his path to the door was clear, he raced toward it. Once free of the room, he went left rather than right, which led to the main gate, the direction Simon would assume he had gone. But Finn knew his castle and headed for the secret tunnel which would take him under the moat and beneath the field, to come out on the edge of Brighton Forest. Only those of his house knew of it and so it would be his best chance of escape. Soon enough he came to what appeared to be a dead end. Turning the torch set high on the wall operated the mechanism and he pushed the wall before him inward a fraction, just enough for him to squeeze through. The door swung back into place after him and he made certain it locked. Even so, he did not stop running until he could no longer hear the distant sound of the moat above.

****

Hours later Finn approached the camp. On foot and rather filthy from the fight and the dark dank cave, he knew he must be a sight.

"What in the name of all the gods happened to you?" Thomas asked by way of greeting.

"Simon never intended to let me go. I had to fight my way out, even under a flag of truce," he explained as he proceeded directly to his tent.

Joan, who had rushed up to join them, gasped. "The fiend!"

"Indeed. Where is Lyssa? I want to speak to you all about our next move."

"She's in her tent. I'll fetch her," Joan offered.

Moments later, Joan and Lyssa joined them.

She gaped when she took in his disheveled appearance. "What on earth happened to you?" she asked, unconsciously echoing Thomas's words. "Are you hurt? I was beginning to worry when you had not returned. It seems I had good cause."

In a few words, he told them about his conversation with Simon, the resulting attempted capture and his escape.

"So what now, majesty?"

"Now, Thomas, we will have war. Prepare to move out at dawn."

****

In the fading light of the sunset, Finn slowly

259

approached his castle for the second time that day. *His* castle, by all the gods. It belonged to him once and would again. This morning had been the time for a strategic retreat, yet there was one more thing he would do before meeting Simon on the field of battle. He would give his people every chance.

With this purpose uppermost in his mind, he watched the drawbridge rise in its graceful gradual motion and when it closed, he began to speak. He did not shout, but pitched his voice so those on the ramparts could hear him. "I am Finn Hale, your rightful king. Most of you know me. As I see it, each and every one of you has four options. The first is pardon. Not surrender, but pardon for mistakes made and the opportunity to live life in peace once this destructive conflict has ended. The second is exile. If you no longer wish to live in a kingdom of your own making, then far be it from me to keep you here. I will not stop you going, only wish you godspeed. The third is joining the right side. The last is death. No man has ever been a more accomplished liar than Lord Simon Fairfax. He altered reports of unrest to cultivate your fear. He told you I was dead and took steps to make you believe it. He would make this lie into truth with his own hands if he could. Far worse than any of that, he would subjugate you to his own will and deny you your power. Do not let him get away with this.

"To stay and fight alongside Fairfax, traitor and lunatic, will only bring death. That I promise. Know well I have no wish to shed the blood of my people. I offer you a peaceful world, power and freedom, but most of all I offer you the balance back. The snow queen is here with me and the balance we have craved for decades is already being restored. Does Fairfax offer the same? Can he deliver the same? I think not, but you must each ask yourselves these questions and consider well before deciding. I grant all of you, even those who support him now, this final chance and beg of you to take it. Know this, I will not beg again. If a full and free surrender does not arrive by dawn three days hence, I and all those with me will fight and we will win."

Then he turned his horse toward Brighton Forest.

****

Joan was ready to go foraging with the hunting party when a very disheveled but familiar young woman approached the camp. Surely it was Sal, she decided and rushed forward. "Sal, is that you?" she called. The girl's head swung in her direction and Joan could see her dirt-streaked face more clearly. It was indeed the young maid who had tended her and Joan held out her hands to greet the girl.

"My lady, you're here!" The smile Sal gave was a tired but radiant one. She put her hands in Joan's.

"I am and now so are you. The queen mother got you out as she has so many others, I see."

Sal's smile faded. "No, my lady," was all she said.

"No? What do you mean? Nothing's happened to her?"

Now Sal looked uncomfortable and would not meet Joan's eyes. "No, nothing yet."

"Nothing yet? Sal, what's happened? I expected to see your friend Edith long before now and yet she has not appeared. Now you tell me the dowager queen may be in danger. What is going on?"

"Edith is dead. Simon, that miserable traitor,

261

murdered her."

"Oh no. That bastard," Joan muttered. To Sal she said, "I'm so sorry."

Now that the first words were said, the rest of the story tumbled out. Sal told Joan everything that happened with the dowager queen, Simon, and Edith on that awful day. Soon tears ran unheeded down her face. Remembering her own escape, sympathy welled up inside Joan for the poor girl and all the pain she went through.

"So you see," Sal concluded, "after a threat like that, after I'd seen what he was willing to do, I was determined to get out and to avenge Edith, but I could not accept the queen mother's help to do it."

"So you faked an accident and made your way here."

Sal nodded then accepted the handkerchief Joan offered.

"It's good you did." She patted Sal's shoulder. "You are not the first, as you know. Hopefully you won't be the last. Already so many have arrived for so many reasons. Come along, we'll find you a place to sleep for the night and get you cleaned up. Then we'll get some food into you. You'll be safe here, I promise."

"I don't want to be safe. I want to fight," the girl stated.

Joan took the girl's arm to lead her toward the tents, patted her on the shoulder again. "Of course you do. Believe me, we'll all be fighting soon enough. There's time enough for you to rest first."

Mere hours later, more began arriving. Starting from just after sunset and on into the dead of night they poured into the camp. As they did, Joan heard countless stories. Many wished only for safe passage. They had no desire to be part of a war. Others, once they found out all Simon did, wanted to join the fight on the other side. Some had stayed with Simon because with the king gone, they believed they had no other option. With his miraculous return, however, they now had a choice and took full advantage of it.

Not everyone deserted Simon, however. There would always be those who are drawn to power, Joan knew. To further their own ambition, they would do anything and follow anyone who could make that happen. With power comes the freedom to do whatever one might desire with nothing and no one to check the cruelty. Some were cowards living in fear of the malignant force beyond their control that was Simon. Still others were victims without the strength or the will to break free. It was these broken innocent ones that Finn pitied the most. It was these he would give his life to protect. And Joan vowed, so would she.

Chapter Seventeen

From his private terrace, Simon could see Finn's army massing in the fading light. He had to admit to surprise at seeing so many. Early scouts had confirmed Finn's army was fifty thousand strong, but seeing it with his own eyes, it brought home what he faced. Without turning round, he said to the soldier behind him, "With seventy-five thousand troops of our own, the odds are good. Even if by some small chance we are defeated, we can withstand a siege for as long as a year. The gods are surely with us. Tell the commanders there will be no quarter. We attack at dawn."

"Very good, my liege." The man bowed and departed.

He was not sure how long he had stood, contemplating the field of battle when Adriane burst in. She came to him with her usual purposeful stride. Once she stood before him, however, her demeanor was quite different than usual. The only time he had seen her this excited was when he showed her the fake signet ring.

"What is it?" he demanded by way of greeting.

"He isn't there," she blurted. "As far as we can tell he isn't on the battlefield. I can only conjecture he's seen sense at last. Or that he is finally showing himself to be the coward I always took him for."

Simon's entire body chilled. Sick fear skittered down his spine. "Finn isn't on the battlefield? You're certain?"

"As certain as we can be. According to our spies and to what we can see through the new spy glass we have used to study them from the battlements, he is not there. Why?" Adriane's eyes narrowed.

"I know this man. The last thing he is, is a coward. Nor would he ever see sense. No, he's planning something and it's big. We need to find him. Now."

Adriane nodded then clapped her hands to summon his top three lieutenants. When they knelt before them, Simon ordered, "Alert all troops to be on watch for the king. One hundred gold pieces to the man, woman or child who brings him to me alive or dead."

"There now, we've done all we can."

Simon shook his head. He addressed the battle-hardened lieutenant nearest him. "Pick your best men. I want patrols along the outer walls and battlements. I want another contingent patrolling inside. I want Finn Hale found."

The man looked shocked. "But sire, we're about to go into battle, detailing these men to some other duty..." His voice died away and he cringed.

"Do it."

The soldier saluted and scurried away.

Simon turned to Adriane. "*Now* we've done all we can. I just hope we find him before he springs whatever trap he is setting."

****

As the first rays of the sun glinted over the horizon, Thomas took position at the head of the royal army. The morning was cool and a mist lay over the clearing that was their chosen battleground. Astride his favorite horse, his fingers grew stiff from the taut grip he kept on the reins. He caught a whiff of fresh mint, even over the more pungent smells of men and horses, and reckoned there must be some growing nearby. The periodic gentle clink of armor and chainmail could not drown out the birdsong some distance away.

In his field of vision, Thomas could see both armies spread out before him. In front of him at the head of the royal army were the archers, who would shoot first to break the enemy line. The infantry was next and they would storm the walls while he would lead the cavalry close behind. Siege engines such as trebuchets and belfries were placed equidistant from one another, manned and ready. It was an awesome sight, months in the planning, and Thomas couldn't help but appreciate its awful beauty.

Joan was close by as always having a last word with the other lieutenants and that offered tremendous comfort. Yet for the first time that boon was not an unmixed one. Facing danger with her beside him when he cared so much about her was both blessing and curse. Even so, he could not imagine it any other way. Going into battle without her beside him would be like going in naked, unarmed and without the use of one of his limbs. He was not a man who often prayed to the gods, but he prayed now. "Hold her safe in battle, oh god of war." In his mind, he repeated the phrase over and over, hoping it would act as a talisman. Such things had power, he believed.

As he waited, out of the corner of his eye, he saw her take up her position beside him. Without looking directly at her, he murmured, "Joan, you're with me. Stay close."

A half-smile played on her lips. "Always, my lord.

There is no place else I'd rather be. I'd follow you into hell without you even having to ask."

In spite of what they were about to face and the fact that they had quite an audience, he pulled her to him and gave her a fierce kiss. When he let her go and she just stared at him, trying to gather her wits, he grinned.

While every soldier waited on his word, with tension mounting, the army stood silent. Or at least as silent as so many men could be. Thomas found himself adding to his prayers. He begged the gods for victory and in some small part of his heart, he pleaded that he himself might be held safe so he could have a life with Joan, and see their children grow up.

Simon's forces started forward first. This gave the royal army leave to move at last. With the sun well and truly risen, Thomas placed himself where everyone could see him at the head of his king's troops, then lifted a hand in signal. As he lowered it, he bellowed, "Charge!"

Thousands of men rushed headlong toward each other across the open field before the castle. When the two armies met, the clash of swords and bodies and armor was deafening.

****

The sun's first rays streaked the sky and the sound of the cathedral bell filled the air, as Lyssa executed step one. With this signal, she knew Finn would begin his progress through the castle. She dug deep inside and prayed that all Finn had taught her would help her accomplish the first part of the plan. With a deep breath, she raised her hands high and sent a great column of ice straight up into the cold clear air.

In spite of the fighting, many stopped, some in mid-blow, transfixed by the sight.

It was also a welcome distraction the royal army took full advantage of. Dimly she heard Thomas's voice shout over the din, "Forward! For King Finn and Ravenstone!"

The foot soldiers raced ahead, the cavalry galloped behind and together, they beat back the opposing forces and rushed the gates.

****

The dank secret passage leading into the castle was dark as midnight. Finn and his fighters marched through the halls as silently as possible; the only sounds the gentle clink of chain mail and the dripping of water from stone. It was vital that they be in the chief corridor leading to the west wing just after dawn. This route would bring them to the main audience chamber, which they would then promptly invade, surrounding the enemy on all sides and achieving their ultimate goal. This was a simple but effective military strategy which would only work if they were in position and remained there undiscovered until the proper time. Getting even twenty men inside in as silent and clandestine a manner as possible had been a challenge but his warriors had met it. He'd assigned only the best, the most highly trained of his troops to this detail. Others he considered highly valuable he sent with Thomas. So he divided his fighters and left the rest in the hands of the gods and the snow queen.

In position at last, Finn had only to wait for Lyssa's signal. But the waiting was, as always, exquisite torture. He and his men far preferred action. Finn's body was poised for battle. This interval of enforced stasis was driving them all mad, but Finn most of all.

At least the torture would have an end. In exactly one hour, when the cathedral bell tolled to commemorate the dawn, the forces outside would attack and so would they. Lyssa would send a great burst of ice straight up into the sky to distract the enemy. For a moment, he was held mesmerized as he always was by the scene he envisioned in his mind's eye of her power, then he blinked and refocused on the task at hand.

After what seemed like an eternity, he heard the first peal of the bell. "It's time," he told his men. With one brief gesture, he indicated they should move out. "Strike down any in our path who offer resistance."

With the battle raging outside, there was no more need for stealth, so they quick-marched through the castle with Finn in the lead. Initially soft, their clatter soon escalated into a cacophony. At first they encountered little resistance, as many of the soldiers were up in the battlements or out in the field. Yet even so, the castle was far from empty.

A young soldier stumbled into their path first, stopping short at the sight of them. Little more than a boy, he turned tail and raced ahead down the corridor. It became apparent he was unfamiliar with the section of the castle he was running through, when he abruptly fetched up against a dead end. He whirled, attempted to go back, but found his path blocked. A wall made of men obstructed the passage and kept him from going anywhere.

"Give yourself up, boy," Finn advised, voice as calm as a lake on a still summer day.

The soldier's gaze darted round, searching for any

means of escape. Finding none, he turned his head and spat on the ground, the gesture one of utter contempt, but then he dropped his sword and held up his hands in surrender. Two men of the royal army stepped forward and took him into custody. They gagged him and bound his hands then kept him under close guard as they continued on.

Those they met next were far greater in number and far more prepared to challenge any enemy, even their king. Soon it all blurred. Finn used fire and sword to bring blood. He shouted commands until his voice hoarsened then was gone. When his voice failed him, he used hand signals. When his sword arm faltered, he used his other. There was always his fire, which never betrayed him. Unbowed, unbent and unbroken, he tore through the castle and all fell before him.

With more self-confidence than he'd ever experienced before, he directed half of his troops to the east wing. Achieving three goals was paramount. First, his fighters must infiltrate every corner of the castle then open the gate. Second, his mother must be protected. Third, Simon must be captured or killed. In spite of his role as king and general, Finn had made this his personal mission. One he intended to carry out no matter the outcome of the battle. Whether they were victorious or defeated, he would not allow Simon to remain at large. Such an insult was not to be borne. Nor would he face the fear of Simon returning to wreak havoc.

****

Every last soldier lurched forward in an organized chaos the likes of which Lyssa had never seen. Following her own personal battle plan, the one she and

Finn had concocted and practiced ad nauseam, she rushed forward with the great mass of humanity. Her next goal was to complete stage two and reach the moat as soon as possible.

Fraught minutes later, on the edge of its brown waters, she lifted both hands and sent her power down into the murky depths. It froze solid within seconds. Men rushed across the moat immediately. She allowed herself one unforgettable instant to savor that triumph then continued on. The stairs of ice she formed helped some of the men scale the wall. For weeks she had practiced creating a set of steps that were solid enough for many men to walk on. Strapped to the soles of their boots were leather strips with metal spikes attached, something cleverly designed by Joan.

Lyssa was happy to see that the time spent had been worthwhile. Eventually the ice would melt and the steps would grow too slick even with the shoes, but it would hold long enough for many of the men to get to the top of the battlements.

As her own troops climbed, enemy fighters atop the battlements let loose bursts of fire and pots of boiling oil. With a gesture, Lyssa froze the streams in mid-air. Her heart pounded so hard that she was surprised it still remained in her chest and a gasp caught in her throat. The oil missed the warriors below by mere inches. Trembling, she comforted herself with the thought that almost doesn't count. Yet looking at the carnage around her, the realization that she could not save them all hit her with the force of a lightning bolt. The screams of a man hit by another pot of oil, one that she had not been in time to stop, underscored the point. By all the gods, she would save some, she resolved. She would save as many as she could.

The fear she had lived with for so long left her at last. As she successfully attained her second goal, a certain strange confidence permeated her being. She could do this, she realized. Ghastly as it was, atrocious as it was, she could and would do as much as possible. She could protect and defend, just as Finn had said. At least she knew now she was capable of that much. At least she hadn't run. Somehow she knew she never would.

Even so, it was not easy and it was not pretty. She used her powers to get the soldiers to the gate, but the struggle was long and bloody. The peculiar scent of blood mixed with burnt flesh and filth filled her nostrils and made her stomach queasy, but she bore down, determined to keep fighting. It all became some hazy living nightmare she was afraid would never end, yet she did not give up. She kept moving and prayed to all the gods there would be peace soon.

****

Joan had not realized it, but she had never been in a true battle before. Her previous experience consisted of mere skirmishes, nothing more. A true battle was far dirtier, much louder, and of course, considerably bloodier. Still, her techniques remained the same, if of necessity a trifle faster. She used every skill she had ever learned, from sword fighting to hand-to-hand combat to improvising as the situation required, and of course, there was her bow.

As always, her primary aim was to watch Thomas's back, knowing he would be doing the same for her. He fought with a savage ferocity downright beautiful to look upon. She met and she matched him as she always did, but even more so now. It seemed she knew his every thought, his every movement. Ever since she became his lover, she was attuned to every nuance of his body.

****

Joan fought with a cool precision he could always count on. In seamless sync with her, Thomas bent to thrust his sword into the man in front of him, while she challenged the man at his back then ran him through.

She wrenched her sword from the body of the first man, pivoted and lopped the head off another inches away from stabbing Thomas. "Are you all right?" she yelled out over the noise of battle. She wiped blood out of her eyes and panted heavily.

"Thanks to you I'm as well as I can be expected," Thomas replied. He shrugged, but he turned his head a bit to grin at her, suddenly feeling exhilarated. "You?"

She laughed. "I'm good. Let's keep heading toward the gate then."

"I am with you," he assured her.

****

Finn and several of his strongest and most skilled compatriots rushed toward Rowena's rooms. Securing his mother's safety was paramount; nothing mattered more, not even the capture of Simon.

Five burly soldiers belonging to Simon were doing their best to break down the door to Rowena's chambers. It was only a matter of time before they succeeded.

"That's my mother's door you are damaging. I'm sure she is already most distressed. What distresses her, distresses me. So, as your king, I'm ordering you to stop."

The men obeyed, but then their commander stepped forward.

"Now walk away."

"No. I am the ranking officer here. My men and I will be going in there and when we do, we will do whatever we like to the former queen mother. And I do mean whatever we like." His lascivious expression was unmistakable.

"Really? I don't think so." Finn gave the soldiers a look, one which had often made grown men tremble and beg to do his bidding.

To a man, they stepped aside and stood quietly by while the royal soldiers, who outnumbered them three to one, disarmed them.

"Later you will pay for your crimes, rest assured, but for now I have more pressing matters to attend to." Addressing his troops, he ordered, "Get them out of here. Take them to the dungeon and lock them up."

Once the perpetrators were gone, Finn stepped back several paces and took a deep breath. With a running start and with one shove of his shoulder, he broke down the already damaged door. Inside, he fetched up inches from a sword that might have pierced his heart. He gasped. "Mother!"

Rowena's eyes widened as the sight of her tall bloody son registered. The sword she held in her trembling hand clattered to the floor. "Son."

Three steps and she was in his arms. For a long time, Finn simply embraced his mother, so grateful to see her alive and whole after so long.

Then concern had him easing back to look her over. "Mother, are you well? Are you hurt?"

"I am fine. I'm not hurt. In fact, I'm on the mend."

"Not quite completely recovered though," he observed. "I have never seen anyone so pale and you are shaking like a leaf. Sit."

She smiled at his commanding tone but did as he ordered, dropping down in a nearby chair covered in the attractive green and gold brocade she favored.

"What of you, my dearest boy? You are filthy and I can see some of that blood is yours. Are you badly wounded?"

"No, it's nothing, not to worry. I've returned and I don't want you to fear anything anymore. I will find Simon and stop him. I am taking back my kingdom today."

"Good." She nodded her approval. "How can I help?"

"Mother, you have already helped so much. You got people out. You sent supplies. You helped organize an army. All you need do now is rest."

"You want me to rest? Stay cozy and warm in my bed while you fight? No. And what of after? You will need help restoring—"

He cut off her protest. "So I will, once the battle is won. For now, much as I hate the idea, I must leave you in the care of my men. You will be well guarded and no one will hurt you, I promise, but you must stay here and remain safe. I will not risk you. I won't have him using you as a bargaining chip, not after all we have been through. Not when we are so close to defeating him. Mother, Simon has to be stopped and the time is now. I cannot manage it if you are not safe."

Rowena studied her son for a very long time. Moving stiffly and slowly, she got to her feet then placed a hand on her son's forearm. "Very well, I understand. I swear I will remain here until this battle is won. Help me back into bed then go kill that bastard."

She surprised a laugh out of him before he left to find the man who usurped his throne.

Chapter Eighteen

When Finn entered the main audience chamber, he did it alone, although it was clear from the noise that a great portion of the royal army was mere seconds away from gaining entrance to the castle.

From the far corner of the room came Simon's voice. "Hello, Finn, I can't say I'm surprised to see you. No, on the contrary, you and I have been hurtling toward this moment for years. This place and time would make a fitting end to our rivalry, I suppose. Still, to be here now, to challenge me now, is a risk. Why would you take such a chance?" he demanded of Finn. "Particularly when the battle is all but lost."

"Nothing is lost while I have the strength, spirit, and heart to hold it. As I told you before, I am here to take back what is mine."

"What is yours?" he scoffed. "This kingdom is not yours. Not anymore. I have taken all that belonged to you and made it mine: land, castle, family, and kingdom. Accept it, Finn."

"And if I do?"

Simon shrugged. "A quick death shall be your reward."

"Kill me then, if you can."

They began to circle each other, two fighters gauging the strength of their opponent before striking.

"You are so bloody arrogant, even now when you

are beaten, Finn. The simple fact of the matter is, I am better at ruling than you are. Strategy, combat, swordplay, governing, book-learning, I have made certain to excel at all of it. Yet even that isn't enough for you. You still think the cursed power you were born with can get you anything you want. You still believe a bit of inherited magic will insure you keep hold of all you desire. I am happy to disabuse you of that notion at last. If it takes killing you myself to prove that to you, then believe me, I'm happy to oblige."

"You are jealous and you are weak. You have always wanted what I was born with: ability, intelligence, looks, privilege, even my kingdom. Admit that the reason you have made yourself so good at all of this is to compensate for the one thing you wanted most that you couldn't have: the fire."

"Yes!" Simon roared. Sword raised, he hurtled toward Finn in a mad rush.

He parried the thrust of Simon's blade automatically. A heartbeat later, he regained his wits, pivoted and used Simon's momentum against him to send him stumbling away. Yet the older man's recovery was all but immediate and soon they circled each other again.

"Truth at last," Finn continued as if there had been no interruption. "I have always been able to see right through you, but it is nice to have some honesty between us finally. Your façade has never deceived me, not for one instant. Just another reason you have always despised me."

"I have so many reasons to hate you."

"So why not drop the pretense and tell me?"

"Why not? What harm could it do when you won't

live to see another dawn? Since I fully intend to kill you with my own hands anyway, what does it matter? You and your kind destroyed my world. I have spent my entire adult life making sure you would never rule what was left of it."

The distant sounds of fighting grew closer and when his own men entered the chamber, Finn shouted, "Keep back! I want to take him myself."

His soldiers obeyed.

When Simon's men rushed in as well, he ordered them away. "Finn Hale is mine. Do not interfere. As for the rest, kill them all."

Simon's fighters took their king at his word. Finn's troops had no choice but to defend themselves and soon the room rang with the sounds of combat.

Finn had no compunction about using every advantage he had, his fire included, but he began with the sword. Slashing out, he missed opening Simon's gut by inches. Undeterred, he continued thrusting, blocking and parrying until he miscalculated. Simon followed through on a blow to his side which missed, then executed a well-concealed feint and cut into his sword arm. Finn turned aside too late and the blade sliced into his flesh from shoulder to elbow. Cursing, he raised his sword to block Simon's next blow. Or tried to. His weakened arm shook, then buckled and the sword flew from his hand. Triumph lit up Simon's face as he repositioned himself for the killing blow.

His victory was short-lived, however. When Finn shot flame at his opponent's face, Simon fell back with a cry of pain and alarm, right cheek burning and hair quickly catching as well. Screaming in desperate agony, he staggered away then used the thick sleeve of his tunic and bare hands to snuff it out before his entire face was engulfed.

"I don't need a sword. You should know that by now." Tired of the games and more than ready to end things one way or another, Finn took his power up a notch. Wherever Simon moved, Finn's flame was there first. With slow deliberate tactics, he forced Simon into a corner. That done, he directed a slender stream of flame at the hilt of the usurper's sword. In an instant, the hilt was hot enough to take off a layer of skin, but Simon did not release his hold. No sound came but Simon's face set like stone and grew steadily redder.

This went on for longer than Finn had ever dreamed possible until Simon bellowed in agony and let go of his sword. He crashed to his knees, cradling his injured hand. For long minutes, he remained in that posture, panting and whimpering, all but weeping.

Finn extinguished his fire, but still held a hand outstretched and ready as he approached. "Yield and I vow I will spare you and yours. You will live a captive, but you will live. Yield!"

"Not while I draw breath. I won't live chained and I won't stop, not ever. You and yours will never have a moment's peace. If I can't rule it, I will watch this whole world burn. I swear it by all the gods."

Shaking and a little nauseous, Finn raised a trembling hand, conjured fire in his palm. "Do not force me to do this."

"Force you?" Simon gave a bitter chuckle. "I can't force you to do anything, especially not right now. I'm at your mercy."

"You bastard."

"Oh come now, Finn. There's always a choice; you

know it as well as I do. So make one. Do it," Simon spat. "Or do you lack the courage?"

With an almighty primal sound of pain and rage, Finn released all that was in him and directed it toward Simon. Flame shot from his hand straight to Simon's black heart. With a whoosh it engulfed him and burned the traitor to ash. The sight would haunt his nightmares for the rest of his life, Finn knew.

Finn collapsed to his knees, panting. He did his best to pull himself together and remember his pride and station. When he was able to observe the happenings around him again, he noted that his own people had been triumphant, at least in this small skirmish. He rose from his knees and retrieved his sword.

Once he was sure his voice would not shake, he gave his people his orders. "This is a great victory, but this battle is not over yet. We have to make our way to the front gate as planned. The rest of our force is depending on us. All of you, to me."

At his command, each of his remaining comrades fell in beside him and he led them down the hallway to the front entrance of the castle.

****

Joan and Thomas joined Lyssa just as she froze the gate. With a sound just a touch softer than thunder, the gate cracked into two large fragments. They fell in opposite directions with a resounding crash. The soldiers rushed in with Lyssa, Joan, and Thomas in the lead. Ready for the next stage of battle, they charged, only to come face-to-face with their king.

"Halt!" Finn roared hastily.

"Halt!" Thomas bellowed in his turn.

For a moment every last person froze.

Then the king raised his sword and gave another roar, this time of triumph. "We are victorious!" he declared.

Every soldier in the royal army cried out their affirmation in response.

Lyssa lowered her magic-filled hand and extinguished her power. With a sound between a laugh and sob, she rushed toward Finn's open arms. Held tight in his embrace, she let the tears of mingled joy and sorrow come. Somehow, his lips found hers and the kiss they shared brought some peace to her troubled heart.

When she found a moment to look about her again, she saw that Joan and Thomas had had the same idea and were still kissing. Locked together, arms encircling one another, they celebrated the triumph of the royal army and the simple fact that they were both still alive.

Chapter Nineteen

After a time, everyone sobered and looked about them at the carnage. The damage to the castle was extensive. The main gate was broken in half and would have to be repaired at the first opportunity. Small fires needed extinguishing before they got out of control and burned-out areas would need cleaning and restoration.

In the battlefield men lay dying, some screaming in agony from burns, others sliced by swords. Still more were injured by the razor sharp tips of arrows. Altogether, the suffering was tremendous.

"Let us not ever forget the cost of this victory as we tend our wounded and bury our dead," Finn advised the soldiers and the townspeople.

Under Finn's direction, order was restored.

"Trying to be everywhere at once will do no good. I will have to prioritize," he muttered to himself. His first task was gathering Thomas and Joan to him; Lyssa had never left his side. "Thomas, Joan, there may still be some alive and well enough to offer resistance. Find them and bring them before me. Use whatever uninjured troops you wish to help you."

"Yes, majesty," they both replied.

****

As Lyssa listened to him hand out other duties, she wondered how she might help. She realized she could use her power to heal. Her ice could be used to soothe burns and cool fevers. Once Finn was free, she put out a hand and grasped his forearm to gain his attention. He turned to her and she gestured to the many requiring assistance. "I thought I and my power might be of some use. There are so many injured." With a twist of her hand, she produced a small icicle.

He looked down at it, then at Lyssa's determined face and understood in that instant what she meant to do. "Ah…I see." He considered for a moment. "Yes, do what you can, but stay within calling distance of our troops. Go nowhere alone."

In one swift motion, he drew her to him and kissed her, one brief touch of lips, then left her to her duty while he went to his.

****

Sometime later, Lyssa walked the field in a shocked daze. The death toll was low but the number of injured men extensive. Facing the destructive consequences of war affected her just as much as the battle had, if not more. When a wounded man called out for water, she snapped back enough to heed the request. Others cried out for mercy or for their mothers so far away. It seemed natural that she should comfort these men who fought so hard for their freedom. She chose another man at random, assessed his condition then did all she could to aid him.

So many with injuries of all sorts, she mused. Her ice was good on many of the burns the men sustained and she did her best to ease those and other hurts. She tied bandages and staunched bloody wounds as well as anyone. As in the battle, she tried to be everywhere at once, but she could not manage it now any more than she had then. Her heart broke more with each moment.

By the end of that long day, she was exhausted, all but spent in fact. She was as weary in body as she was in spirit and barely made it to her new quarters before she dropped. Without even bothering to undress, she fell into a dreamless sleep as soon as she lay down upon her bed. Deep in the night, Finn wrapped his strong arms around her. Half-awake, she turned to him, content. In the morning, he was gone.

The next day held more of the same. Some of the wounded men died, others improved. From time to time she glimpsed Finn going in or out of the main audience chamber or walking among the troops. Aside from one or two searing moments of locked gazes, which Lyssa felt contained every emotion it was possible to experience, they said nothing to each other. This time, however, when she dragged herself to her rest the next evening, Finn was waiting.

In spite of her dispirited state, her heart leapt at the sight of him and she offered a shaky smile. He sat on a stool but when she entered he rose to greet her. As soon as she got a good look at his face, it was clear something was very wrong. Even as he took her hands in his, she wanted to reach out and comfort him.

"You look dreadful," she informed him bluntly. "What can I do?"

"There's nothing you can do. There's nothing anyone can do."

For the first time she noted the all but empty wineskin set beside the stool and the goblet on the small table beside him. "Perhaps if you spoke to someone about what's troubling you?" When he shrugged and said nothing, she added, her tone sharp, "Well, drinking enough to kill a horse will help nothing. If that's what you intend to do, you can do it elsewhere."

For a few minutes she waited, hoping for some response, but when nothing came, she made an impatient sound deep in her throat and made to leave.

She had gotten to the entrance when he said in a quiet voice, "He was never going to stop."

Once she seated herself on the bed, he told her of his encounter with Simon. She did not interrupt but let him spew, knowing he would be the better for it, like lancing a pus-filled sore. When he finished pouring out the story, she mulled over all he told her before speaking. "You are right. He was never going to stop," Lyssa assured him. She used his own words, hoping they would have a positive impact. "He said it himself and you know he spoke the truth for once in his miserable life."

Finn poured more wine and tossed it back as if it were water. "I know. I had to end it. The things I had to do in battle were bad enough, but he's made me a killer. I've killed men in combat before, of course, but I never truly wanted to murder a man until I confronted him. Certainly, I have never wanted to dispatch someone personally, with my own bare hands. I could have tried to stop him, to contain him. I didn't."

"You couldn't take the risk. Your sole motive was to protect. To do that, you had to kill him. You are not to blame."

Finn shook his head. "It wasn't just that. I wanted him dead. For everything he did, for everything he might do, I wanted him gone."

She took his hand in a firm grip. "And who could blame you after all the damage he did? Treason was the least of it. Political intrigue and a military coup aimed at you personally, murder, and at the last, open war. All of this was intended to take you out of power and put himself in. Right then, right there it was him or you. I for one am glad you defeated him."

"Thank you." He squeezed her hand hard for a moment then let it go. "But it isn't that simple. My motives weren't all noble. I wanted him gone for my own reasons. What's more, I wanted to be the one to do it. I wanted to be judge, jury and executioner. No complications, no threat to anyone anymore. Just done. Over. When I tried to negotiate, Simon asked me a question that has haunted me since. How am I any different from him?"

"Answer me this; if there had been any other way to stop him, would you have done it? Much as you wanted to, would you have let yourself kill him?"

"Even when I look back over all the happenings of the last months, even when I consider each and every incident, every insult and all the good and bad that resulted, I still can't say, not for sure. I'll never truly know, but I don't think I would have. If there had been another way, I think I would have found it and used it. Much as my own desire might have been otherwise. But there was no other way."

She lifted their joined hands and kissed his fingers. "I concur with that assessment. I know you better than anyone and I think—no, I know—you did, if not the right thing, what had to be done."

"It's comforting to hear you say so, even if I can't quite believe it myself."

"I think you will, in time." She sighed and prayed she was right. "In the meanwhile, you are exhausted and so am I. And believe me you look it. You are far too pale and there are lines on your face that weren't there even days ago. Let's rest."

With a grunt, he nodded and rose.

She took his other hand and led him to her bed. There, with arms wrapped around each other, they slept.

****

Thomas and Joan were tasked with rounding up all the enemy soldiers and imprisoning them. Many were injured and most were broken men. There were some who, even knowing defeat, denied it and became all the more desperate and determined.

"Will we ever find them all, do you think?" Joan asked Thomas a bit plaintively after four solid days of mopping up the remnants of the enemy.

"I don't know. I hope so. I think we're close."

Joan snorted. "That's what you said two days ago."

Over the previous days, they and a full squadron of others hand-picked by Thomas, Joan and the king, searched the surrounding woods, which everyone agreed would be the best place to go to ground. Some sixty miles east, Brighton Forest ended a quarter mile from the southern coast and the port town of Lees. The forest was not square in shape. Instead it formed a most unusual half-circle with the sea running parallel with its southern edge. With the castle at its western end and Spencerville at its east, anyone wishing to avoid detection could lose themselves in the forest, proceed along the circumference of the woods, then arrive at Lees town, the busiest port in Ravenstone. From there it would be a simple matter to take a ship to anywhere in the world.

"Yes well, it's a bit difficult to judge these

things—"

Thomas's voice cut off and Joan's gaze shot to his. He signaled her to the left in one curt motion and rotated a finger to indicate she should circle around the perimeter then stay put, concealed. She was reluctant, but following his orders was second nature, so she did not question him.

Less than a minute later, a rider appeared, coming in fast. At a gallop, there was no mistaking the skill of their prey. No matter, the rider hadn't a chance against Thomas.

Breaking from cover, Thomas was through the trees and beside the rider in seconds. Catching up with the rider then matching the pace was easy enough considering the disparity in the quality of their mounts. Thomas rode the best stallion in the king's stable, while their target, in spite of having an excellent seat, rode a nag stolen from some farmer. Joan was surprised anyone was able to coax such speed out of the poor old thing.

In the blink of an eye, Thomas dragged their hapless victim out of her saddle and over his so she was sitting in front of him. Without the encouragement of a rider, the old cart horse dropped from a gallop to a canter and was soon contentedly cropping grass some distance away.

As soon as Thomas halted their headlong rush, the woman lashed out with a blade previously concealed in her boot, only grazing his thigh when Thomas deflected the blow. When she squirmed and twisted to get a better angle to try for his gut, a loud voice stopped her.

"Be still or you will get an arrow through the head." Joan backed up this statement by emerging from the trees, arrow nocked, ready, and pointed at the woman's skull.

She took in her situation with one glance and held up her hands, then opened the one holding the knife and dropped it to the leafy ground. Thomas forced her to face forward in the saddle again then bound her hands behind her with a handy bit of leather cord. That done, he threw his captive to the ground and followed after her. She hit dirt with a distinct feminine *oof* then rolled and got to her knees.

Standing before her, he threw back the hood of the cloak. His eyes widened. "Well, well, look who we have here. A woman and not just any woman, Adriane Wentworth." He hauled her unceremoniously to her feet, uncaring of any discomfort or injury she might suffer in the process. "You were ready to go home, Joan? Now's our chance. I'll bring this one in personally and enjoy it."

Adriane shot him a glance full of loathing and rage. "I am a queen. You will never be able to hold me."

Thomas laughed aloud with genuine amusement. "Won't we? You committed treason against the rightful king of Ravenstone. You tried to have him assassinated. As for being queen, your own claim to that throne is more than a little shaky. I wouldn't rely on that to save you."

Adriane shot him one last filthy glance then turned her face away.

****

Over the next weeks, order was restored throughout the entire kingdom. The council was reinstated much as it had been before the coup. Law was reestablished. It was with great joy and no little trepidation that Lyssa became a part of that effort.

"Are you certain about this, Finn? Perhaps this should wait. So soon after so much upheaval, your people may not take well to yet another change." Lyssa dawdled outside the council chamber and fiddled with the sapphire pendant she wore on a thick gold chain.

Finn gave one emphatic shake of his head. "I will start out as I mean to go on. You are to be my wife and will rule at my side from today."

Lyssa raised her eyebrows at his unwavering tone. "Well, when you put it that way." She took a deep breath and followed him in to meet with the newly elected council.

Most were aware of the part Lyssa played in the conflict and so she was far more readily accepted than she would ever have predicted. Taking her place beside her betrothed, still a bit bewildered by such an unexpected turn of events, Lyssa tried to focus on Finn as he stood to address the council.

Having gained the attention of them all, he spoke. "To begin, each member of the enemy force who participated in the battle will be required to give an account of themselves to the king and his council. We will assess their particular conduct. Then and only then will every man and woman be given a choice: exile or surrender. If the person was instrumental in perpetuating the conflict, however, he will not be given a choice and will be imprisoned. Some few, including Adriane Wentworth of Minden, are hereby branded traitors and shall be publicly executed. She is even now awaiting my pleasure, having been captured by our most trusted advisor, Lord Thomas Marbury." Finn gave them a moment to digest this, then lifted his voice again. "Does this meet with the council's approval?" Every voice rose in affirmation and Finn let out a satisfied sigh before he continued, "In that case, let us discuss the particulars."

Since much of the rest was mere details and easily decided, it was done much as he decreed. Adriane Wentworth was beheaded at dawn on a fine April morning exactly as he ordered. When he witnessed her execution, he observed that she went to her death silent and unmourned.

****

Six months after Simon was deposed and what people called the battle of the succession was won, a formal summons from the king was delivered to Thomas. The tedious but necessary business of the trials was at last over and Thomas had expected some respite from his duties. Time enough he had hoped, to finalize wedding plans with his betrothed. To receive such an order from Finn, particularly without some explanation attached was rare, though not without precedent, so Thomas's curiosity was piqued. He gave up thoughts of his marriage for the moment and presented himself outside the main audience chamber at the appointed time. When he found Joan waiting as well, his interest reached new heights.

After a most affectionate greeting between them, he sat beside her in the brocade chairs provided for those waiting to have an audience with the king then asked, "Do you have any idea what this is about?"

"None. Do you?"

He shook his head. "All I can say is that I am intrigued."

They were not kept waiting long. Soon a palace

guard opened the doors and bade them enter. "I've called you here because I have a task for you both."

Joan and Thomas exchanged a glance and smiled. Thomas spoke for them. "We are at your command, sire."

Finn smiled in his turn then nodded in acknowledgement. "I want you to search the world for all those with ice powers. There are others like the queen, but after the plague, they scattered to the four winds. Who better than the two of you to find them?"

Thomas lifted his eyebrows. "You want us to what? How?"

"Lyssa and I have some ideas on that. Don't worry, we won't send you out empty handed," he told them with a cheerful grin.

"Assuming we can even find them, then what?" Thomas asked.

"Bring them back here if they wish it. If not, take an accounting so that we can have an accurate number. I want you to pick a small team of no more than twenty. Only those you trust. Take the lead, organize them then send them out in every direction. Once you have all that in place, I would also have you go out yourselves."

"Searching the entire world will take more than a bit of time. How long do we have?"

"You have as long as it takes. There is no limit. But we do have ways to narrow the search. We'll discuss that later as well. I know it's a lot to ask and I will miss you both more than I can say, but this is how you can best serve your kingdom. Will you do it?"

"I'm not sure I feel comfortable leaving you so soon after you have regained your throne. Things are still a bit precarious yet," Thomas commented thoughtfully.

"All the more reason for you to go. The balance between fire and ice is slowly being restored. We must do everything possible to facilitate this process. The balance and the kingdom are intertwined and the fate of one is inextricably tied to the other. Again yet another reason to maintain and strengthen both. Having Lyssa here and taking her as my queen is the most important step, but there is more, much more. It is a massive undertaking. Lyssa is, of course, imminently suited to this task, but she is my queen and my wife and I cannot spare her, nor can I go myself, at least not at this critical time. Bearing all this in mind, this is a task I could entrust to no one but the two of you. So, will you accept this charge?"

Thomas made a derisive noise. "Massive undertaking is right. It will take years."

"I know. Are you up for it?"

Thomas glanced over at his betrothed. "Joan?"

"Why not? Travel, adventure and a most congenial companion? What could be better? So long as we can return to see the two of you married."

Thomas grinned. "You heard the lady. We are at your majesty's service." He bowed with a great flourish.

****

Six months later

On a warm spring day, they wed. The morning dawned as bright and beautiful as Lyssa could have wished. The cathedral was decorated with her favorite flowers, soft pink roses and pure white baby's breath, the arrangements draped over the end of each pew, with larger ones on the altar. Light poured in from the enormous windows and even the chilly church was comfortable. The whole effect spoke of the magnificence and joy of spring.

Her dress was made of a rare white silk and cost more than anything she had ever worn. The royal seamstresses had outdone themselves with the pearl beading and lace. Her veil was affixed to a tiara of her own design made of ice. As her attendant, Joan wore a rich forest green silk only slightly less costly which suited her very well.

Waiting in the vestibule at the back of the church, her heart was full to bursting. She could barely wait to be Finn's wife. When the music began to play, she recognized her cue. Joan headed down the aisle first then Lyssa stepped out.

Her prospective husband looked wonderful in his wedding clothes. Brown pants and a green tunic the same shade as Joan's dress paired with black boots polished to a gleam completed his ensemble. Thomas wore a similar outfit, if not quite so fine.

As she walked, her train trailed behind her and all those in attendance gasped in awe at her loveliness. As for her, her eyes were for Finn alone. If she had ever had any doubts, the radiant joy on his face put them to rest for good and all.

As she climbed the steps to the altar at last, she held out her hand to him. His palm clasped hers and she took the last few steps to stand by his side. They promised to be together forever and always, husband and wife.

Chapter Twenty

One year later

They worked together in their private study and talked quietly, discussing this and that regarding the kingdom. Finn paced as he spoke. In the normal course of things, Lyssa might have been on her feet as well, but a heavily pregnant belly prevented her.

When he paused, having come to a natural stopping point, she asked, "Any word from Thomas and Joan yet?"

"Not since their last communication from Brewton. With any luck, they have already arrived in Lees and we will hear from them soon. But they are making their way back and should return in good time for the birth."

She rose ponderously to her feet, waving off Finn's help when he offered assistance. "Oh, I do hope so. I want everyone I love with us when our child is born. My life is so full. I never guessed I could grow to care about so many. That I have is a constant joy and wonder to me. I want our daughter to be surrounded by all that love as soon as she takes her first breath."

"You're so sure we're having a girl? We could have a son, you know," he reminded her.

"We could but we're having a girl. I feel it in here." She placed a hand over her heart.

He took her hand in his, placed his other over his

child. "Daughter or son, as long as you and the child are healthy. I ask the gods for nothing more than that." He smiled as he felt their offspring give a healthy kick then frowned at the strange tightening of his wife's stomach. Her gasp of pain made him speak more sharply than usual. "Lyssa, what's wrong? The baby—"

She patted his hand which still rested on the mound of her belly. "There's nothing wrong with the baby except that it's ready to be born."

"Oh, it's ready to be…" His voice trailed off and his expression changed from relieved to puzzled to a combination of excited and terrified in rapid succession. She'd never seen quite that expression on his face before and it made her want to smile. Knowing now was not the time, however, she kept her lips straight.

"Are you in pain? Stupid question, of course you're in pain. You should sit down." He took hold of her arm and guided her to the nearest chair.

Never had she seen him this flustered and again she fought the impulse to smile. Hoping to calm him a bit, she sat then grasped his hand. "I'm fine for right now," she assured him. "I'm not in any pain at the moment, but if you could pour me a glass of water then fetch the midwife, that would be a tremendous help."

Grateful to have a task, he did as she requested with alacrity.

****

The midwife and her assistant shooed Finn outside. With little choice in the matter and reluctance in every step, he retired to the study.

Hours of waiting with nothing to do but listen to her screams put him more than on edge. His hands clenched and his entire body tensed with the need to go to her. He was in agony. Not as much as she was, at least not physically, but every cry of pain tore at his heart and hurt worse than any physical wound. Knowing there was nothing he could do to help her drove him mad. If he could just be there to support her…and why couldn't he? He was the king after all, tradition be damned. He set down his glass of brandy and rose.

"Majesty, are you well?" the attending servant asked.

"No, but I will be once I'm with my wife and child, which by the grace of the gods will be born at any minute."

"But that isn't how it's done," the man protested.

"I don't care how it was done. I'm king and I say how things will be done." He turned on his heel and hastened to his wife.

After a brisk preemptory knock on the birthing chamber door, he did not wait for a response but entered. A young midwife-in-training was the first to see him. She gasped and nearly dropped the clean linens she had in her hands.

"Betty, I need that linen. What are you about?" The midwife, Elaine, snapped and turned. Her eyes widened at the sight of him, but then her jaw firmed. "Majesty, I am afraid you must not be here."

"I am not leaving until my child is born. I will not leave my wife to go through this ordeal alone any longer."

Lyssa lay back, eyes closed as she rested between pains, but at the sound of his voice, her head shot up and her eyes opened wide.

"I assure you, your grace, women have babies

every day. She will be fine."

But he wasn't even listening; he only had eyes and ears for his wife. As he pushed farther into the room, Lyssa stretched out a hand to him. He stepped forward and took it without even thinking.

The midwife sputtered and threw up her hands in dismay. She didn't have much more time for consternation, however, as another contraction gripped the queen. "Betty, the linen." She snatched the clean sheets from the girl then turned her full attention to Lyssa. "All right, your grace, it's time for you to push."

Lyssa's grip on Finn's hand tightened so much that he was certain the bones rubbed together. Tears and sweat streamed down her reddening face. Loosening her grip just slightly, but not letting go of him, she panted like a bellows then gasped, "I can't."

"You can," he contradicted her. "You can do anything you put your mind to. Now, our child is waiting to meet us."

"Our daughter," she corrected.

Finn laughed a little and kissed her forehead. "Yes, our daughter. Now, when Elaine tells you to, you push."

Lyssa nodded and soon enough Elaine ordered, "Push."

With a tremendous effort, Lyssa bore down with the next contraction and the baby came fully into the world. While Elaine cleaned up their new offspring, Lyssa waited, holding out her arms.

At long last, the midwife turned and presented them with a child, expertly swaddled. "Majesties, you have a beautiful healthy daughter."

Once Elaine placed the small bundle in her arms,

Lyssa said through her happy tears, "I knew it! I knew she was a girl."

Finn laughed aloud as profound relief filled him. Then he looked down at his precious daughter and awe swept away every other feeling. "So you did. She is the prettiest little girl I've ever seen. What shall we call her?"

"You are right. She is absolutely the prettiest girl I have ever seen too," Lyssa said, kissing the top of the small head. "What do you think of the name Eleanor?"

Finn considered a moment. "I think it's lovely and I like it very much, but let's ask her shall we?" With one gentle fingertip, he touched the baby's cheek. "What do you think? Do you like the name?"

The little girl fixed her gaze on her father and sighed.

"I think she likes it," he whispered.

"Eleanor Hale, princess of Ravenstone, our beloved daughter. Yes, that sounds perfect." With a gentle sigh which echoed her daughter's and her child in her arms, Lyssa dropped off to sleep. Finn watched over them both until dawn, just as he knew he would for the rest of his life.

A word about the author…

Shirley grew up in Baton Rouge, Louisiana and started writing at an early age. Always talkative, when she was eleven she began to put her thoughts on paper, writing stories inspired by some of her favorite writers, Laura Ingalls Wilder and Madeline L'Engle. Recently, her novel *If The Shoe Fits* was published by The Wild Rose Press.

Shirley graduated from Nicholls State University, where she majored in History and minored in English. Since graduating she has worked at some of the best libraries in the Baton Rouge area. She makes her home there and enjoys spending time with family members.

Visit her at http://www.shirleypmccoy.com